Murder by the Book

By

Pamela Malz

W & B Publishers
USA

W & B Publishers

For information:
W & B Publishers
Post Office Box 193
Colfax, NC 27235
www.a-argusbooks.com

ISBN: 978-0-6923123-3-9
ISBN: 0-6923123-3-1

Book Cover designed by Dubya
Cover Art by Pamela Malz
Printed in the United States of America

Dedication

This work is dedicated to Tyler.

Chapter One

Jess Auberdine unlocked the door to her modest yet chic interior design business, still gushing over the fact that it was her own, although it *had* been for nearly two years now. She could still envision the huge red ribbon tied across the glass doors, stenciled with her name and logo; the giant pair of scissors provided by her adoring husband, Bob – she could officiate the grand opening *the proper* way; the bottle of Crystal and the expensive kind of caviar. It was a dream come true. Jess knew it would never become customary to see her name in lights, so to speak. *Auberdine Designs*: the logo, showcased below the company name and created by her hairdresser, was a swirling bouffant of red hair and a mega-watt smile - Jess's trademarks. Originally, Jess pointed out to her hairdresser that the design business had nothing to do with her appearance, despite how adorable the sketches looked. After time and deliberation, she decided to use the logo, coming to the realization that it was her mark, her stamp on the world, much like her own business would be. She was well known for three things after all: the outlandish tint of her hair, a smile any dentist would endorse and her sense of style.

After setting her bags on the reception desk, she locked the door behind her, knowing she had plenty to do before the store opened for business. One of the first things on her agenda would be to remove the coffee stain from her dusty-pink Chanel suit. She had worked too hard for that suit, even if it was on massive mark-down. But it was no knock-off. Jess had heard club soda worked wonders on stains, but she didn't have any handy. She turned down the corridor toward the restroom, which had just been redecorated. *Water can't hurt*, she thought absently, removing her jacket and exposing the stained portion of her sleeve. The pipes wheezed as she turned on the faucet. Something else to add to her around the office to-do list. Nonplussed by anything awry at Auberdine Designs, Jess was too intent on patting-not-rubbing her Chanel to notice the other sound.

The water seemed to be helping a little, at least to dull the stain; but she wondered if she ought to run it across the street to the drycleaner just to be safe. The problem was that they weren't opened yet and furthermore she was wearing a shabby old tank top beneath her coat, having been under the impression that it wouldn't be necessary to remove the coat at all today. The tank had a nice neckline and was soft and comfortable, but she would never wear it to work as a stand-alone item of clothing. She decided to call Bob and see if he was still home. If he hadn't left yet, he'd be glad to bring over another pants or skirt suit. Then Jess could drop the stained one at the cleaners, where they would hopefully be able to make it as good as new. En route to the phone, she also decided that if Bob was still at home, she'd ask him to bring her a second muffin.

The lobby was empty, of course, but it felt . . . different. "Hello?" called Jess, suddenly feeling foolish. Of course there was nobody there. Bob was right. She had been watching too many creepy movies lately. That and her wild imagination were a lethal mix for a woman who spent so much time alone at the office. She had two assistants who worked for her, but she opted to only have them here during operating hours. It cut costs, plus it gave her more time to get the creative juices flowing. She skittishly laughed off her temporary feelings of trepidation and walked into her office to use the phone. The reception desk phone had been right there, where she had been standing, but instead she went to her desk phone. She knew this was because she had in fact seen too many horror movies. *Then why didn't I shut the office door behind me?* Jess thought, as she heard a faint rustling sound coming from the opposite end of the building. The onset of the ringing on the other end of the line startled her, but she felt a sense of relief when Bob answered her call on the first ring. "Oh Bob, thank God," she began, then realized she sounded a bit dramatic. As doting and wonderful a husband as he was, she didn't want to be teased anymore about her movie watching habits. It made her feel like a child who was doing something wrong when he went on and on about how cute she was when she was scared. *Those movies are for big girls*, he'd mock. Well she wouldn't give any fuel to his fire, the big lug. She quickly tacked on, "It's my Chanel suit! Silly old me, I spilled my Starbucks blonde roast all over the sleeve. Will you be a dear and grab my black suit off the hanger in the hall and swing by with it? It's with the other things just dropped off from the cleaners, including your dark shirt for tomorrow night."

"Anything for you, Darling."

"Then how about another one of those chocolate chip banana muffins while you're at it?" she smiled. Just being on the phone with Bob had put her at such ease that she had all but forgotten about being scared. Jess sometimes didn't know what she'd do if she hadn't met Bob, or if anything ever happened to him. He – along with her passion for design – was her everything. Excited about seeing Bob again this morning, the prospect of a stain-free suit and a second sinfully delicious muffin, Jess hung up the phone after sending her love. She was so sated at that moment that she actually sighed. Yes, life was good. She left her desk, suddenly aware of how cold her bare arms and shoulders felt. It was almost as if there were a draft. Jess shivered. She thought for a split second of putting the stained coat back on, just until Bob got there, but then she remembered that the sleeve was nice and wet.

The heating unit was on the wall on the way into the storage room, used for stashing furniture items used in shows and model homes and long cylindrical rolls of Persian carpets. There were yards of material and piles upon piles of swatches. It was well ventilated, so as to keep the integrity of the furniture. This was no warehouse, but it was lofty and vast and cold . . *and poorly lit and spooky*, she thought. Jess rubbed her arms in an effort to quell the goose pimples before flipping on the heat switch. She heard what sounded like cranking gears and could feel the heat pouring in from the vent above. Thank goodness. She flipped on the coffee pot deciding to go for an unprecedented second cup today. It would go great with that muffin. She heard a thumping noise behind her and expected to see Bob knocking on the door when she turned. Instead she gasped. There was an intruder in the store, his face covered with a ski mask. Jess gasped, stifling a scream. "Please," she began, taking a step back. *Keep your cool, girl.* Her mouth ran dry. She had heard of things like this happening all the time on the news. It was probably a drug addict looking for a quick chunk of change to satisfy his habit. He looked terrifying, but she needed to keep her grip on reality. She *could* be a big girl. She would reason her way out of this and live to tell about her brave fight for her life. *Bob will get a big kick out of this*, she thought. *Bob!* He would be here any minute with her change of clothes.

"Please. Just let me get you the cash from my purse," Jess said, calmly as if she were talking to a class of kindergartners. "The store has nothing but checks and credit card slips but I take those home each day. I won't even call the police." The intruder simply and slowly nodded his head side to side. "No?" mouthed Jess. "No, you don't want money?" Tears began to stream down her cheeks. Her trademark smile was nowhere to be found. She looked as the man reached into his coat pocket and pulled out a huge butcher knife. "God, no! Please!" Jess started to run, but the man stationed himself near the front door in a matter of steps. The lock on the bathroom was already added to the *things to fix around the office* list, so she had nowhere to run but the storage room. It was dark and scary, but nothing could match the fear of seeing the masked man standing there, staring, lips curled into a sinister smile. She skidded into the warehouse feeling the strap on her excessively high heels digging into her ankle. She wished she could yank them off and use the dagger-like heels as weapons. Of course there was no time for that. There was no time for anything as the predator was fast on her heels. She had the advantage of knowing her way around the room, but he was too close for her to even stop and hide in one of the many shelves or nooks. She could only continue running, until she reached a dead end. When she did, it would be the end of her. If only she had her cell phone with her. She might be able to call for help. Then she remembered everything she'd ever heard about being in a perilous situation involving an attacker. Scream for help. He was already planning to harm her, obviously, so it wouldn't hurt to try and save herself. *Bob! Bob should be here by now*. She began yelling, screaming for her husband, as she reached the wall. The dead end. All Jess could do was brace herself against the cold unfinished concrete, arms flailing, screaming her last words, a plea for help. She knew it was too late when the blade circled her shoulder and created an unearthly warmth. It didn't even hurt really, but when she looked down and saw what was happening, she passed out.

Chapter two

"Keeley! I finally got you on the phone!" shrieked Leah.

"Hi, Leah!"

"Congratulations, New York Times Best Selling Author! Ahhhhhh!" squealed an excited Leah! Keeley yanked the phone away from her ear, smiling at her old friend's reaction to her success. "Stop screaming and I'll send you a signed copy," Keeley joked.

"You think I haven't bought out every newsstand within a five mile radius of my house! You're a famous writer. *He Knows You're Alone* will be on every bookshelf and nightstand if I have my way. I'm giving them as gifts to everyone I know. And since you offered, signed copies would make even better gifts!" gushed Leah.

"Take a breath! And thank you. I'm excited too."

"Excited? You're living the dream, Keeley! You own a gorgeous antique book store, which will be absolutely *famous* now that your book is taking off; you're a best seller; you're dating Ben, who is just the most adoring man alive. . . "

"I have more good news," gushed Keeley. She couldn't resist indulging her loyal friend. "Ben proposed," blurted Keeley, almost afraid of the reaction she might elicit. In anticipation she drew the phone three or four inches away from her ear, which was still throbbing.

Screaming ensued, which made Keeley beam. Her *own* good fortune was not lost on her. She *was,* in fact, living the dream. She had scrimped and saved every penny in order to buy the vintage building that looked more like a museum than a bookstore. She did her research and recreated a renowned old bookstore, complete with bookshelves lining entire walls, annexes, rolling ladders and a grand staircase creating a precipice in the center of the store. It was an architectural gem that shined even brighter after proper restoration. After restoring life to the building, Keeley began the next endeavor, which was stocking the immense shelves with precious literary works: the rare, the unique, the one-of-a-kind and original manuscripts, along with modern day finds. Books, she once thought, could make her just as happy, if not happier, than any human being ever could. That was of course before she met Ben. Somewhere between the time she created her dream store and met the man of her dreams, she began trying her own hand at writing. It was a long shot - that she knew, but *Dream Catcher* caught the eye of an up and coming publishing company, resulting in a book deal and some minor publicity for Keeley. After that she wrote *He Knows You're Alone,* and the rest is history.

Once Leah's hysteria began transitioning into actual words, Keeley rested the phone back against her ear. "You're such a good friend, Leah. You've always supported me."

"Does that mean I get to be in your wedding?"

"Of course it does! But don't start trying on dresses yet. Ben's firm is taking that deal in Australia. We're going to be on opposite sides of the world for a while yet. I guess that's why I haven't officially announced the engagement. It's kind of bittersweet." Keeley bit her lip.

"Oh, . . . so there's a flaw in the life of perfection after all?"

"No, that's not what I meant, Leah," she began, feeling guilty. "I'm so blessed and so appreciative. I know I don't have the right to complain."

"I'm just ruffling your feathers. Does your brother know about the pending nuptials?"

"Bob? Of course." Keeley's brother Bob was nearly twenty years older than she and acted much more like a father than a brother, especially after their father's death five years ago. She sometimes felt that he was too overbearing, more so than their own father, but he meant well and could always be counted on. "Speaking of the devil, Leah, I'm getting a call on the other line from Brother Bob right now. I'll have to call you back." Keeley lamented having to end the blissful conversation she was having with her dear friend, but her brother always came first. Bob had a way of always making her feel like she was his top priority too. He had that effect on everyone, but Keeley knew it was sincere. Bob would go to the ends of the earth for her, so she made sure to make him feel the same.

"Bobby!" she announced, gleefully, sure he was calling to once again congratulate her on her windfall of glorious news.

"Keeley . . . I lost Jess," said the unfamiliar voice.

"Bob? Is that you?" Keeley was more focused on the flat, glum-sounding voice than the actual words that had been spoken. She hadn't heard *what* he had said, only how he had said it. Bob never sounded like this. In fact the idea of Bob sounding so glum and impersonal was so foreign, so preposterous that she didn't believe for a minute that it was he.

"Yes it's me, Kee. Jess was killed." Then he began to wail with a sound so guttural that it reminded her of the first time she'd heard a catfight or a pack of howling coyote pups, a sound so unnatural and horrific that she doubted for a moment that it was real. Then finally his words broke through; the meaning of Bob's words finally registered . . . *Jess was killed.*

***

The drive to Bob's was forty-five minutes when you weren't fighting rush hour traffic. The bridge was not only uncongested, it was deserted. Keeley couldn't help but glance over her shoulder, several times during the drive. Nightfall had a way of adding a subtle feeling of apprehension to most situations, not that this particular situation wasn't dour enough. But Keeley was flat out frozen with fear. Not only was losing Jess devastating, but, having mulled over Bob's words . . . it sounded that Jess had not only been killed, but that Jess had been ravaged. The horrid details were echoing through her mind; she actually covered her ears with gloved hands at one point, as if she could silence her thoughts. *Her arm was taken completely off. Her face was barely recognizable. I was too late to save her. Poor Jess. Poor Bob.* But that was an understatement. Bob would never, ever be the same. Keeley knew Jess's murder would, in some way, be the end of her brother as she knew him. It was impossible for *anyone* not to love Jess. She was over the top, tacky and smelled of Aqua Net and menthols, but she had a huge heart and Bob just adored that woman to pieces . . . *Pieces . . . Torn to pieces.* Keeley suppressed a wave of nausea.

The adoration was completely mutual, of course. Keeley was always in awe of their tremendous love for one another. It was the kind of love that made others want to gag, but it was true and pure and yes, gag-worthy. They had met each other later in life, after several failed attempts at love under each of their belts. Bob was "too nice" and Jess too larger than life for most men's egos. They met at a gathering to sponsor the opening of the City Life Art Walk, both being enthusiasts of culture and art. Bob was hit hard by Cupid's arrow, saying right off the bat that he had finally found his purpose in life. Keeley and her mother were wary until they too met and subsequently fell in love with Jess Auberdine. Jess was strong, confidant, loving and had her own money. Bob seemed to have a hard time separating those who were more interested in his wallet from those interested in his heart. Jess was the total package. She was beautiful, in a Texas pageant sort of way; was involved in charities; and had a relatively new business that seemed as trendy and popular as Jess herself. So why would someone take that away? Keeley stuffed some tissue into her coat pocket as she put the car in park. She stared up at Bob's expansive brick colonial. It looked dark and vacant, the same way she knew Bob would appear from here on out. Keeley braced herself. She knew this would be one of the most trying moments of her life, including the deaths of both their parents. It was like being in a sinking hole. Keeley wiped her eyes, stung by guilt, suddenly realizing she was currently mourning the loss of her brother, not Jess. She knew she would buckle when Bob opened the door and she saw his face. Blue eyes, always so full of light and cheer would be empty and lifeless. Keeley would miss her sister-in-law dearly, but the pain she was pushing through was for Bob. His life had turned into a death sentence. The voice on the phone was merely some *man* on the verge of losing it.

Bob had asked her not to bother coming until this evening because he would be dealing with the police. She also figured that perhaps he needed a few hours to digest everything, or maybe that wasn't true. *When you were in Bob's spot, after losing mom and dad, you didn't care about holding it together. You couldn't possibly rationalize things, or make sense of anything. She* sure as heck couldn't comprehend any of it. Jess had been tortured . . . Fun-loving, big-hearted Jess. Disgusted with her vivid imagination, Keeley thrust the images from her brain. *Damn you, Stephen King*, she thought, suddenly realizing the vivid and vulgar imagery had been created by *his* mind's eye. The book . . . *It*! Stephen King's *It* had a sequence where a character's arm had been torn right off, torn off by a monstrous entity. That novel had *terrified* her as a teenager, sticking with her through her own career in the horror genre. She felt the bile rise in her throat, but fought it back when the front door slowly opened. There stood Bob, looking peaked, gray and frighteningly forlorn.

***

The tea was cold and bitter, but she drank it anyway. Bob had insisted she have some, so what could she do? Growing up, tea was her family's cure all. Headache? Have some tea. Nauseas? Try some tea. It worked for cramps, bruises, bad break ups . . . and yes, even heartache. Bob was already moved out of their parent's house before Keeley was even born, but he was always present, a mainstay in all her childhood memories. Sure it was different than if they had grown up under the same roof, but they had a solid relationship never tainted by rivalries, sibling bickering over toys or attention, or whatever else was standard issue for growing up under the same roof. Mourning over tea, however, *was* standard issue for these siblings, who lost both parents within a matter of years. Keeley knew it would ultimately happen while she was still young since they had had her so late in their lives. But it wasn't like they died of natural causes, the way she had so sorrowfully anticipated while growing up. They were taken from her too soon. Once she had made the mistake of referring to her *premature* loss of both parents and how it wasn't fair that she hadn't much time to spend with them. Bob had corrected her, saying that it was a devastating loss no matter how long she had the chance to be with them. She figured that it was his way of rationalizing and maybe giving credence to his own loss of their parents. Yet despite his words of wisdom, Keeley couldn't help feeling once again that love had ended too quickly; this time for Bob and Jess. He was the happiest he had ever been; and, sadly, it was so short-lived.

"Thank you for the tea," Keeley sipped tentatively, still not sure of what to say. For how bonded they were, this moment was about as intimate and familiar as a blind date. Sitting across the coffee table, Bob seemed miles away.

"Tea heals all, right?" asked Bob, attempting a smile. *Not this time*, Keeley longed to say. She felt like she was doing a disservice to her brother by avoiding the topic and making ridiculous small talk on the worst day of his life. But what else could she say? What was left to say, really? Most of the information about Jess's murder was provided by the policemen assigned to the case. Keeley had hugged her brother for what felt like an eternity after the officer left them alone. What was left? Certainly she was being helpful simply by being present. At least she knew she would feel if she were in his shoes. Having lost so much of her family so early on, she knew that if, God forbid, she found herself in a similar spot with Ben, she'd find solace in Bob's presence. Instead of aggravating the wound or continuing with extraneous gibber jabber, Keeley leaned forward, touching her brother's knee. "I'm here for as long as you need. Let me do all the foot work, the phone calls, the planning - short term and long term. Please, Bob."

"I might just take you up on that, Kee. I just don't see how I'll be able to keep . . . plugging along. I also don't see how I can cry anymore. I'm like a tapped well." Bob's attempt at humor only resulted in an eruption of more tears. Keeley hugged him and played mother to him after years of his playing father to her.

By the time the fire had died in the fire place and the tea kettle was empty, she led her brother upstairs to his room. He told her he wouldn't be able to go into the master; not anymore. So they walked down the hall, arm in arm, to the far guest room that seemed to exude even more Jess than the master. It was decorated primarily in pink roses and framed pictures of country cottages. Some were photographs taken by Jess on various road trips of bed and breakfasts dotting the countryside where Jess always liked to spend the long weekends. Of course there were pictures on the wall of family members, including her and Bob's parents and several candids of the happy couple, a few of which were taken by Ben. Keeley figured Bob chose this room because it was as physically far from the master bedroom as one could get in the vast house. Keeley's temporary room, which was downstairs, already had her suitcase laying on the comforter. She didn't do anything other than place her bags inside yet, so she didn't get a good look at the room's decor. She had always stayed in the *rose cottage* room when she was a guest at their home, not *their* home, now, but his home. Bob, like their father once was, is now a widower. The thought was jolting.

Keeley prepared for bed, brushing and flossing her teeth, rinsing her tear streaked face and changing into her most comfortable flannel pajamas. She swapped her contact lenses for her glasses and settled under the covers. The gory account of Jess's murder melded with the images conjured up from the King novel. It was horrid to have a visual account of what must have happened to poor, helpless Jess. More horrid, was Keeley's inability to block the images out. Her morbid thoughts evolved into morbid nightmares. The combination of what happened in the novel and the officer's account resulted in the famous evil clown Pennywise from *It*, hunting down and slaughtering her sister-in-law. The clown had blood streaming down his contorted face and fangs. Keeley darted up in bed, stifling a gurgling scream. She was dripping with sweat, desperate to forget her dream. Was it actually a monster, like Pennywise, who had taken Jess's life in the early hours of the morning? Of course it was a monster. What *human* with a heart could snuff out the life of someone else, and Jess of all people?

Chapter three

It was after midnight when Harper Middleton arrived home to her condo. She was counting the seconds until she could put a down payment on a home of her own. Her life was falling neatly into place and she couldn't be happier. The evening had gone better than expected, but Harper found herself wondering if he could really be "the one." She hadn't let on for a second to Carson that he might *not* be "the one." From the outside, her life was cookie-cutter perfect. There was a point in her life where appearances were everything, but she wasn't so sure if that was enough anymore. Yet marrying Carson would mean having her dream home even sooner, a cozy little savings account and a constant companion. It would mean never having to be alone. It would mean being *mostly* happy for the rest of her life. What were the odds that she would ever meet another man so personable, handsome and well off whom she liked *even* better than Carson? And then she'd be sacrificing her chance at true love, like that of her parents and her grandparents before them. She knew women who would kill to be in her shoes. Trying to decide if Carson Beckman was good enough for her; *Champagne problems*, she deduced.

Harper removed her heels and sat on the edge of her bed. What a night! It was the launch of Carson's firm's newest project. She, along with Carson, schmoozed with all the head honchos, making one good impression after the next. Harper was in her element. She knew she'd be a great asset to a powerful business man like Carson. She was by no means a gold-digger. She worked hard for what she had and she'd be fine with or without a leading man. They always had a good time together, and they had plenty in common. What was she so worked up about? She was being too picky, that was the problem. Yes, Carson would make a wonderful spouse. They'd be lucky to have each other. She decided to stop second-guessing herself and reminded herself to live in the moment. She knew she really ought to be enjoying herself more.

Replacing her strappy heels for a pair of fuzzy socks, Harper walked straight into her closet and removed her dress. She held it up, admiring the cut. That dress stirred up plenty of attention tonight, and it certainly warranted it. It cost a fortune and fit her like a glove. Carson had admired it when she tried it on for him the other night. It was more of a come-on than a complement, actually. He had said, "I like it, but it would look better on the floor." Harper rolled her eyes at that comment. She knew it was innocent flirting and that she should be flattered, but the comment rubbed her the wrong way for whatever reason. It was little things like that, innocent remarks, superficial glances, tiny things that no one else would ever notice. Only Harper *did* notice. She knew her standards were so high because she was so in love with the idea of being in love. It had to be perfect. But despite what her parents have, they're not perfect. *That's an unattainable dream. Perfection doesn't exist, even in fairy tales*, she had to remind herself. So, if the worst Carson could be charged with was making a cheesy or perverse comment, she shouldn't sweat it. Translation, get over it.

When Carson had kissed her good night, the poor guy had had no idea she'd spend the next ten minutes scrutinizing his every move. Harper emerged from her reasonably-sized walk-in closet wearing her favorite night shirt and flannel pajama bottoms. It wasn't until then that she noticed the rose petals decoratively creating a trail toward the bathroom. Her heart leapt. *Carson, you devil, I'm so sorry for second-guessing you,* she purred. What was this? What could be waiting for her at the end of the trail of petals? Smiling, she arched her head around the corner. She pulled back, not disappointed, but more confused. The rose petal path climbed the one carpeted stair leading up to the sunken tub. The tub was full, water steaming and brimming with bubbles. On the ledge of the tub was a cosmopolitan glass, not hers, with a pink striped stem, containing pink liquid and an orange wedge. Of course it was a great gesture, but it seemed odd. Also, the bath couldn't possibly be steaming. Carson had just dropped her off. He knew people in high places, but that would be ridiculous to call in a favor by having someone fill up her bath tub. Unless . . . *was Carson here?* Did he sneak back in somehow, because he was planning to propose to her tonight or something? But there was no legitimate back door entry to her condo unless you were Spiderman, and she had locked the front door - no dead bolted it - behind her. Still stunned with confusion, Harper rubbed her furrowed brow. She turned, deciding to go to the source. She'd call Carson and find out what was going on. *One more little oddity, dammit.* Feeling her frustration return, she backtracked and picked up the glass. She could use a drink, but after just one swig she realized she'd made a mistake.

Her throat tightened as if to push the liquid out, then she began gagging violently. Her skin was slick with sweat, she was convulsing and her throat felt like it was on fire. She staggered to the hall, retching, then slipping on her own vomit. She hadn't had the mind control to release the glass after the first gulp. It landed, shattering on the tile just as her skull smashed the side of the tub. It was all over in a matter of seconds. The cyanide cocktail worked wonders on Little Miss Perfect.

***

Once the nightmares subsided, which wasn't until the wee hours of the night, Keeley actually slept soundly. She woke up feeling okay, until the bitter memory of the day before crept in. It would probably be years before Jess and Bob didn't occupy her waking thoughts. Glancing at the clock, Keeley was startled to see that it was nine fifteen. She hadn't slept that late in who knew how long. Her thoughts immediately went to Bob, knowing there was no way he would have slept in so late under the circumstances. He was alone. She hurriedly pulled on a sweatshirt and opened her door. The house was quiet, but of course it would be. There would be no clanking of dishes as Jess made waffles and bacon. No whiff of her vanilla roast floating down the hall. No off-key but charmingly endearing humming would ever fill that kitchen again. Keeley hoped that Bob was still upstairs, sound asleep and oblivious to his bitter world.

The kitchen was empty. Bob must be upstairs, she thought, but if he was asleep she didn't dare wake him. Unsure of what to do, she went back into her quarters and picked up her cell phone. Ben would want an update on how Bob and the investigation were doing. Of course nothing had been accomplished yet with the investigation, but hopefully they would get more news today. *The news.* Keeley dropped her phone and practically ran to the front door. She wanted to intercept the morning paper before Bob woke up. She knew the media would be having a field day with Jess's murder. Of course she wouldn't keep anything from her brother, but it wouldn't hurt to be able to soften the blow, or at least anticipate the questions he might have. And there was, of course, the possibility that new information had surfaced.

The morning air was cool and crisp. Not at all what you'd expect when the world had been turned upside down. She snatched up the paper and closed the door, pleasantly surprised to see that no one was looming outside the house trying to catch a glimpse of the grieving widower.

Naturally the front page was all Jess. The photograph of her was one that Keeley had never seen before. She looked the same as always, eyes sparkling, brilliant smile. This alone would destroy Bob. She sat on the couch in the front room and began reading.

Murder in a Small Town.

Early yesterday morning the posh community of Drakesborough lost one of its most beloved patrons, Jessica Auberdine Travis. Travis was a local business woman who was actively involved in several noteworthy charities and was perhaps best known for spearheading the renovation of the city's fine arts scene, including The Drakesburough Art Walk and the centuries old Carlson Museum of Ancient Artifacts.

Although no one has been apprehended for Travis's brutal murder, the police are actively searching for any leads in this devastating case of foul play. The murder scene was Travis's place of business, Auberdine Designs on Fifth Avenue, right in the heart of Drakesborough's business district. The lock on the front door was found to be tampered with, but her husband, Robert Travis, CFO of a manufacturing conglomerate, states that Travis had a working alarm system, which was found unarmed the morning of the murder. Travis's husband also pointed out that she sometimes neglected to use the alarm system while she was on the premises.

"Is that from this morning?" asked Bob over her shoulder, causing her heart to skip a beat. "Sorry, I didn't mean to startle you." He looked awful. Keeley averted her eyes.

"No, it's okay. Just a little on edge," Keeley attempted a smile. "It is today's paper." She offered it up to Bob, who begrudgingly accepted it.

"Anything pertinent in here?" he asked. She knew he wouldn't want to pour over all the details again unless it was worth his while.

"I didn't get too far with it, but please, let me read it for you." She turned to see Bob, the new Bob, tired, drawn and empty.

"No, I can do it. I keep thinking about how I might find the one detail . . ." He removed his glasses and began reading the article. Leave it to Bob to think he is responsible for finding who Jess's murderer was. He wouldn't make it through to the other end if something didn't get done fast.

After what seemed like an eternity, Bob pulled the paper away and placed it on the table. Before he could comment, the doorbell rang. Both Keeley and Bob jerked up and walked cautiously to the door. It could very well be the beginning of the predicted media frenzy. Instead, relief washed over Keeley when she saw Bob, after staring through the peephole, release the deadbolt and turn the knob. She stepped aside and was actually comforted to see the same two police officers who had been there yesterday.

"If you have a minute," began the older officer, Detective Dean, "we wanted to ask a few more questions and share something else that might be of interest to the case." He displayed no smile, but had a friendly face. He looked exactly like what a police officer looked like in the movies: Handsome, graying temples, a paunch belly, yet in relatively good shape. Keeley felt comfort in his presence. He somehow seemed detached and empathetic, so that you somehow managed to keep it together around the guy. Yet he seemed compassionate and genuinely concerned. They were in good hands. Keeley made a mental note to mention that to Bob once they were alone again.

The other officer was young and seemingly uninvolved emotionally or otherwise. He had managed to avoid eye contact with her during their entire last visit.

"First off, I see you've already seen the morning paper. There really shouldn't be any surprises in there. We've kept you in the loop as much as possible, Mr. Travis."

"And I appreciate that," uttered Bob on what looked like auto-pilot mode.

"So that's why we're sharing something else with you. It's another case, which we believe to be unrelated. The sole purpose is just to try and get as much input as we can from each of these tragedies. If something stands out to you, anything at all, please bring it up. It's proved helpful in past cases. Sometimes when the spouse or someone else close to the victim can see a similar scenario from the outside, it can stir something up regarding their own case." Keeley saw a flicker of light return to Bob's eyes. "Not sure if you remember that case in Dover County 'bout five years ago. Young lady went missing after her car died on the highway. She was picked up by a serial rapist, poor gal." *More of Detective Dean's soft side.* "Anyway, across the state line a little boy was kidnapped, seemingly totally unconnected. After we shared details regarding the abducted woman with the little boy's mother, she felt like the two cases were connected, and she was right.

"What made her think they were connected?" asked Keeley with apprehension, then regret.

"Well, turns out a scorned 'ex' tipped off the rapist to go after that young lady's son. Hers was the only circumstance where the perpetrator broke his M.O. It was a revenge crime that ended up serving two callous, monstrous sons-of-bitches at the same time. We had already cleared the boy's absentee father, but it turned out it was a friend of his who was retaliating for something the boy's mother had done. We tracked down the friend and he was locked up. The young woman from the first crime didn't fare as well." Keeley knew better than to ask about the newest victim this time.

"I'll do everything I can," said Bob.

Detective Dean paused and the younger one, who never introduced himself, studied the pictures and decor hanging on the walls. "Last night a woman was murdered about an hour outside of Drakesborough. Different scene on all levels. This happened after midnight, and the execution was completely different. The victim, although female, was in her twenties. Different part of town, no forced entry. And . . . she was poisoned. The only reason we can speculate that a second party was even involved is because there was no cyanide on the premises." *Cyanide.* Keeley flinched. "Nothing she could have poured it from, and no empty bottle or container of any kind holding traces of the poison. Granted she could have disposed of it before ingesting the world's most toxic cocktail. Lots of suicides are premeditated. But from the looks of things, this young lady was living quite a life. Her boyfriend was getting ready to propose and he and everyone else in her life found it completely out of character, so we found those two little factors pertinent enough to open an investigation. Funny thing is, there is one commonality, come to think of it. Both Jess and the other victim were each said to have had a life that others would envy. That and the fact that they both took an interest in art."

* * *

Keeley was unsettled as she cleared away what was left of their noon time tea session. She had made tea and toast, hoping Bob would receive some nourishment, but she saw now that he had only eaten a couple of tiny bites. It was his way of appeasing her no doubt. Typical Bob, to still be cognizant of everyone else, even after losing his wife. She absent-mindedly tilted her plate, spilling remains of buttered crust on the kitchen tile, realizing she was even more preoccupied than she had been since the news of Jess broke. The officers were right . . . something about the second case, and that young girl's murder, was not sitting right. Of course it had nothing to do with Jess, and it wouldn't crack the case making everything alright. Nothing would be alright for a while now. And the strife she had felt just days ago over Ben's pending trip to Australia seemed so stupid and trivial now. Leah had just teased her about her perfect life.

Keeley knelt, using a paper towel to wipe up the buttery fragments of cold toast. She realized she had yet to update Ben on how Bob was faring. That of course wouldn't be something Ben would have to wonder too much about. He knew what type of deep bond Bob and Jess shared. He had even made a comment when she first called to tell him about Jess's murder. He had said, "I can't imagine how Bob feels. I would just die if anything happened to you." She smiled, her first since Bob's initial call, and felt solace in his words.

After rinsing the plates and stacking them in the dishwasher, Keeley decided to get to work on her remaining phone calls. She had offered to call their friends and business acquaintances once Bob called Jess's family members and dearest friends. Unfortunately word traveled fast and by now everyone she intended to call would have seen the news coverage regarding Jess, who was even more popular in death, if possible, thanks to the news-starved world of mass communication.

Her first call was to Randi Howard, a woman whom Keeley had actually met before. She was a friend of both her brother and Jess, whom they had met through the art outlet. Randi had been at their house for a cocktail party celebrating Jess's store when it first opened. Keeley had remembered her in particular because she was brazenly drunk and kept shouting, *Randi is getting randy.* To which her aging husband replied, "What's new?" The comment was harmless and so was Randy, but Keeley couldn't help but remember her. She answered after the call was picked up by the answering machine, sounding a bit out of breath. Randi said that she was on the treadmill, but Keeley wondered otherwise after her brash exclamation that night at the party. Randi went on to say that she, like everyone else, was dumbfounded that Jess could be the victim of anything other than petty female jealousy, forcing Keeley to once again recall something Detective Dean had said. *What was it exactly?* He had said the two victims were both living a life others would envy. Keeley was desperately trying to cling to something concrete, anything at all that might make a difference in the going-nowhere case of Jess Auberdine Travis. As a result she found that her attention had strayed from randy Randi.

"I'm sorry Randi, could you say that again?"

"I *said*, don't you think it's weird that Jess didn't bother with the alarm system? You know how she was always getting *spooked* about things."

"I know, but Bob said she was probably just too comfortable there. It was her home away from home and she was so proud of it." Her eyes stung as a tear leaked. She wiped it away and tried to think of a tactful way to end the call. She knew Randi was enjoying the venting process – Keeley too had felt a little better discussing the many, many questions she had with the police officers – but now she felt thoroughly depleted and ready for a break. The call had already gone on for nearly ten minutes and Keeley was desperate to take an ibuprofen before her headache got even worse.

"You're right, honey. I'm just grasping at straws," sighed Randi. Their conversation was surprisingly level-headed and Keeley felt like a heel for assuming Randi was anything other than a harmless post-middle-aged woman having a good time at a party. Having a few drinks and acting goofy wasn't a crime. Then, as if reading her mind, Randi finished the conversation with a comment about how she could use a stiff drink. Again, the nagging thought from before popped back into Keeley's head. A drink . . . The girl who had been poisoned. . . A cyanide cocktail. . . *And Then There Were None*! Agatha Christie's mystery novel from the late 1930's. The original title was derogatory and racist, but her bookstore housed a copy with the original title! A character died from cyanide poisoning. That's what had been eating at her, a cyanide cocktail. Another vivid image followed; and this time it wasn't Jess's arm dramatically being ripped off. Instead she imagined a beautiful stranger, choking to death on her poisoned beverage

Keeley willed herself to stop. She was so enthralled with literature that it sometimes consumed her. Her vivid imagination came from years of reading the rich written word of beloved authors, and was honed when she too began to write. Now it was as if the enthralling titles and plots and characters she once loved were tormenting her. Her heart nearly jumped out of her chest when the doorbell rang.

***

Randi Howard hung up the phone feeling a bit slighted when Jess's sister-in-law ended the call so abruptly. She sighed, depositing the phone on its cradle on her bedside table. Her newest boy toy, Sergio, had just left. He asked her for a drink, but she turned him down when the phone began to ring. Her husband was calling at all hours of the day now. She didn't know if he was on to her daytime habits or what, but she would be surprised if he cared. Their relationship was no love story; they were no Bob and Jess, not by a long shot. They played the game, with zealous flirting at charity balls and cocktail parties. It was a big fat game of charades.

After she painstakingly remade their marital bed, pillow upon pillow, sheets tightly tucked, she decided a martini would indeed do her well. She pulled a silk robe over her camisole and headed downstairs. She wondered how much longer she'd be able to pull off having lovers who were in their twenties. Her wealth alone could compensate for maybe twenty five years of her age. She was adding an olive to her drink when she heard a knock on the door. She left the untouched drink on the counter, wondering if Sergio was stupid enough to come running back for more. It would of course be flattering, but risky. It might mean she still had a few good miles on her speedometer, yet she wouldn't put it past her husband to hire a private investigator or something equally outlandish. When she peered through the peephole, she was actually a little disappointed it *wasn't* Sergio for more than one reason. Her enjoyment returned however when she saw how handsome the young police officer was as she gestured him inside.

"Well, hello. This is about Jess Travis, I assume?" she purred.

"Yes ma'am. I'm Officer Penske. Do you have a few minutes for me?" he asked, removing his hat.

"Please! Don't call me *ma'am.* And yes, I'll make time for *you.* Come in, come in." She ushered him into the large sitting room adjacent to the kitchen, stopping along the way to pick up her drink. "Can I offer you anything? I have plenty of non-alcoholic beverages, but they're not as much fun. Wouldn't you agree?"

"I'm fine, thank you," he stated, clearly looking a bit uncomfortable. "I just have a few quick routine questions to ask you which may assist in the investigation." He cleared his throat. "How long had you known Mrs. Travis?" He went on and on for what felt like more than a quick round of questions. Randi was growing bored with him despite his striking good looks. They could have so much more fun if he'd just stop talking. He asked her everything from where she was the day of the murder (ouch!) to what the two women discussed the last time they'd been together. After one martini and several unstiffled yawns – Sergio had worn her out – Randi was off the hook. Officer Penske finally stood and shook her hand, thanking her for her time. Walking him out, she was surprised to overhear the static-enhanced report coming across his walkie-talkie. Someone had said something about a second murder...

Chapter four

"Bob, please try the soup." Keeley was surprised at how sallow and drawn Bob's face looked after only a matter of days. Not exactly a small guy, Bob was built like a well-fed linebacker, muscular but not super lean. Jess was too good of a cook to have a scrawny husband, she'd often joke. She made all those down-home, stick-to-your-ribs kinds of meals. It seemed like whenever Keeley came over there was the inevitable side of potatoes de jour and rolls or biscuits. Keeley would have to remember to try and come down more often and do some cooking to keep her brother in good health. Of course as things stood, she couldn't imagine leaving him at all, let alone returning to cook him a ton of food. Would his appetite fully return? She doubted even that hers would after today's visit from the Drakesborough police. The officers who came today were much less tactful than Dean, refusing to sugarcoat details of Jess's murder, and displaying no discretion at all. It was awful. Bob looked like he might pass out for the duration of the visit, but the poor guy was hanging in there as well as ever. The body had been identified by Bob before Keeley had arrived, but the officer in charge felt the need to throw around several gory pictures, which he required Bob to "take a look at." The whole thing was so draining. Once they left, Keeley found a can of chicken broth and used the remaining veggies from the crisper drawer and the thawed package of chicken breasts in the fridge. While she thought he might actually be ready to eat, Keeley was having to force herself. But, she drained her mug because she knew she needed the sustenance. Bob, looking weary, took an obligatory sip. "It's good," he nearly whispered. "Thank you, Kee."

Keeley asked, "Bob, what . . . what are we going to do about the funeral?" Bob had been sidestepping the issue since the minute she first brought it up. She knew it wasn't because he didn't know whether or not Jess wanted a burial, cremation, or an opened casket. It was because if there was no funeral, it meant she wasn't really dead. She'd had the same syndrome when Mom and Dad died. Again though, she broached the topic, the soup suddenly weighing as heavily in her stomach as a Thanksgiving dinner. It was mostly because she had barely eaten since the ordeal began. She had consumed countless cups of cure-all tea and then only picked at a few snack items found in the cupboards, eating a handful of nuts here, a bite or two of a granola bar there.

"I like the idea of bringing her home to Fort Worth to be with her Grandmother," said Bob.

Jess was raised by one feisty southerner, whom she had lost just over one year ago. While Granny Auberdine was much older, Jess and Keeley had bonded further over losing their parental figures before they were ready.

"Okay. I'll set everything up. Did you want the ceremony to be made public? In Fort Worth, I mean? Or keep it just family and have a memorial back here?"

Bob looked defeated. His face pretty much read, *I don't care. I don't want to do this at all.* She realized she should not have begun an inquisition just yet. However, if they were going to be transporting the body, they needed to get the ball rolling. She did need the details, upsetting or not.

"I guess we'll just do us and Thomas and Janine. Judy Simmons, and Ben of course. I think her cousin in Dallas would want to attend." He sighed and gave a cursory tight-lipped smile. "Then once the dust settles we can organize something for Jess here at home."

"That sounds perfect." Keeley cringed at her word choice. There was nothing even remotely perfect about these plans. She stood, crossing toward the light switch panel on the wall. It had grown gloomy, the sun moving toward the other side of the house. "Bob, where does she keep her address book? I'll need it to get in touch with the others. And her cousin's name. I'll need that too."

"Her cousin's name is Georgina. Last name Auberdine. And Jess kept phone numbers, addresses and everything else in her rolodex at her office." Bob looked worried. He knew - she knew - that no one wanted to go to the office. Not yet.

She shook it off, making it appear as commonplace as heading to the market. "That's fine. I was thinking of picking up some fresh food anyway." *Not that anyone was eating.* "I'll swing by there. I'll call Detective Dean first to make sure someone can let me in." She wished things would stop being so awkward. She knew her brother better than anyone, but this was starting to feel like an awkward interview, practically. She walked up to him and hugged him with volcanic force. He hugged back. They both wept a little, but it felt good. They were both trying so hard to sidestep everything, including their raw and desperate emotion, that it wasn't good for either of them. It was time to get back to basics. They were going to persevere, and somehow that small moment felt like a tiny notch on the grieving scale. "I love you, Bob. We'll get through this. We'll do it for Jess."

Still half embracing, Bob smiled, genuinely this time. "Jess is looking down on us right now, thinking what blubbering fools we are, isn't she?" And then, they both laughed. In that fleeting moment, Keeley knew it would be okay. Not yet, but one day. She smiled and stood up, smoothing out her Capri pants. "I'll just put in a call and head out. I won't be long. Is there anything I should pick up . . . from the grocery store or . . . from Jess's office?"

"I think we're okay."

***

Twenty minutes later, Keeley pulled up to Jess's design shop. She parked right next to the police car that Dean promised her would be there. The officer saw her leave her car and head toward Auberdine Designs and promptly got out of his car. He asked if she was Miss Travis, then fumbled around in his pocket, presumably searching for the key. Keeley felt her head swim when she saw the yellow tape. The glass-paneled walls on each side of the door were covered in a plain white papering, to obstruct the passerby's view of the inside of the store. She steadied herself. This had to be done and she sure as hell wasn't going to make Bob do it. Jess's shop had turned into a bloody crime scene. That she had to acknowledge or she would faint. Of course Jess's body had been re-moved, but would the scene still be intact? Would they have cleaned it by now? Probably not.

"Miss Travis, please allow me to enter first and find the best route to the office." He had read her mind. And she was glad. She didn't want any more details to mentally pin to this scenario. She was already having enough trouble with the ghoulish imagery her mind kept conjuring up.

Seconds later the officer emerged and asked her to please follow him. He also had the foresight to tell her to keep her eyes down on the ground. She appreciated that he wasn't so jaded that he forgot what death looked like to a layman. She did as she was told and they were standing inside Jess's office. Keeley had only been in the office once. When they had the grand opening, she had stood exactly where she stood now, beside the massive oak desk. Jess had sauntered behind it, took a seat, leaned back and placed her high heeled feet right on that table. "This is a good look for me, isn't it?" she had asked from behind the desk. She was one proud business woman. This place meant so much to Jess. What would become of the business? What choice did Bob have though, really? She was suddenly self-conscious of the kind officer hovering next to her. He of course couldn't leave her alone in the office. It was a crime scene after all. She reminded herself why she was there and started eyeballing the large piece of furniture. A rolodex would most likely be on the desktop, but it didn't appear to be at first glance. Keeley looked down to see several oversized drawers and tried the one on the top right first. There it was. A good old fashioned rolodex like her mother once had. She reached in to pluck it out, and did a double take. In the drawer, next to the rolodex was a worn looking paperback copy of Stephen King's *IT*.

***

Keeley slipped into her bedroom after finding Bob asleep on the couch. She knew he probably had gotten little if any sleep since the murder. This would do him some good. Once alone in her quarters, she sneaked out the copy of *IT* from her purse. She knew she wasn't supposed to take anything from the office with the ongoing investigation, but she couldn't help herself. Better, she couldn't control herself. It was a compulsory, stupid move; but once it was in her grasp, she slipped it straight into her purse, unbeknownst to the officer. She second guessed keeping the book in her ownership, but by then it was too late. She was just so taken aback to find the book there in the first place, considering how coincidental it was. She had just compared Jess's horrible attack to the character in the book! She had no choice but to grab it and deal with the possibility of having stolen crime scene evidence later.

It just didn't add up. Keeley tapped the book against her opened palm. Jess was *terrified* of scary things. She would sometimes watch toned-down, aired-on-television versions of slasher films, but only in the sanctity of daylight. And then she'd be paying for it for the next week or so. Bob would tease her and then console her. *He acted like a father figure to Jess as well sometimes.* Jess didn't mind it though. She ate it up in fact. But would Jess really be reading one of the top ten creepiest novels of all time? And while she was alone? At work? Jess worked while she was at the office. Jess didn't just hang around engaging in hobbies. As much as she adored Auberdine Designs, she adored Bob and her play time more. She worked her butt off during office hours, but when the clock struck closing time, Jess was sure to be heading home.

Keeley sat a moment, on the bed, deep in thought. She wasn't sure what she was after, or why she cared enough about it to sneak something from a murder victim's drawer, probably violating several laws at that, but . . . it just seemed too coincidental, way too coincidental. She lay back on the quilted bed, arranging the extravagant supply of pillows so that she was almost lying down. She opened the novel to page one and began to read.

The terror, which would not end for another twenty-eight years - if it ever did end - began, so far as I know or can tell, with a boat made from a sheet of newspaper floating down a gutter swollen with rain. Keeley had goose bumps, as she envisioned the whole scene. The book had terrified even *her*, and she was a true thriller novel fanatic. *The boat bobbed, listed, righted itself again, dived bravely through treacherous whirlpools, and continued on its way down Witcham Street toward the traffic light . . .* Keeley's eyes zoomed ahead. Yellow eyes shining from the gutter, a sympathetic clown holding a brightly-colored bunch of balloons, a little boy cruelly and morbidly attacked in bloodlust. *No way in hell Jess would have had anything to do with this book!* Keeley flipped the top right corner of the novel, looking for a dog-eared page or any clue as to whether or not Jess might actually have worked up the nerve to read this book. She probably borrowed it from an employee at the shop, then realized what she had gotten herself into and shoved it in the drawer. As simple as that. Mystery solved. Keeley tossed the book aside. Then she sat up. Jess probably cracked the cover, deduced the plot, deemed it too scary, then shucked it away. Then, she just so happened to meet the same gory fate that appears within the first few pages of that very book! How often do you hear of an arm being torn clear off? Head spinning,

Keeley curled up near the nest of pillows and fell straight to sleep.

***

Detective Dean had all but turned the residence of Harper Middleton upside down and there was not one iota of information indicating who poisoned her. Her boyfriend and about one hundred party goers from the night before had already been questioned, along with friends, coworkers and family members. No leads whatsoever, which made Dean begin to question whether or not the Jess Travis murder was, after all, related. Two women murdered within a night of each other, both were on the Art Association member list and both had everything to lose. Other than those two criteria, they were as different as night as day. Of course they were from two very different age groups and social circles (minus the art interest). They looked different – hair color, body type, style – and came from different backgrounds and lived in neighborhoods about an hour apart, albeit in the same county. Poisoning someone and slicing off an extremity . . . well, rarely did you hear of even the worst sociopath having such a varied repertoire. They typically liked to stick to the same weapon – guns, knives, their hands. It wasn't as cut and dry as just murdering in general, no matter how you sliced it, so to speak. He stepped over the customary yellow tape bisecting the master bedroom and bathroom from the rest of the condominium. Her bedroom fit the bill of a young woman, semi-fresh out of college who lived on her own. The house was modestly decorated. She had some funds, but it was clear that the furnishings and adornments were Bed Bath & Beyond versus Pottery Barn. The place looked just nice enough for a responsible adult, with a young and modern twist to it. The bathroom counter was strewn with beauty products and the closet was loaded with shoes and clothes. Pictures on footed frames covered nearly every flat surface. Most of them were of Harper and her boyfriend, others were groups of beautiful young ladies, including Harper, and one was a shot of either her parents or grandparents. It was tough to tell. She had a smattering of fashion and decorating magazines across the coffee table in the living space and a small wall unit with a few books and photo albums.

Dean settled in a yellowish beige loveseat and flipped through one of the albums. Poor Harper had it all, one might say. Her boyfriend Carson was beyond devastated. Dean wouldn't have any reason to speak with him again about the murder. There was no way it was him. Poor kid was inconsolable. He was the only one who could be reached from her cellular phone's contact list. Carson was listed under ICE or in case of emergency. This had turned out to be one hell of an emergency. *A young girl's throat had all but been turned inside out, dammit.* Dean sighed loudly and replaced the photo album back where it belonged on the shelf. He'd seen enough this visit. There was nothing more he could do at this very second to save Harper's soul. So he did a last loop through the condo, as he always did, hoping he might leave with a final thought. Fodder for his customary middle of the night insomnia. He hated waking up in the night. It was haunting. His mind punished him for a long career in the business. But more than a few cases had reached a head after one of his midnight reflection sessions. He did a once over of the kitchen, noticing for the first time a bag of Funions cinched closed with a chip clip. How he loved those disgusting things. His wife hated them. Really *hated* them. She actually forbade them in the house because she said they stunk so bad you couldn't brush the smell out of your mouth or wash the stench off your fingers. So he stopped eating Funions. But maybe it was time to bring back an old habit. Maybe she hated the Funions so much because that way she wouldn't dwell on his hellacious job. Well he no longer drank, no longer gambled and no longer smoked cigars. If he wanted to eat a damn Funion, then Funions he shall have.

Dean made a firm decision to swing by a convenience store on the way home. *Funions all the way!* He was just leaving the walk-in closet again when he noticed something on the small vanity that he had missed the first time, much like the damn Funions. It was another book, similar to the worn trade books lining the small shelf in the other room. It didn't take a detective to deduce that she was probably currently reading this book and that was why it wasn't on the shelf, stacked away with all the others. It wasn't the book itself that caught his eye, but the title.

How do you like that? he thought, cringing. *Now there's a revolting little dose of racism.* The book had quite a title. *Wow.* Not sure why; perhaps just to show one of his colleagues, or maybe it would actually mean something, but he grabbed the book and slipped it inside of one of the clear evidence bags. Taking a second glance at the bagged book, he noted the author. It was Agatha Christie, a well-known author, whose books his aunt used to read all the time. He chalked it up to just a generational thing and pocketed the book anyway. No harm in keeping it around, now that it was bagged. Sadly, it was the only piece of evidence they had, minus the shattered martini glass.

Chapter five

Keeley knew she needed to eventually get back to the store at some point, if even for a moment. Summer, her dedicated store manager, was totally reliable and trustworthy. But she was a busy Ph.D. student and, reliable or not, the store was not her responsibility *and* she had a life of her own. Keeley was beginning to feel a bit guilty about the fact that Summer would be expected to basically run the place on her own. Ideally Keeley could hire another student to balance the weight of their ever increasing clientele, since her book hit best seller status, but that would also involve a major time commitment. She felt like she'd be betraying Bob somehow. Currently, there was only one other employee, in addition to Summer, and Regina was a mother of three kids with a limited schedule as it was. She could only do mornings during school hours and filled in on the occasional Saturday or Sunday evening shift. Ben had certainly offered to help out enough, but he had his own rigorous career to focus on and was preparing to relocate to another country.

Last night she had toyed with the idea of temporarily shortening the store's hours of operation. She was hoping that after a week she might be able to have most things squared away and might have more flexibility in regards to manning the store. The funeral plans would already be in full swing and Bob might decide he'd be ready to begin the healing process. If she shortened the hours, then Regina could open and stay until two o'clock and then Summer could come in and close down shop by six o'clock (instead of the standard eight o'clock). Then again, she didn't know if that would be the greatest idea at the high point of her opportunity to really make it big as an author and the owner of an up and coming book store. But what choice did she have, really? It was Bob or the store and she knew what the answer was before she asked herself. Family always came first. She would need to have a quick discussion with the other ladies. If things went well, perhaps Summer would volunteer to conduct a few interviews during her shift, so long as Keeley set everything up. If Regina and Summer could finish up the week, while training a new clerk, then Keeley would have flexibility when it came to traveling to Fort Worth and planning the memorial here at home for Jess. She'd then have more time to dedicate to Bob on his road to recovery. *It just might work.* Keeley felt a sense of relief. Plus, she had actually had a pretty good night's sleep last night, allowing herself to let go of the wild notions of Jess and the copy of *IT*, which was now stashed in *Keeley's* drawer.

She had just started making pancakes with pumpkin pie spice, cinnamon and allspice. Bob liked them. He'd ordered them on a trip to San Francisco her family had taken to celebrate her high school graduation and acceptance to the college of her dreams. On the menu, the seasonal breakfast dish had some corny name, like Falling for flapjacks or something. She wished that he might at least eat a few bites of the cakes today. She was hopeful, and thereby prompted to make them, when she came into the kitchen this morning and saw the empty carton of milk and the plate covered in telltale sandwich remains. He was still sleeping, that she knew. She had tiptoed upstairs and leaned her ear against the closed door and had heard snoring, earlier, while the griddle was heating up. Snoring was something that she didn't hear the night before, also making her hopeful that perhaps he was at least getting some actual sleep. So down she came to finish making a delicious breakfast that might once again lure him to eat.

Keeley tore a corner off the first pancake to test her spicing skills. It was delicious. After making enough of them to feed a small country, she covered them, minus the one she had been picking at, with a cloth napkin and set them inside the microwave. They'd be ready, and hopefully still semi-warm, when Bob woke up this morning. Whatever was not eaten could be stored in the freezer for a ready-to-eat breakfast over the next couple of days. She let out a breath. Finally. Keeley was starting to feel a little bit more like herself and perhaps when she had to go to the bookstore, later today, that would help too. It wouldn't hurt to get Bob to try something from his normal routine, but she knew it was too soon for him. She wasn't the one married to Jess. Keeley loved her like a sister, but again, it was almost like she was mourning the life her brother would have had, versus mourning the loss of Jess. *More guilt.* Keeley decided she would bring a tray of breakfast and a cup of coffee, not tea, up to Bob's room. It was nearing nine-thirty and he never slept this late. She would broach the topic of heading back to the store today. Then again, if he was sleeping this late, it was because he needed it desperately. She decided to head upstairs one more time before barging in on him with a plate of breakfast he probably didn't even want.

Keeley crept on tiptoes, like she remembered doing many a Christmas morning as a little girl when she was trying to sneak a peek at Santa Clause. Once she reached the landing, she crossed over to the guest room where Bob was sleeping and listened at the door. She heard nothing. Total silence. Then she jumped a little when the shower came on in the bathroom. She collected herself and decided to say good morning. She cleared her throat and cracked the door opened about two inches.

"Bob?"

"Hey Sis, just about to hop in for a quick shower. Be right down." He sounded less distraught than lately. That was for sure.

"Okay. I have food if you're hungry. See you soon," she called loudly. She softly closed the door, not waiting for a response. She didn't expect him to heal overnight. This would be a lifelong struggle, but she couldn't help but feeling that things were at least moving in the right direction. She had been a student when Dad died. She was about to begin grueling mid-terms at the time and she had told herself that she couldn't do it. She couldn't possibly focus on her studies in her condition, but she also felt wrong about thinking of anything except Dad. Again with the guilt. A psychiatrist would have a field day with her. It was Bob and Mom who had told her she had to continue with her studies. It was important, she had worked so hard during the semester, Dad wouldn't have wanted her to throw away her budding future, etc. Begrudgingly, she had listened to them. Of course she never stopped mourning her dad and her final exams left something to be desired, but she had persevered; and quite frankly, it was much easier on her that she had attempted, though coerced, normal life. Routines, patterns . . . what keeps the mind stable. Soon Bob would come down and she'd mention that she needed to head to the store at some point, optimally today. Although he'd decline, she'd offer to bring him along to enjoy the ride and the change of scenery. Of course she'd be back before dark, and he might even enjoy the solitude; but he had plenty of that with the current trips upstairs. She was trying to find a balance of spending time with him (moping together) and giving him space (moping separate). Today though, she decided that her moping would be coming to an end. She would be there for him: a good example of a whole, healthy, functioning person. She would be there for him and she would be ready for when it was his time to heal. That was the best thing she could do for him; stay level-headed and stay prepared for whatever mood he was in. If he needed time, she'd give him time. She would be there as his still shaky, but solid, shoulder to cry on.

"Morning. What do I smell?" asked a strangely chipper Bob, entering the kitchen.

Keeley couldn't hide her surprise. "It's pancakes. I tried to copy the ones you liked so much in San Fran. Are you feeling alright?" she asked, reaching for the tray in the microwave.

"Yes. Well, under the circumstances I am. I finally ate and I finally slept. I won't get over Jess, ever. But I just know it's not the way she'd want me to behave. I'll take it one minute at a time, Kee, but right now I'm okay." *Wow!* This was certainly not what Keeley was expecting. She liked his positive attitude, but it was almost eerie. It seemed like he was laying it on too thick. Possibly the stage of denial?

"Well . . . great then. I'm happy for you." She hugged her brother quickly and decided to bring up heading back home while his mood was so pleasant. "I was thinking I might try and tie up a few loose ends at the shop. Be there two hours tops."

"Sure. Of course." Bob sat at the bar stool against the nook.

"Any chance you want to take a ride with me? We could have a small bite to eat, get some fresh air?" His face was unreadable. "But of course I understand if you would rather lay low," she went on, "and take a rain check."

"I don't know, Kee. I just think I'm not quite ready. Plus, you know I'm not one to give a hoot about what other people think, but I'll bet the people around here are just waiting in the wings for me to emerge. I'll wait. I'll wait and I'll be *fine* here. Don't rush." She studied his face. It was worn and his eyes looked like fresh tears could still brew at any moment. She felt like a clod. It had been less than forty-eight hours. *Stupid.* Of course, though it was important to ask. To give the choice . . . to give him the option to deal with whatever choices, emotions and anything else he might be experiencing. And she did, and that did not make her an insensitive sister. *Then why do I feel so lame?* she thought.

She stood and kissed his cheek. "Then I'll throw myself together so I can be back here soon. Because I want to. Love you." Bob attempted a smile, and Keeley went off to the bedroom to get ready.

Chapter six

The cabin was a good forty miles or so outside of her hometown, Drakesborough. She loved spending time here; but, if it weren't for the family tradition, she probably wouldn't be picking up everything and heading off to the woods just when things were starting to get so busy for her and her family. Tranise Gray was a full-time mother and a part-time model. She had been modeling since the ripe age of five and spent the height of her career, during her late teens and early twenties, in Milan. She had continued with steady modeling after getting married, then sporadically throughout two births. She was now "forty-something" and the gigs were few and far between, but nonetheless, there were gigs. She was very satisfied with how her life was going. She was even looked upon as a local celebrity by her affectionate, tight-knit community. She was currently the prime candidate for a new designer's "it" girl, so the diet began along with squeezing in the early morning workouts. The girls had already adjusted to the school routine, but with fall around the corner, and Tranise had foolishly volunteered to be "the cookie mom" again as well as the unofficial class parent for her oldest, things were slowly adding up.

So today, while Jeff took the girls to the baseball game, Tranise was setting up the cabin – clearing the spider webs and dust, running the water to flush the pipes, stocking fresh linens, and adding touches of home. The house would be ready for them when they came up next Thursday after school got out. She actually really enjoyed this part. She loved being there. She loved the outdoors, the fresh air, the idea of getting away from it all, and she especially loved the memories. Her grandfather had built the cabin, with the help of her own father and so the tradition began. She shared the cabin with her brother and his family and her parents still came down once in a blue moon, but they never came alone since setting up was becoming difficult for them as they grew older. The cabin was an actual log cabin, with wooden floors and built in wooden fixtures, all at the hands of her hard-working granddaddy. She smiled as she pulled up to the cabin. It was a very impressive structure. Whenever she told people about the cabin that Grandpa built, they assumed it was a modest little shed or something. Not even close. It was quite large: two-stories, three bedrooms, a full kitchen, two bathrooms and a family room. There was a wraparound deck that spanned the entire cabin. It was gorgeous. And perhaps her favorite parts were the blue and white checkered drapes her grandmother had sewn, adorning all the windows. It was quaint, yet chic, and Tranise was very proud of it.

She got out of the car and grabbed two handle bags from the backseat. She walked up the path and braced herself for the musty odor that was unavoidable after months of having been vacant. She was glad she had remembered to pack a few of her favorite candles. The door creaked opened and she was pleased to see the place. It didn't smell too stuffy, actually. Tranise parted the curtains in the family room and kitchen, allowing some of the mid-day sun to seep in. That reminded her she needed to power up. *Let there be light!* She set down the bags and her purse on the leather loveseat, and left the cabin to go around back to turn on the power switch. This was the part she always had trouble with. More times than not, Jeff ended up dealing with the stubborn old switch. If she couldn't manage it, she'd just have to beat the wavering sunlight and wait until Thursday for Jeff to do it.

She stood beside the box, noting that she was standing on an ant hill. She scooted to the side while flipping the switch to open the box. The master switch looked more rusted than in times past. *Come on old guy. Help me out, will you?* she pleaded. She pushed with all her might, feeling as if the switch might snap off before it would ever budge. She tried futilely a few more times. Her fingers began to burn. Suddenly she began to wonder if she was wasting her time on this. The cabin was certainly well lit enough to do a few household chores in, especially if she didn't waste any more time on this. All things considered, it would be like an adventure. A game – "Beat the Clock," or "The Real Housewives of Yore." She smiled at the notion and grabbed the last few bags before entering the cabin again. As soon as she crossed the threshold she knew something was awry. She stooped to deposit the bags on the wooden floor. She tilted her head and took a few steps forward. She was tempted to call out, "Hello?" But that would be stupid. Who would be here? Then she heard it. The floorboards over her head began to creak. She stopped. There was nobody here. There couldn't be. There were no other cars parked nearby. And you couldn't just walk here from the main road. It was really off the beaten path. Maybe there was an animal trapped in the cabin, but how would it have gotten in here in the first place?

Her first thought was to get the hell out of there. She scanned the pile of bags she had deposited on the floor. None of this was anything that couldn't wait til Thursday. She began retreating, then stopped herself. She had driven all the way out here, and nothing pleased her more than seeing the delight on her kids faces when they arrived and saw the cabin with all the personal touches of home. She even had planned to prepare a goodie basket for the girls this time. She bought books of mazes and word searches and paper dolls for Malia. Nonpareils and chocolate peanuts, and a travel-sized game of checkers. She had to push through. The only reason she was worrying was because the house wasn't exactly brimming with light. It was an irrational fear and she'd have to get over it. She made her way over to the stairs, carrying a garbage bag full of bed sheets and light blankets. She would make up the bedrooms first, then go downstairs where the light would be stronger. She would only stay as long as she felt comfortable. There. She knew she could do it. She was a sensible human being. She clenched the top of the bag, then hugged the bottom of the overstuffed bag with her other arm. *A soft, cuddly shield of protection. Get over it.* She was half way up the steps when she heard another creaking sound, only this time it seemed to be coming from downstairs. *Okay, that just proves it's your imagination. Houses creak. Especially old ones that have no working electricity while you're by yourself.* She continued up the stairs, then let out a deep breath when she reached the top. Master to the left, girls' rooms to the right. She went to the left, thinking that wing of the house would lose sunlight faster. With fear-driven speed, she made the bed in less than two minutes, then scurried down the hall. She was more afraid than she thought she would be. She was turning her head at every juncture, her heart booming within her chest. Arriving in the master room, she tossed the bag of bed linens onto the large footboard at the end of the bed.

"Tranise," someone whispered. She screamed. When she turned, there was no one there. "Tra-ni-se," sang the menacing soft voice. She positioned herself in the corner of the room, desperately whimpering. Then, the intruder made himself visible, emerging from the small hallway leading toward the bathroom. He wore a black ski mask and a coat. Tranise was literally paralyzed with fear. He was holding a large butcher knife and although she couldn't take her eyes off the gleaming, razor-sharp blade, she couldn't help but notice something in his other hand. A paperback copy of the legendary Edgar Allen Poe novel, *A Tell-tale Heart.*

***

Tranise was bound and gagged, lying in the corner of the family room, which was now almost completely shrouded in shade. When she saw her masked assailant meticulously sawing away at the wooden floor, she knew his exact game plan. Just like in the renowned novel, he was planning to dismember her and bury her remains under the floor boards. In the book, the killer was so insane and stricken with fear after stashing the body under the floor boards, that when a police officer came to inquire about the missing person, the killer believed the murder victim's heart beat could be heard through the reassembled floor. Tranise was more than familiar with the horror novel, and in fact owned a copy herself. It had terrified her when she read it in fifth grade and again as an adult.

When Tranise first put two and two together, she fought. She fought hard and ended up with an ostrich egg-sized lump on her forehead. She swore her skull had been cracked. The pain left her beyond moaning and writhing and she was very surprised that the fight in her had died so quickly. But she had so much to fight *for*. Her whole life, she had flourished under pressure. All those pageants and scholarships and her career, even her babies. She had struggled so long to have those babies. Tears ran down her face, her throat retching with hard, violent sobs.

"Shut up," he uttered as matter of factly as if he were commenting on the weather. She did. She wasn't exactly sure what the plan was, but she knew there had to be one. She wanted to fight. She would fight.

She had exhausted the possibility of loosening her bound feet. Her toes were raw from trying that over and over. Thank God she had the time he was using to cut up the floor as a chance to make an actual plan. She thought for sure he would have used the knife by now. Instead it sat, gleaming beside him. He was a monster. He was desecrating her family's cabin, while she sat, waiting to die. He was a total nut job. He looked so spooky, sawing away wearing that mask that she could barely force herself to look at him. But she needed to look at him. She had to gauge her time.

***

Keeley was going eighty miles per hour on the highway when she glanced down. She immediately slowed herself down. The last thing anyone needed right now was for her to get into an accident or even to be pulled over for speeding, even. Bob was going to be fine. Keeley was simply making up for lost time because there had been major construction on the Number 5 freeway. It was like a parking lot for nearly forty minutes what with the freeway being condensed down to one lane and all the lookie-loos who needed their fill of excitement. But luckily she was nearly ten minutes away from the store now. She would be in and out and back on the road again soon enough.

When she turned onto Maple Oak, the beginning of the revamped shopping district, she noticed it was awfully crowded for a lazy Sunday. There was a new wine bar opening up, but she didn't know whether or not that was this weekend. It was amazing how quickly she had fallen out of her daily routine. It felt like weeks instead of days since she'd been here. Keeley finally parked on the street a block and a half away from the shop. Life went on for everyone else. The quaint community was lively. Couples sipping lattes were shopping for antiques, trendy overpriced apparel, home decor, and . . . well, hopefully books. Keeley couldn't help but smile when she pushed open the door to her charming little establishment. It was a definite comfort to her. The smell was warm and rustic – *leather-bound books meets reheated bakery muffins*, she thought. She always hoped her customers felt just as welcome as she did when they entered.

"Hi, Boss," joked Summer, who smiled, then stopped herself. *She forgot*, realized Keeley. "How's your brother doing?" Summer asked, sheepishly.

"He's as you'd expect, but he's . . . fine. Thanks for asking." Keeley went behind the counter and washed her hands, while Summer engaged her in shop talk. After helping herself to a warm muffin, Keeley scooted a chair next to where Summer stood behind the register.

"I'm planning to hire someone else to help out, Summer. Then you can get back to your normal schedule."

"Keeley, don't do that. It won't be long before you're back and I swear I'm fine. I sit back here and study when the store's empty. Granted, I should be dusting and straightening," giggled bubbly Summer. "But seriously, I'm okay with working more hours. My most demanding course this semester is an on-line course with open hours of attendance. My other classes are in the morning during Regina's shift. If you hire someone else, that's money you could just be paying me, your first and favorite employee." Summer flashed a playfully coy look Keeley's way.

"Summer . . . if you really want the hours than this is a no brainer. But I thought you had night classes," said Keeley, biting into her muffin.

"I was just signed up for study groups and tutoring an underclassmen. If it comes down to it I can ask Regina to do a night or two. She probably wants to get away from the kids here and there. Besides, if it's cool with you, I can have classmates meet up here. It might drum up business, not that you need much help there. We've definitely expanded the clientele. So . . . what do ya say?"

Keeley looked at her friend. Increasing Summer's hours was definitely the best route to take. Keeley wouldn't have to go through the screening and hiring process, or end up having to hire someone that might not be trustworthy. Summer had an amazing work ethic and an unmatchable loyalty to the store and: Keeley. In the end, nothing else made sense. This would be a lot less work for her and one less reason to be away from Bob more than she had to be. She stood up. "If you're sure, Summer. And if things change, don't hesitate to tell me." She gave Summer Bob's home number, then decided to browse the store before happily heading back home earlier than planned.

She climbed the enormous staircase, never losing that sense of awe she had the first time. It was so beautiful and reminiscent of something you might see in an old Hollywood mansion. Keeley perused the shelves, making sure things were in order, as well as searching for a bit of reading material. In her haste she hadn't thought to bring a book. Of course, and she knew it would help her sleep at night if she had something to rein in her brain at bedtime. She crossed over to the used book selection, after finding the new section in perfect order; Summer underestimated her own handiwork. The used section was to the left of the staircase and housed a ladder that moved along the wall sized set of shelves. It was actually her favorite part of the entire store, minus the grand staircase. Not only did she love the look of the expansive bookshelves and the moving ladder, but she loved used books. She loved the history, the idea of reading something that someone else had owned at some point. Plus, in her opinion, you couldn't beat the classics. Not necessarily turn of the century classics, but books written forty plus years ago. Keeley honestly hadn't found any "new" books to catch her eye in a few years. So she combed the familiar titles, pausing at her standard favorites. *It might be nice to have a familiar read right now,* she thought. *Something I don't have to work too hard for.* The thought alone of an old favorite already seemed to calm her nerves. She began a small pile on one of the small tables positioned in the used wing. Her first pick was something she'd read half a dozen times, but it had been a while. She figured she was due, so she plucked *The Cradle Will Fall,* by Mary Higgins Clark, and then added Harris's *The Silence of the Lambs,* before remembering the recent bout of nightmares and putting it back on the shelf. She couldn't resist a couple of her favorite James Patterson novels. She felt like a kid in a candy store. Fred Mustard Stewart's *The Mephisto Waltz* . . . then she saw it. She saw Agatha Christie's novel, with its original offensive and derogatory title, right there on display. The new title, *And Then There Were None*, was much more becoming. She added that to her stack too before heading to the checkout counter. Not sure why she wanted to again relive the poisoned cocktail scene, she decided to read that one first. Tonight, once Bob had gone to bed, she wanted to do a little research.

***

Tranise was in excruciating pain by the time the floor was excavated to her attacker's liking. Her extremities were well beyond numb since the ropes were so tight, and her head felt like it was split down the middle. She was certain she was not getting enough air through the gag in her mouth.

The man turned and stood. His mask curled near the exterior, signifying to her that he was smiling underneath it. She gagged at the sight. He walked over toward her after first stooping to grab the knife. He reached with his free hand and pulled the gag from her mouth. "Don't make a sound," he instructed. Then he moved the hatchet-sized knife in her direction. She suppressed a yelp when she realized he was simply going to slice off the bindings from around her wrists. There was no doubt about the fact that he was going to kill her; it just wasn't going to happen this second. If it weren't for the blatant display of the Poe book, she would have figured he was here to rob her, or even rape her. The floor boards might have ultimately tipped her off that he had bigger plans, but still . . . she was thankful for the warning he didn't seem to realize he had given her.

As soon as he slit the ankle binding, Tranise jolted her foot into his flank with all her might. It was with such force that she surprised herself. He lost his footing and tipped to his side. Quickly she jumped up, her feet and legs numb. She shoved over the small tiered shelf that stood against the wall on her way to the door. She reached down and grabbed her purse by the long strap and began fidgeting in the front pocket for her keys. He was less than two steps behind her and she would need more than that to make it to the safety of her car. She found the keys as she tumbled out the front door of the cabin into the lazy late afternoon. In a last desperate attempt to save herself, Tranise gripped her oversized purse where the straps met the purse itself, swung her arm back to her right, and turned, literally knocking the guy off his feet for a second time. She jumped into her Mercedes SUV, slammed and locked the door and fishtailed out of there.

Chapter seven

Keeley pulled up outside of the house at a quarter past four. The air had a chill and the sun was on its way out, but it was before dark, like she had promised. Of course Bob didn't care whether it was dark out or not. He even told her not to rush. *She* was the one with the sudden phobia of night. She grabbed her handle bag of scary books off the passenger seat and decided maybe the genre *was* a bit inappropriate. Suddenly she was acting like a kid who just saw their first horror flick, for Pete's sake. Keeley slammed the car door, then manned the alarm. She stopped beside the car. Something felt off. The air was still, but some fallen leaves danced in the late day shadows accumulating by the side of the house. "Oh my God!" Keeley yelled when the neighbor's cat unexpectedly leapt out of the shrubbery. Keeley steadied herself, then laughed. Clearly, she was on edge. She glanced at her bag of books and wondered if it was such a hot idea to read them, let alone at bedtime. She heard the lock click, then Bob opened the door, solemn as ever.

"Keeley, I hoped that was you. Come in."

She felt immense guilt pour over her. He *hoped* it was her. He must have *needed* her and she wasn't there for him. How stupid to leave him all alone. Her guilt turned to genuine concern when she saw the frantic look on his face. He led her by the hand toward the couch. His hands were shaking.

"There was another victim!" He looked delirious. Keeley wondered for a minute if he was having some sort of grief-induced uncertainty. Maybe he had only *now* allowed himself to acknowledge the recent poisoning of the young girl. But that notion left quicker than it came when he went on.

"Another woman who lives here in Drakesborough. She's also a very prominent woman. A former model and according to Detective Dean, a client of Jess's several years back. Something's going on here, Kee," his voice trailed up at the end. She began feeding off Bob's fear. She had never seen him like this. He looked terrified, but continued. "This woman, Tranise something . . . she got away from him. She saw the killer. He was wearing a mask."

Tears trailed Bob's cheeks. Keeley's mind went into overdrive. *Jess truly was the victim of a serial murder? Why the hell did they have to tell Bob her killer was wearing a mask? He's going to worry even more about what Jess went through! And what about the fact that both women who were killed shared their murder scenes with famous works of fiction? It wasn't a coincidence? And the copy of* It *that she stole from Jess's office drawer . . .*

"Okay, Bob, just relax. I'm here for you." His brow was slick with sweat and he looked like he might actually explode with emotion. "Tell me exactly what Dean said."

"It was awful, Keeley." All of a sudden she noted the glass of hard liquor on ice that sat beside him on the end table. "Dean says that Tranise believes he was trying to duplicate a famous murder scene. One from Edgar Allen Poe."

Keeley went pale. She just sat, unable to say a word; unable to let any of it register. Her hair-brained theory had been correct. She knew what she had to do.

Bob went on: "I think it might have been a short story. Anyway," he paused to take a sip of his drink, "he had her tied up! And she waited while he hollowed out the floor of her family's vacation cabin. He had a knife, but somehow she was able to fight him."

They both knew what Bob was thinking. Jess hadn't won the fight. Knowing her she put up a good one, but in the end it wasn't good enough. This woman had gotten away though, and she would help to nail the killer.

"I found something in her drawer, Bob."

"What do you mean?"

"I found a book in Jess's office drawer. Another horror novel, and . . . a scene in the book I found . . . well, it rings true in Jess's situation. And I took the book from the desk while the officer wasn't looking." She cringed, studying Bob's face for his take on her bizarre rant. Would he be scared? Angry?

"What book?" he asked, numb, staring into space.

"*It*. By Stephen King." Keeley gulped, hoping Bob wasn't familiar with the cult classic's gore.

"I've only heard of it. Did they, the character I mean, have something happen to their arm?" He looked pale.

Yeah, their arm was ripped clean off, by a chameleon-like monster, brought to fruition by human fear.

"Yes," was all she said. There was no reason to elaborate. Keeley was struggling with the flood of emotion. There was a killer out there, murdering unsuspecting, prominent women, and they were using famous works of literature as their inspiration. She stood and headed to the kitchen on autopilot. If there was ever a time she needed tea to "cure all," it was now. As she left the room she heard Bob call out that she ought to let Detective Dean know what she had found.

***

After getting off the phone with Dean, Keeley was ready for bed. It was only a little after six o'clock, but she was spent. The day had been so emotionally draining. She and Bob had concluded that Jess was part of a serial slaying, with a gimmick no less; Keeley was probably considered a suspect after telling Dean how she was not only privy to the killer's M.O., but that she had stolen evidence from Jess's crime scene; and now she was scheduled to meet with Dean and the escaped victim, Tranise Gray. Dean told her she could be his right hand gal on this because of her literary expertise and all. She was pretty sure she sealed the deal when she announced the breakthrough about Harper Middleton's murder also being borrowed from a famous novel. *Perfect.* Just what she was hoping for. A prime seat on her sister-in-laws murder case. As if things could get any worse in terms of parading Jess's murder through the paparazzi . . .

***

They had finished off the chicken soup for dinner and passively watched Wheel of Fortune. The silver lining in the update was that Bob seemed distracted from Jess's death, even though it was by the bigger picture of Jess's death. He sipped soup and stared into space. "Did you know? I mean were you pretty sure about what was going on when you grabbed the book from her desk?"

"I thought it was a real coincidence, but I never thought it would turn out like this." Bob had also told her how Dean had found the Agatha Christie book at the scene of Harper's murder. "I guess I wondered enough to take the book, but at that point I just thought it was just some morbid curiosity. I . . . didn't put two and two together until you told me about Tranise. Even then, I still didn't fully grasp it. Now I have. I'm glad Dean is asking me to help. At first I wasn't. I mean, I want to help in any way I can, but it . . . I have my Master's in literature, I am the most avid reader I know and stocking and running the store will make me an invaluable resource if I don't say so myself. I know everything there is to know about alternate titles, alternate endings and countless ways to kill off a character. I think I can actually help here, Bob. I'd be in my element."

"Then by all means, go get 'em, girl."

Chapter eight

Detective Dean didn't need his alarm this morning. He'd been up half the night going over the bizarre murders and what the connection could be to the choice of victims. The idea of recreating fictional murders was one thing. The perp was obviously out for notoriety and fame, which of course he would receive. The case would be sensationalized, the perverse community would gossip over which book *and which victim* will be dramatically played out next. The whole thing was about to explode and they had nothing to go on, nothing but a few old paperbacks and a librarian turned detective. Dean was happy to have her along – he was the one who asked Keeley to help, but a criminologist at least would have been a little more appropriate. Still, with budgets and red tape, Keeley would have to do the trick.

Finally, Dean rolled out of bed and started his morning routine. Coffee, coffee, coffee. He made a piece of toast to go with his coffee, and was eating it slowly at one of the center island barstools in the kitchen, still deep in thought, when his teenaged daughter came up behind him.

"Morning!" she chirped.

He turned and saw her standing there in her cheer uniform, looking more like a woman than his little girl. *Where did the time go?* She was beautiful. Same baby face, though. She still had a couple years before she'd be going off into the world. He forced a hug on her and told her to be good and stay safe. His constant parting words for her. "Daddy, I'm just going to school," she rolled her eyes.

"Then be extra careful," he teased. "That place is loaded with danger. Boys, peer pressure, bad kids . . . should I go on?"

"Please don't!" She grabbed a brown paper bag from the fridge. "Besides, I'm always careful. And all those boys you worry about . . . they've all met *you*, ensuring that I will probably spend my whole remaining high school existence alone!" She tossed her sweater over her shoulder and winked on the way out.

"I'm glad those teenaged heathens are scared of me. One for the good guys!" he yelled out, jokingly behind her.

In her wake came his wife, Terry, wearing a robe and slippers. "Who are you preaching to now?" She poured herself a cup of coffee.

"Zoey just left. And she left *damn* early too," he said glancing at his watch.

"She likes getting there early. She studies."

"Yeah, she *studies*. That reminds me – I've got some cliff-side property for sale that you might be interested in."

"Very funny! But I'm not the gullible one. You're the one that just let her walk out the door and hop in Ryan Walton's convertible." Terry gestured toward the window where a convertible Mustang could be seen squealing away from the curb.

Dean was showered, dressed and ready to go fifteen minutes later. If he had his way he'd be pulling up to Palisades High to nail Ryan Walton for speeding and thinking who knows what about his little girl. Instead he was heading toward the home of Tranise Gray. This would hopefully be as easy as it was in the movies. Someone had escaped the throngs of a lunatic and would then be able to tell you exactly where to find them. But things were never like they were in the movies when it came to criminal investigations. That's why he couldn't bear to watch any of that nonsense that came on TV every single night it seemed. Terry liked watching those shows. Dean suspected she liked the simplicity and the cookie cutter endings. It probably made Dean's job less real. Maybe he ought to give those shows one more try. It might be nice to see the bad guys get nailed within an hour period for a change. Yeah, that would be nice alright.

He glanced down at the GPS system and saw that he was right around the corner from the Gray residence. The houses on this side of town were beyond mansions. Seconds later he pulled up and was pleased to see his little helper was already there. She was cute and sweet and reminded him of his Zoey. With her book smarts, maybe she would in fact be the game changer.

***

To say that Tranise Gray was gorgeous was an understatement. She was intimidatingly tall, slim, yet curvy and with cocoa-colored skin and hazel eyes. Breath-taking might have been a better word. Keeley knew it might be emotional meeting with her. The woman had been through hell and back, including escaping the monster who murdered Jess. It was a lot to take in.

Tranise held tight when shaking Keeley's hand. Her eyes were full of understanding. The first thing she said was, "I'm sorry for your loss," then she welcomed them into her home. For having just recently escaped death, Tranise cleaned up well and seemed very together.

Once they sat down though, Keeley saw her hand shaking as she reached for her water bottle. Clearly, she was not okay, she just kept a good facade going. How *could* she be okay? She had almost been a victim of a cold-blooded murderer, now less than twenty-four hours later she was about to endure the Spanish Inquisition. Again. No doubt she had been questioned to death. Keeley was simply the sister-in-law, came hours after the murder took place, and she was drowning in questions after she first arrived to Bob's house. But these questions might be different. The type of questions given to the survivor of a murder would definitely be different than the questions given to a family member of a murder victim. This woman's family still got to have her around. This would become a distant, albeit painful, memory. Actually, it would at some point be looked at as something to celebrate. For she and Bob every year it would mean one more piece of life without Jess. It would constitute an annual trip to the cemetery in Fort Worth. Flowers being placed on her grave, maybe. A heartfelt sharing of special times spent with Jess.

But for Tranise, with all due respect, a little therapy and a fresh outlook could hopefully put an end to the incident all together. Keeley hoped so. She didn't want to feel bitter toward the brave and heroic woman she had just met, and she wouldn't. She needed to be rational and focused. They stood a chance at nailing Jess's murderer which is more unbelievably gratifying than they could have ever imagined when this whole thing began. Not that she or Bob was into the whole vengeance thing or anything. It was about the fact that no one would have to go through that again – at least at the hands of this particular scumbag.

Tranise's husband brought coffee on a tray with mugs, cream and sugar. He too seemed to be holding it together quite well. The kids were at her sister's in Dumont. Tranise's husband, Jeff, joined the group, his arm around his wife, protectively. Dean stood, signifying that it was time to get down to brass tacks.

"Mr. and Mrs. Gray, thank you very much for allowing this. I believe that Miss Travis here, being the relative of another victim, as well as the first person to nail down the fiction novel aspect of the case, will really be an asset here."

"We're both very eager to do whatever we can to help in the case. Of course, Tranise stands by what she said about the mask. Not only did that keep her from knowing who he was, the body type and voice were completely unfamiliar. There's only so much to go off here," said Jeff.

"Look, I'm not a lawyer," said Dean. "I'm on your side. And I know this is extremely wearing and tedious. Trust me. But we need to keep hammering away if we want answers. I think that all of us have something to gain by getting answers, don't we all agree?"

They all were in agreement. Keeley was suddenly painfully nervous. The collective tone of the group was miserable at best. Morale was going downhill fast. Keeley sipped her coffee wondering if this might not be such a great idea after all.

***

Summer was dismayed that Regina had called in sick, but what choice did she have? She promised Keeley she'd take charge of the store, even it meant having to skip one of her morning classes. Summer never personally skipped work *or* school if she was sick, but it sounded like poor Regina had two sick kiddos as well. She didn't have anyone to take care of them if she came into work, sick or not. So Summer would do what she promised and take care of the shop. It was only temporary. She wouldn't trade places with poor Keeley *or* Regina at this point, so she was happy to stick it out for her co-workers in need. The store would open at ten o'clock, meaning that Summer had about fifteen minutes left of study time now that her drawer was counted and the other opening tasks were completed. *The exciting world of ancient ruins awaits.* Summer positioned herself behind the counter and pulled out her course text and notebooks. She scanned the counter searching for her favorite pen before remembering she had balanced it behind her ear. She laughed out loud, decided a muffin would complement Mayan structural design, then ultimately lost the battle to stalling, so she began to take notes. *The ancient civilization's earliest ruins have been dated to 500 BC. That I knew. Blah, blah, blah . . . The only known, fully developed written language of pre-Columbian era – did not know that. . .* Summer jotted notes and was surprised when her phone alarm begin to go off. *Darn!* She'd had a good pace going. *Oh well.* She crossed over to the front door, key in hand and unlocked the door and flipped the sign to *open.* Typically there wasn't exactly a line formed at the front door, so she could easily get back into her study groove. She wasn't totally shocked to see two patrons waiting out front though. Business had kicked up a bit since Keeley was coined a best seller. And sadly, Summer believed, business picked up when the news leaked Keely's connection to Jess's murder.

"Good morning! Welcome to 'Buy the Book'." Summer stepped aside and allowed the man and woman inside. She noted they were not together when they each went a separate direction after entering. "Please let me know if you need help in finding anything," Summer added. She went back to her studies and five minutes later the woman, a blonde in her twenties, came up to the register with a stack full of predictable reads: *Eat Pray Love, Summer Sisters* and *Marley and Me.*

"Did you find everything you needed?"

"Yes." The woman looked anxious.

"Are any of these gifts?" asked Summer.

"No, all for me," she answered, sounding rushed. She looked over her shoulder, then leaned in after brief hesitation. "That man up there. . . he's acting really weird."

Summer bristled. "Weird?"

"Yes. I . . . wait, has anyone else come in the store?"

"No," said Summer, confused.

"Then he was talking to himself." The woman chuckled. "There was no phone, I looked."

"A blue tooth maybe?" suggested Summer.

"No. I saw him front on. At first he was making this sick kind of laughing sound. Then he sounded like he was threatening someone, talking through gritted teeth. That's when I looked up. He looked kind of irritated when I did, so I wrapped it up." The lady signed her credit card slip and said, "thanks," before abruptly leaving. Summer barely had time to slip the receipt in her bag. She let out a deep breath, not exactly thrilled at the concept of being alone in the store with some psycho. After a good ten minutes, she decided to check in on him. She recalled the lady saying he was upstairs, so she climbed the staircase and sure enough, he was in the horror section. How apropos. He had a canvas shoulder bag and it looked full. He turned when the floor creaked under Summer's steps. He smiled and looked actually quite handsome. "I hope you don't mind that I'm putting the books in my bag. I fully intend to pay for these," he joked, patting the bag and showing off a killer smile. He wasn't crazy, thought Summer, he was gorgeous.

"Oh, that's fine," smiled Summer. "People do it all the time. Avid reader?"

"Very avid. You?" He walked closer to her. She was shocked she hadn't notice how striking he was when he first walked in. She guessed she had been preoccupied.

"Well, right now I'm kind of left without a choice. I'm a history student. All I do is read, so. . . it's sort of lost its thrill." She shrugged her shoulders, coyly.

"Reading against one's will should be outlawed. I believe it should be done *strictly* for pleasure. And it should always, always cause a thrill." His flirtations were so blatant that it caused Summer to blush.

"Tell that to my professors." Summer was disappointed when she heard the bell, meaning a customer had entered the store. "I'll be up front if you need any help."

Two customers later, Summer decided to check on Mr. Avid Reader. He'd been up there for a while, plus he was much more *thrilling* than the Mayans. She jogged up the stairs and turned to the horror section, which was vacant. She walked the corridor leading to action, mystery and pre-owned novels. No one. Not that there was ever anyone in the western section, but she tried there too. It was possible he had come downstairs without her knowledge, but odd. The sweeping staircase was the focal point of the store. Perhaps when she was ringing up her last customer . . . she checked all over downstairs, smiling a little when she entered the romance section. She stopped, feeling stumped. Avid Reader was gone. But she would have heard the bell if he had left. You could hear the bell from anywhere in the store, including the employee restroom.

Summer climbed the stairs two at a time. When she reached the end of the hallway she saw the small window was opened. It was no bigger than a few feet tall and a few feet wide and Keeley never opened it. They used a central temperature control unit. Summer glanced out the window and saw a tiny ledge with a rudimentary fire escape. Avid Reader had fled the scene.

***

Half an hour in and Keeley was feeling much more at ease. Tranise's husband, Jeff had even started to relax a little. Keeley knew he was just looking out for his wife. Any protective husband would in this situation, but she could tell Dean wasn't a huge fan of Jeff's need to shield his wife quite so much. She knew Bob would never again let Jess out of his sight if she had survived. Who could blame the guy after all? He'd been given a second chance.

Tranise explained how she knew right away about the Poe book, having read it before and of course the subtle hint of his holding the book and carving out the floor. She admitted that although she was planning to escape, she never believed she could do it. Little pieces of information continued to flow from the woman's mouth, but nothing ever seemed too substantial. Keeley detailed everything she knew about each book and had even brought along the copies of *It* and *And Then There Were None*. She was surprised to see how she was able to focus on the content without picturing Jess anymore. It was just like any other job; she remained detached from the fact that Jess was involved, acting stoically and competent. Thank God she was able to keep it together. Tranise only lost control one time during her account.

By the end of the session, everyone just looked tired and haggard. They agreed to collect their thoughts and meet up again in a few days, and of course to contact Dean if anything should stand out. Dean also said that he would hold off on releasing any of the information about the murderer being a fictional copycat as long as he could. He hoped it wouldn't get out before they had any better leads because it would be a media sensation. It would be nice to have a piece to work with in case they were lucky enough to be able to question anyone beyond Tranise or Keeley.

Once Keeley was in her car, she pulled her cell phone out of her purse. She had two missed calls and a voicemail, all from Summer. She didn't bother with listening to the voicemail, and called Summer at the shop right away. Summer answered on the first ring.

"Hello? I mean, 'Buy the Book,' may I help you?"

"Summer? What's going on?"

"Didn't you get my message?"

"No, I just thought it would be better to call. Is everything alright there?"

"No. I mean yes. I'm not sure."

"Just relax, Summer. Are *you* okay?"

"Yes. I'm fine." Keeley exhaled. "There was a guy in here. He had a bag of books and a woman customer told me he was acting strangely, so when I went to go check, he seemed totally normal. We made small talk, then a new customer came in, so I left him. Much later I went to see how he was and he was gone. I never heard the entrance bell and I combed the entire store. Then I saw that the upstairs window was opened."

"He left through the window?"

"Yeah, carrying a ton of books. He had his own bag. I'm so sorry."

"Did you call the police?"

"Yes, but they argued their way out of coming. They said if there was no alarm or forced entry . . . I had no way to prove anything. And when they asked what I suspected was stolen, I told them that my guess was about ten paperbacks. The calculated sum was too low to even file a report without their being an actual person detained."

"You're kidding." Keeley sighed. "Oh well, at least you're okay, Summer. That's not a big deal. Petty theft is the least of my worries. It might be time for an alarm system though." *Especially with her female employees working alone at night. And especially after Jess, Harper and Tranise.*

"Thank you, Keeley. And I'm sorry. I guess after that lady warned me I should have kept a better eye on him."

"It's not your fault. I just think it's a mockery of the legal system that there will be no justice over a formality - being that books are too cheap to waste their time. Does this mean now there will be no complaint registered?"

"I guess not. Too bad, though. Maybe we ought to start marking up the thriller novels, huh? Poetic justice," smirked Summer.

"Thriller novels?" echoed Keeley.

"Yeah, a whole bag full," answered Summer. Keeley got the chills. A whole bag full of *thriller novels*. Stolen. Right after the connection had been made to the murders and attempted murder. It didn't feel right.

"You wouldn't happen to know off hand any of the titles? Or could you possibly tell what was missing from the racks?" Keeley certainly knew she could, with her keen eye for books. She didn't know if Summer coveted the titles as much as she did. And no matter how diligent they were, the books were always getting moved around, compromising perfect alphabetical order.

"I saw him put one in his bag when I first ap-proached him. And I do know a few titles that are miss-ing. I just dusted there last night. Why do you ask?"

"Curious I guess. Plus I'll need to restock." She wanted to yell at Summer to hurry up and spit it out . . . and that if there was any slim chance in hell that this was their guy, that women's lives were in jeopardy . . . but she didn't. She played it cool. After all, there was nothing to get worked up over. This was just a stupid coincidence.

"Okay, *Silence of the Lambs*. Also, *Cycle of the Werewolf*." *Another by Stephen King,* thought Keeley. "And I think it was *Dracula*. I can go check. Oh! Almost forgot, he took *He Knows You're Alone. That's* the one I saw him holding. You've officially hit star status! People are actually stealing your books from the shelves!"

Keeley was reeling. Her book, too had been stolen? Keeley knew the only reason Summer was being so flippant about it was because she didn't know about the connection between the novels and the murders.

"But don't worry," continued Summer, "between you and me, this book thief was a hottie!"

Keeley was stunned silent. Of course this had to be a coincidence, but she would definitely relay this to Dean as soon as she hung up with Summer. "Keeley? You're okay, right? I know it's scary that we were robbed, but it was just some petty nonsense. Petty theft. You said so yourself. You have bigger fish to fry. Don't let this ruffle your feathers, because I swear I've got things under control. Promise."

"I know you do. Summer, . . . did the guy seem like he might not have had the money for the books?"

"Not with that outfit. He was wearing *some* designer. My guess is he wanted some kind of adrenaline boost." Summer paused, "The whole thing was just . . . odd. But he did tell me how much he loved books. He seemed so *harmless*. He's probably just a little unstable." *Harmless and unstable*. Keeley swallowed hard.

"Why don't you close up a little early today? Before sundown, okay?"

"Keeley . . . "

"Please do it. Alright, Summer?"

"Sure, boss, if it makes you feel better. But I promise, everything's going to be fine. This guy won't be coming back here again. And if he does, next time I'll call the police."

Chapter nine

After recounting everything that transpired to Detective Dean over the phone, Keeley did something she never thought she'd do. She pulled up outside of Drakesborough's local 'Book Barn', competitor at large. She needed to get her hands on the books Summer had listed and she didn't want to drive all the way back to her store to do it. She had read all of the books at some point, naturally. They were all top rated novels within their genre: *horror*. The idea that it was a big fat coincidence that those titles were stolen from her store was fading. *It, Tell Tale Heart, And Then There Were None, Silence of the Lambs, Dracula, and Cycle of the Werewolf,* were all list toppers for thriller novels. Even her book's recent recognition of Best Seller fit the bill. This was either a huge fluke or . . . well, she hoped that's just what it was. She exited her car, and stepped right into what she hoped was a spilled smoothie. *Darn*! The tip of her boot was covered in a bright pink blob. She reached in her purse and pulled out her bottle of water, pouring a small amount onto the leather. It did the trick for the most part. Satisfied, she entered the store. The thought crossed her mind that she was entering enemy territory, but for some reason it felt a whole lot safer than the idea of entering her own store right now. The small window that he supposedly left through was small and dangerous. It wasn't meant for human passage. She shuddered.

"May I help you?" asked an attractive silver-haired clerk.

"No, thanks," replied Keeley, realizing she sounded offensive and abrupt. She flashed a smile to make up for it. It wasn't her fault that Keeley needed to go to another book store, despite the fact that she owned her own bookstore and would be paying someone other than herself for merchandise that she already had. Especially a copy of her own novel. She was pretty sure she had all the books on her home shelves as well, but what choice did she have?

"Well . . . let me know if I can help you." Now she was the one who came across as harsh. Snooty, actually.

"Thanks." Keeley started off toward the back of the store and immediately saw the mystery and suspense headings and knew thriller was probably tucked in there somewhere.

She found three books within a short time, but didn't find *Cycle of the Werewolf*. In her store, the story came in two editions: a stand-alone, shorter novel and as a part of a compellation of short stories. She searched again for Stephen King compellations and horror story compellations, but it didn't turn up. She could always go ask Snooty Pants, but for some reason that felt like a non-option. She scooped up her pile of books from the carpeted floor beside her, but as she turned to stand, she crashed right into someone and the books scattered to the floor. "I'm so sorry," uttered Keeley, just as the young man also apologized. Then they both bent to grab the books at the same time and ended up bonking foreheads. Grabbing their heads and laughing they managed, between the two of them, to get the books restacked and into Keeley's arms.

"Thanks," she said, still blushing. She couldn't tell if she was still embarrassed over the ridiculous scene they'd caused, or because he was so ridiculously handsome. He'd be perfect for Leah. *You already have a wonderful fiancé of your own,* she had to remind herself. What was it with her? She never checked out other guys. It was most likely that she missed Ben. And her poor emotions were all over the place lately.

"I'm Josh by the way." He stuck out his free hand. The one that wasn't holding three horror novels of his own.

"Keeley," she said, starting to walk away. "And thanks again . . . Josh."

"No, wait! Can I . . . buy you a scone or a coffee? Coffee and a scone? For your troubles I mean."

"Caffeine only adds to clumsy, but thanks." Again, she started to leave.

"Okay. I know. Meetings like these only happen in dumb romantic comedies. Guy and girl in bookstore . . . they bump heads while reaching for the same book . . . in the end they wind up sole mates. I guess I'd better work on my pickups. Have a great day . . . Keeley." He flashed her a mega-watt smile and turned the corner. For some reason, her heart was beating a hundred miles an hour.

Keeley decided that a coffee did sound good. Maybe even a scone too. She would buy two of each and see if she could coax Bob into eating something more. It was nearing lunch time. Naturally, when reached the end of the line, Josh was there. Standing right in *front* of her. How could she be so oblivious? Now it looked as if she were following him. She decided to slowly sneak out of line before he saw her. Of course, it didn't work. "Hey. You changed your mind!"

"No, I just . . ."

"How's your head?" He laughed. "Cause mine's a little sore. I'm not gonna lie." Now Keeley laughed. He was so darned charismatic that her rapid heartbeat returned. Same with the blushing. *This was wrong.* She had a fiancé, whom she loved very much, and here she was inadvertently sending a message to another man. And he was flirting with her in public!

"I have a fiancé," she blurted out. More blushing.

"Oh. Alright, well . . . then I guess we aren't movie-caliber sole mates after all." He gave his million dollar smile and snapped his fingers. "I'm still getting coffee, though." He was still smiling. He was so damn charming.

"Sorry. That was weird," she began awkwardly. Keeley was never good at flirting. "I just don't like the idea of sending out the wrong message is all." She cringed. It was Josh's turn to order. "I understand," he said advancing forward. She couldn't hear what he ordered, but he smiled as he walked passed, Styrofoam cup in hand. "Enjoy the books." Then he paused for a minute. "I love thrillers too." The smile that inappropriately sent her heart into hysterics was not there this time.

Keeley ordered her food and drink and then headed toward a second line, to purchase her books. She was careful to check first that a wounded Josh wasn't already in line. She tried her best to ensure this, lingering over cream and sugar at the condiment table, then leisurely making her way to the checkout line. Things had been awkward enough already. Her plan had worked. There were two people ahead of her and Josh was not one of them. Looking down at her books while she waited her turn, she remembered that before she bumped into Josh she was thinking of asking where she might be able to find *The Cycle of the Werewolf.* Asking for help from Snooty Pants would beat *bumping into* Josh again any day. She stepped out of line and headed toward the circular desk in the center of the store just as an elaborate alarm system started beeping. Snooty Pants whooshed past. Keeley had seen it a million times. Someone had left a scanner on at a department store, a small child had accidentally carried a toy out of a store, or the alarm mechanism was malfunctioning. But not this time. Employees were ushered, a security guard from the strip mall had entered the store. This was a legitimate alarm. Keeley looked around. There were at least a half dozen customers between the bookstore and the small cafe in the corner, and it was still very unnerving knowing a robbery had just taken place. Poor Summer had been alone in the store when this happened to her. *How terrifying for Summer and how coincidental for me . . . my store was robbed, then a second bookstore that* I *was in was robbed. . .* Keeley felt her heart rate climbing again. And she was wondering if once again it was because of Josh.

***

Once the alarm drama had died down, word around the store was that someone *had* compromised the system, but no one seemed to have known who it was. Keeley mentioned to the manager that she had been behind Josh in the coffee line, but that she didn't see him after that in the book purchase line. The manager scoffed at her, acting like she had just offered up the most monumental time wasting piece of information ever. She didn't worry about it, knowing she'd confide in Detective Dean later on. She also made a mental note to finally have a good heart to heart with Ben. She wished she'd thought to meet up with him while she was back home, but she'd been far too pre-occupied. It seemed like a hundred years since she'd seen her fiancé. Keeley hoped she could coax him into coming out to Bob's place tonight if things weren't too crazy for him at work. Maybe that would liven things up a little. At least Keeley had gotten out of the house. Poor Bob would have to get some fresh air at some point. Her mind was made up. She'd ask Ben to come for a late dinner tonight, and she'd try and take Bob for a picnic lunch tomorrow down by the lake. That sounded good. Right now though, she was waiting while an employee searched the back room, in a last ditch effort, for the copy of *Cycle of the Werewolf* which his computer informed him *did* exist somewhere in the store. Unless of course it was stolen just moments ago. *I love thrillers too*, he had said. Much like the thief who had invaded her own store.

Keeley was itching to start reading one of the books she was holding. She cracked open *Silence of the Lambs*, read two sentences, then closed the book. She couldn't focus here. What she really wanted to do was go home, with or without the book. She wanted to see Bob and put on comfy clothes and curl up with one of these cursed books. *But If Ben comes over, he might stay late*, she thought, the guilt returning full force. *What do you think? You're going to read about a murder in one of the many books some random guy stole and somehow find a way to save a life? Fat chance.* She had read too many books.

By bringing these books home, she was simply go-ing to . . . *to what?* She wasn't sure. She had some shred of hope that something would come to her, she guessed.

She was also regretting giving the copy of *It* from Jess's drawer to the department because some part of her wanted to go over the edition with a fine toothed comb. There may have been a tip, hidden somewhere in there that held the key. *The key to what? To the padded cell they'd be sure to lock her up in if they knew how certifiable she sounded right now.* The clerk who was helping her came back empty-handed. "It's just not here. The computer says we have a copy, but I've gone through the whole place and I can't find it. I'm sorry."

Chapter ten

Tranise was so happy to see her girls that a fresh flood of tears gushed out. Thank God she was here to hold them. Thank God for everything. Tranise hugged them and they hugged back. They didn't know all the details of what had happened to their mommy, but they knew a bad person tried to hurt her. Once they returned to school she was pretty sure the truth would come out, so she and Jeff did their best not to stray too far from reality. The girls were young still. Too young to hear that anyone, especially their own mother, had been the victim of an intended murder. She was all about telling the truth and showing examples of powerful women to her girls, but this was not the time. Chrissa was only in third grade. Malia was in fifth. They were planning to have the kids out of school next Friday, so instead they were keeping them out today and tomorrow. The girls would return on Wednesday and hopefully they could remain untainted by reality for as long as possible.

Obviously, the cabin trip was indefinitely on hold. Tranise didn't think she could ever bring herself to return there, despite the rich family history and memories. She sniffed back the tears and released her hold on the girls. "I have an idea. Who wants to bake cookies?"

"Me!"

"Me too!"

"Then let's go. I need a chocolate chip taster to make sure they're still good." Tranise reached into the cabinet and pulled out the gigantic yellow bag. She glanced back at Jeff, who marveled at her attitude.

"You know, Tranise, you don't have to try and be super mom right now," he smiled, noticing how pretty she looked without make-up.

"Try? I thought I was," she teased back. "Truth is," she cupped her hands to her mouth and whispered, "I just really want some junk food."

Jeff laughed, following her into the kitchen. "Look out girls, I wanna be the chocolate chip taster." He picked up Chrissa and playfully moved her aside, then fended off Malia, while reaching for the bag of chocolate chips. Tranise crossed her arms and smiled, taking in the beautiful scene. She realized that she might be alright after all.

The first tray of cookies was just placed in the oven when the phone rang. She knew the call was inevitable, but couldn't help but scowling. Yet, she felt thankful for the time she had with her family where she was actually able to forget, even if just for a little while. She psyched herself up for the call, promising herself a warm cookie once the call was over.

"Hello?" She expected to hear Detective Dean on the other end. Kind hearted, but direct. Instead, silence. "Hello?" she asked again. Jeff looked perplexed from across the room and walked toward her. She held the phone out and shrugged her shoulders. "No one's there." She replaced the phone on the receiver. She turned to see a disgruntled Jeff facing her. "What?"

"Don't answer that again, Tranise." She didn't even think that it might have something to do with her attack.

Her few minutes of family bliss had placed her dead center in oblivion.

"Oh my God, you're right. Should we call the police?"

"No. Not yet. But if it happens again we will."

"You think it could have been . . . him?"

"It could have been. It also could be that someone knows and thought it might be funny to poke a sleeping bear. Let's just wait and see. You go rest." Tranise walked away and Jeff unplugged the phone from the wall. For a moment he had to lean against the table. What if it wasn't over yet? What if whoever went after Tranise in the first place was planning to come after her again? And what if they didn't stop until they got her?

***

Keeley was gathering trash from dinner, Bob was taking a quick shower. Ben was on his way with a bottle of "good wine," that he was sure Bob "could use." She didn't have the heart to tell him that Bob most likely wouldn't drink it, but then again he was drinking hard alcohol yesterday. Maybe he would, maybe he wouldn't.

She was glad to see that Bob ate the muffin she brought for a mid-day snack, then he took her up on her offer to pick up some "brain food" at the greasy drive-thru just a few miles away. She scooped up balled-up napkins and empty boxes from the burgers and fries. They both ate everything they ordered. Keeley knew she could use all the energy she could muster for what lay ahead. She recounted for Bob every last detail from the second she arrived at her own store until the second she left the neighborhood bookstore. She was glad to see that he didn't think she was a paranoid nutcase and neither did Detective Dean. She was glad to see both of them take her information in and try and make sense of it.

Dean wrote her statement and promised to have someone follow up with Summer at her store. Now she just had to sit back and wait until something came to Tranise, Dean or even her that might actually be useful. Until then she would just try and relax and be there for her family. She promised herself not to invest too much into the missing titles from the store. Reading those books wouldn't help in any way. Unfortunately, they would only be relevant if the murders did take place. Then she could recognize the scenes

. . . . and agonize over them in her sleep. She shuddered at the mere thought. That wouldn't happen. They would catch the lunatic murderer before anyone else suffered a cruel and bizarrely staged fate. She had to keep reminding herself that there was an entire police squad working on the case, not just her and Tranise. But everyone was banking on them to use their inside expertise. Maybe it wouldn't hurt to read those books.

Just as Bob came down the stairs in a casual outfit, there came a knock at the door. Ben. Keeley was overcome with happiness. She really missed him. Ben had a way of making her feel safe. Of course that was always Bob's role, but right now, Bob was taking care of himself. Keeley wanted, no needed, to see him. She didn't realize just how much she needed to until she heard his voice today on the phone. She was thrilled that he was able to make the time to drive out and visit. She walked in wide strides to the front door. Her heart was heavy. She glanced through the peephole just to be certain and of course there was Ben, her knight in shining armor.

"Ben! Thanks for coming." She embraced him, then stepped to the side so he could greet Bob. The two hugged, no words necessary. They liked each other and had gotten along since day one. They seemed as different as night and day when Keeley first met Ben, but then she slowly realized there were in fact many similarities, probably all the traits that drew her to her future husband.

"I'm just sorry I couldn't make it out sooner." They stood momentarily in the foyer, then Ben produced a bottle of wine and a small bag of groceries from the boutique market down the street. "Keeley said you guys would have eaten by now, but I just brought some extras in case." A baguette stuck out of the top of the bag. Keeley reached out to accept the wine and the bag, but Ben declined, saying he'd pour up some wine.

Bob didn't object, but simply nodded and sat on the chaise lounge while Ben followed Keeley into the kitchen. Things felt different somehow. Of course she knew why. There was a sadness here that would take a long time to lift. When Ben reached the counter and set everything down, Keeley reached for him fiercely. She didn't want to let go. She needed to have someone console her for just a moment. She wasn't used to being the rock for Bob, or for anyone really. He hugged back and rubbed her back. "Tough day?" he smiled.

"The worst." Flashes of Josh crashed through her mind. She felt that same guilt, then fear. She took a breath, forcing the tears not to flow. "I already fell better. Thank you for coming."

"Will you stop saying that?" smiled Ben, grabbing the bottle opener from the bar top and expertly opening the bottle. "It makes it look like I wasn't thinking of you guys. It's all I think about." *God, what an angel.*

"Well I'm still going to say it. Thank you, Ben." She planted a kiss on his forehead, then walked to the cabinet where the wine glasses were. She grabbed three and Ben poured deliciously fragrant wine for the three of them. Frankly, Keeley knew she could use a drink after the last few days. One glass would be perfect. It wouldn't be enough to cloud her mind, it would just help her to let go a bit.

They carried the glasses into the sitting room, only to find Bob fast asleep with his chin tucked into his chest. They exchanged knowing smiles and retreated to her guest room. She knew if she woke Bob now he'd feel forced to play host and to placate them into thinking things were fine. Keeley suddenly felt bad, like maybe it wasn't such a great idea to invite a friend over, even though they both considered Ben family long before he proposed. Keeley sipped her wine as she settled on the right side of the bed against the pillows. Ben slipped off his shoes, then he joined her. He linked his socked feet with her barefoot ones and she giggled. Just like old times, only not.

If they were at her house or his townhouse, they wouldn't be lying in bed, fully clothed anyway, at this hour. On a Monday night, they would be sitting on Keeley's deck if weather permitted, staring at the stars, or in Ben's beautifully decorated game room. They would be watching a comedy or playing pool or darts or a board game. They would have finished a late meal prepared together of course, and then sat unwinding at the end of their separate busy days. Keeley scooted closer to Ben and he enveloped her in his arms. "How's the big guy really doing?" he asked, kissing the top of her head.

"Better, I think. I think these new developments have served as a good distraction, actually." She sipped, wanting to share more information with him. He was all caught up on the robbery at her store, but she hadn't had the chance to tell him about Josh and the second robbery and her possibly irrational fears that somehow it's all tied in and that she has no way to stop the murders! *And reading the God damned books won't do one thing about it.* She glanced over at her stack of books that she had already removed from the bag and placed in the order in which she wanted to read them.

"I'm glad. Penny for your thoughts, though," smiled Ben. Good old Ben. Quite possibly the kindest man to ever live. He was faithful and caring and patient and wonderful. She would miss him immensely, and that's what she told him; that she would miss him; that missing him was what captivated her to silence right now; another lie. Well, another lie by *omission*, but that somehow seemed worse. She decided to tell him about Josh. All she would be *omitting* was the part about her blushing profusely as he flirted. She couldn't help it if he was flirting - if he even was. Maybe that was just a part of his weird scheme to rob the store. Assuming it was even Josh, if that was his real name, who robbed the store. More than likely it was the same street rat hoodlum who had stolen from her and Josh had just gotten in a quick line while she dawdled and had made a quick exit. Why didn't she think of that before? Because since Jess, everything has become sinister, that's why. Realizing the silence had gone on painfully long, she spoke.

"So after the whole thing at the store today, I went to the local bookstore. I wanted to take a look at the book titles that Summer thinks were taken from my shelves.

Call it morbid curiosity I guess. Anyway, suddenly an alarm went off and it turned out someone stole some books, but they never saw who." Feeling better about the fact that the Josh thing was probably just a mental red-herring on her part, she decided to leave him out of the story all together. Suddenly she felt foolish for even bringing him up to Dean. Then again . . . Summer made a comment about how attractive her thief had been. And Keeley hadn't remembered being so flustered around a man since she met handsome Ben. *Just drop it*, she scolded herself.

"It sounds like quite a day for the criminals. Unless of course you think it was the same person? On a thieving rampage?" Ben seemed to take pleasure in teasing her. That stung.

"Actually, I had thought so. And on top of that, I wondered if the fact that horror plots are being mimicked, somehow ties into all these stolen thriller novels." She sat up, feeling surprisingly defensive.

"Hey, it's okay. I didn't mean to upset you. It's actually not that farfetched an idea." Keeley smiled and let her back rest against the headboard again. "I'm serious. You ought to tell the detective you've been working with."

"Oh, I already did. As soon as I left the store." Ben looked stung now. She told Dean, but then not her fiancé, her confidant. She's only telling him the information right now. Clearly, he was hurt. "Sorry. I called him right away and then" . . . *don't lie again* . . . "I wondered if I was being too rash, so I decided to drop it." It was partially true, except she didn't realize she might be being too rash until just now. But if Ben is giving this theory credence. . . . maybe it's not just a dumb idea.

"I know you're going through a lot, but I'm always here to listen, even if you think it's nothing, okay?" *And the Boyfriend of the Year Award goes to . . .*

She felt satisfied with Ben's response. She didn't feel like a lying cad anymore. Ben was such a genuinely good person that he had a way of making everyone else feel good too. They finished their wine and Keeley turned down a refill. She was ready to finally call it a day.

Ben declined her offer to stay the night and left just before nine o'clock. Part of her wanted to plead him to stay, to serve as a security blanket, yet part of her, despite the fact that her eyes were growing heavy, wanted to glance at the books. She took the top book off the stack, *Dracula*. She hoped to God no one would be mimicking this mode of death. Draining one's body of blood was indeed a monstrous, gruesome approach, but so were those used on Jess and Tranise. She knew it was in vain, but she opened the book and once again nestled in the abundance of pillows. Suppose the thief was the actual killer. She didn't know what other books had been stolen (they only knew a *few* titles from her store, *none* from the local store, and who knew how many other shops had been vandalized). And from the small collection she held here, minus *Werewolf*, she had no idea which one would be attempted first. If this was even a valid theory . . . so many ifs.

And if for some oddball twist of fate this was actually playing out in the way she imagined, again, what could she do about it? Warn people against vampire lookalikes? Futile. It was all futile. Nonetheless, she liked Bram Stoker and she could use a good read. It would take her mind off the day. Or would it just plant even more suspicion and fear in her over churning brain?

She ended up reading the first two chapters, which were excerpts from the character, Jonathan's, journal. He found at the end of chapter two that he was a prisoner in Count Dracula's castle. She closed the book and set it aside. She decided to just rest for just one second before going to brush her teeth and prepare for bed. Of course, she fell asleep immediately, entering the first of a series of fitful and terrifying dreams. Ben starred in the first few, falling prey to both the bloodthirsty Count Dracula and also Pennywise the Clown from *It*. Next up were poor Jess and Bob, the two being tortured and terrorized by a monster, no doubt the elusive werewolf. She finally forced herself awake when she could no longer stand it. In her last dream, she was being chased through some sort of thorn-laden labyrinth by Josh. He was yelling to her that she dropped her book, much like she had done in the actual store. When he finally caught up to her he had fangs and a set of knives for fingers, ala Freddy Krueger. She was drenched in sweat and very afraid. So afraid, that she didn't climb out of bed even though she needed to use the bathroom.

Chapter eleven

Keeley and Bob were waiting in the Dallas-Fort Worth International Airport at the luggage center. The last couple of days had been a whirlwind. There had been an immediate opening to have a ceremony and so the siblings literally dropped everything and fled out of town. They were going to check in at their hotel, where they would stay for only one night, meet up with the other few people who would share in bidding farewell to Jess and have a small, no-frills dinner at one of Jess's old haunts. The following day they would attend the small ceremony and take the next flight back home.

Bob's demeanor had gone from bad to worse as he progressed through the stages of grief. Tuesday morning, Keeley was awakened to Bob crying in the backyard, going through a box of mementoes. He was so out of it that she wondered for a minute if he was sleepwalking or even drunk. He was rambling on and on about how it was his fault that Jess was murdered and that he should have never let her out of his sight. That same evening he was confiding in Keeley that he still couldn't believe she was dead and that he was still waking up in the middle of the night wondering if it was all just a terrible nightmare and that maybe, somehow, Jess could come back. It was devastatingly sad; even more upsetting than her initial visit to see Bob. At least then he was still sort of in shock. Now there was no doubt about the fact that it had set in. Keeley was nervous to see the other friends and family members tonight. Bob had taken no visitors, minus Ben, and now seeing other people with feelings toward Jess . . . well it would make things a whole new real for him. Tonight would be hard.

Her second and last piece of luggage made its way around the circular.

"Ready to go?" asked Bob, gripping his small suitcase.

"Yup." Her palms were sweating. Everything was much harder than she imagined it. She had hoped the trip would bring closure, but right now the tension and feelings of desperation were so palpable that she thought she might be sick.

They caught a shuttle for the ride to the hotel. It wasn't too far and the accommodations were nice. They sat in silence for the whole ride, both afraid to break the silence. Plus, there were two others in the back of the van. The driver pulled up alongside the hotel's entrance and opened the sliding door. The Texas air was humid and thick, but it was a nice contrast to the arctic blast of artificial air inside the shuttle. The fresh air also provided a nice break from the stench of smoke-ridden leather and cloth.

They grabbed their bags and headed inside toward the check-in line.

"Welcome to Mesa View, do you have a reservation?"

"Yes, it's under Robert Travis."

"Yes, and would you and your . . . guest each like a key?" This was standard routine for Keeley and Bob. People didn't know whether to think she was his daughter or younger wife, but for some reason they never settled on sister.

"His sister would love her own key," piped Keeley. She and Bob shared a smile. The highlight of the trip so far.

After signing for the room and accepting two keys and a folder of information, they were ushered toward the elevator. The room was on the top floor. It was a suite, of course, nothing but the best when Bob was around; so they each had their own sleeping space. Keeley had brought the remaining books just in case she had any trouble falling straight to sleep. She didn't dare read the books on the plane. For whatever reason, they had become her own dirty little secret, a guilty pleasure. She supposed she felt self-conscious about putting so much stock in those stupid books. And she felt like it would be too morbid to read them in front of Bob on what was already going to be an extremely tough couple of days. Instead on the flight she opted for a small stack of gossip magazines. Bob plugged into the airline headset and listened to music and took a nap. The flight was the easy part. Now, they had a little time to burn before meeting up with Jess's cousin and a few others.

They each unpacked their small amount of luggage and prepared their living areas for the next twenty-four hours. Keeley kept the books hidden underneath the small attaché case that she would keep beside her bed. It held her glasses, contact lens case, saline solution, lavender sheet spray and a bottle of aspirin. After hanging her skirt and blouse for tomorrow, she went to the main area to wait for her brother. The room had a large attached balcony with a vast patio. She stepped closer and parted the sheer drapery. It would typically be a great asset to any hotel room, but this trip no one would be lounging around enjoying it; no late night stargazing, no mindless chitchat over morning coffee. The view would go ignored, along with all the other mundane activities of life. At least for the next two days. Keeley hoped that the closure she had been waiting on would present itself once everything was said and done, once they had said goodbye to her. She sighed and turned away from the glass door. The kitchen was also pretty impressive. A full-sized fridge, an oven, a sink, a small wet bar and a vase full of silk flowers. There was even a dishwasher, although it was about half the size of a standard model. Upon opening the cabinets and drawers, she saw that they too were fully stocked. Glasses, plates, silverware and various cooking utensils. It was quite a nice room. Out of curiosity, Keeley even opened the refrigerator and was surprised to see a bottle of champagne. She leaned in to read the label.

"It's got everything," said Bob, emerging from his room, tying up his necktie. No, not everything. Blatantly missing were both of their significant others. Otherwise, yes, the room had everything. Everything for the perfect weekend getaway. A couple's retreat. But this wasn't the perfect weekend getaway. It was a funeral weekend. Keeley was a bit surprised that Ben was unable to skip out on his recent work case and join them. While it was such short notice, she couldn't help but feel a little hurt. Of course she told him that it was fine and not to worry, that he could pay his respects at the ceremony back home, and that they were fine – he shouldn't go out of his way; but truthfully, she believed that he should have gone out of his way. Once again she felt bad. Ben was perfect. But she couldn't help feeling like he should read her better by now. No, it wasn't okay that he wasn't there. She needed him. Why didn't he know that? To his credit, he told her he could probably move some things around, pull a string or two, but he made it sound like he would be jeopardizing his position. She was sure when she objected that he would push. But she was wrong. She should have just told him how she felt. But they knew each other better than that, didn't they? Or was she being the typical female stereotype, angry that her mate didn't read her mind?

"It is a nice room. Are you hungry, Bob?" She realized she might have been opening the fridge because her subconscious mind was realizing they hadn't had much more than the complementary bag of peanuts on the flight over since breakfast.

"A little, but I can wait until tonight. Let's order something for you though, Kee."

She noticed that he had lost a few pounds over the past couple of days. His clothes seemed to hang from him, rather than fit him. Keeley was hungry. She was accustomed to eating several snacks each day, in addition to regular meals.

"Maybe I will." She was suddenly feeling a little light headed. She didn't want to spoil dinner, but she really did need at least a little something. She walked over to the pile of standard leather-bound books on the table. She found the room service menu right away. Bob sat down across from her and put his feet up on the ottoman. She saw breakfast, lunch and dinner, then found "appetizers." That would be better. Despite her normally hearty appetite, it had whittled down over the past couple of days. A full meal a couple of hours before an already dreaded dinner wouldn't sit well.

She opted for the mozzarella sticks. Protein. Plus there would be extras to share in case Bob changed his mind. She requested two orders plus a Sprite. They quoted her twenty minutes, so the two of them just sat and stared at the mostly obscured glass door. Bob was the first to break the silence.

"I think we ought to try and push the second ceremony back a few weeks."

"Whatever you want to do, but why?"

"Well," he began, "It just seems like maybe it will give us a chance to digest everything." *Translation, it's all getting to be too much.* She understood perfectly.

"I'll support whatever choice you make, Bob, but I have to point out that . . . the longer this drags itself out, the longer it will take you to get closure." There was that word again. "I just think that it will be too hard to relive this again once . . . you've begun to heal." She hated saying those words. To the person mourning a fresh loss, the worst idea ever is that it will pass. It would signify that the person wasn't foremost on their mind anymore and right now, for Bob, the thought was probably unimaginable.

"I know what you mean, but . . . I just don't know if I can do it. I don't know if I can do tonight, Kee. I remember it being difficult with Mom, and with Dad, but . . . " He didn't finish his sentence.

She didn't know if he was going to conclude with, "but this is different," or "you expect to lose your parents at some point," or "they had lived long lives," but it all meant the same thing. This was his wife and it all sucked to high heavens.

"I know tonight will be hard. I'm not sure how I'm going to make it, so I can only imagine how you feel. I'll go with your wishes one hundred percent, but promise me we'll get through tonight before making any decisions. And we will make it through. Promise."

"I know. I know we will. Thank you so much for everything. All you've done for me . . . I think another good reason to wait is so that you can get back to that life of yours for a bit. You've barely got any time left before your *new* fiancé is going abroad. You need an engagement party – *and* a bon voyage party. And we've barely even begun to celebrate the new book!"

Leave it to him to worry about her beginning a life while his wife's just ended. He seemed genuinely concerned that she might not get a few pats on the back out of her recent good news.

"Bob, I have the rest of my life to . . ." That it was a poor choice of words would be an understatement. She swallowed hard. Jess thought she had the rest of her life. Heck, *Bob* thought he had the rest of *his* life. "I'll be fine and I can do any of those things whenever I want. This is about doing what feels right for you. Don't do anything because of anyone else right now. Let's see how tonight goes."

"Thank you."

"These people love Jess." *Loved.* "And they love you."

After eating the mozzarella sticks – which actually took thirty-five minutes to deliver, they freshened up and changed clothes and headed out the door.

Dinner was actually a lot more cheery than Keeley had envisioned. There were the initial tears when everyone reconnected, but overall it turned out to be a great opportunity to remember a great and spirited woman. There was even laughter as they swapped stories. Keeley subconsciously kept taking peeks at her brother, but overall he looked intact. He ate a normal amount of food and even opted for dessert – Bananas Foster.

Chapter twelve

Adrienne Torero listened again as her stomach growled. She fumbled with the keys, then dropped her purse, spilling everything. She cursed, then gathered lipsticks, a pack of travel tissue, her already cracked cell phone, her wallet and two candy bars she had hidden there the other night during a weak moment. She paused by her front door, tempted for just the briefest moment. *Don't do it, Ade*, she chided. *You were the heaviest one at the meeting tonight. It's not worth it.* Adrienne had never really cared about weight. She was told her whole life that "she wore it well," or that she was "voluptuous." She had even heard the famous reverse-compliment about how she had "such a pretty face." But the catalyst for joining Weight Watchers came in the form of a wedding proposal from Peter. She had been waiting longer than she would have liked for the proposal. She was not used to having anything in her life beyond her control. Not that she was a control freak. Clearly the tipping scale tonight gave that away. No, she had no control when it came to food. And, until a couple of weeks ago when she stepped foot into Amore Bridal Boutique, it still wasn't an issue. Peter loved her for who she was, a respected professional in the community. Her size was simply not a blip on her radar.

She stood up, shoving the candy into the front pouch of her purse and zipped it shut. No way would Blair of Amore Bridal get the best of her! The woman was a sheer billboard for setting feminism back one hundred years. She started off by telling Adrienne that they would have to charge extra to get the dress in her size. She then continued to go on and on about how she might want to make some lifestyle changes before ordering a dress *that size*, once the measuring was said and done. After burying her sorrows in a pint of Ben and Jerry's, and recounting the entire story to Peter, she felt a little bit better. But the next day she had gone to Lila's Bridal where she stood, half clothed in a gorgeous gown, while two straining employees called for a *third* employee to hold the dress together while they tried to zip her into it, which, by the way, never happened. She almost died of embarrassment when two model-thin women snickered and pointed in her direction and then when she saw two other brides-to-be looking dashing in slim-fit gowns. They laughed and smiled as the clerks pinned the heck out of the oversized floor model dresses to fit their trim physiques. How the best news of her life could send her into a downward spiral – and a horridly depriving diet – she never knew.

She collected her belongings and unlocked the door, successfully this time. She greeted her puppy, Pluto, with a kiss once she hung her purse on the coat rack. "Hello, Pluto! Mommy is here. And that scale was rigged tonight at my meeting, I just know it was." She smiled, gently pushing Pluto off her leg. "I'll get you some puppy chow and Mommy can have a nice boring salad." Adrienne walked toward the answering machine, where a blinking, digital 2 summoned her. She knew that one of the two calls would be from Peter. He always greeted her in the evenings when she came home, especially lately. He knew she was feeling down, so he had also ordered a barrage of flowers – one bouquet to her office and two to her house – over the past few days. She pressed play on the machine, then opened a can of dog food. *How pathetic that it actually smells halfway decent.*

"Hi, Hon, it's me. Hope your day was good. Call me." Peter was a saint. His voice was just what she needed to hear right now. She deleted the message and readied herself for the next message so she could delete that one too and call her fiancé. It was a telemarketer. *Delete.* The phone rang a few times before going to voicemail – not unusual – Peter was the head surgeon at All Saints Hospital.

Adrienne grabbed a bag of lettuce from the drawer and dumped a portion onto her plate. Then she opened a can of tuna fish that barely rivaled Pluto's can of food in scent, and added that to the plate. She chopped up a carrot and doused the salad in tasteless diet Italian dressing. Pluto followed her to the couch where she turned on the news. Just as she was growing interested in a human interest story about a local high school kid, the power shut off. The television, the lights, everything. She removed the fork from her mouth and set it on the plate beside her. "It's okay, Pluto," she said, more for her benefit than Pluto's. *Keep calm.* "Let's see. Where are the circuit breakers? Or is there a neighborhood outage? Candles. Let's get candles." The curtains were slightly opened so there was still enough light to get a feel for where everything was in her house. It wasn't pitch dark. Adrienne went to the kitchen and grabbed two candles and a fireplace lighter. She peered out the window and saw that Mrs. Ruffin across the way still had her power. She could see clearly into the house; the old lady was vacuuming. And the Hendricks family had their porch light ablaze. Was it just this side of the street? Or just her house?

"Come on, boy." Holding a candle, Adrienne walked toward the front door. There was less light in the windowless hall. She stepped on the shoes she had left by the door and squealed. Pluto whimpered in sympathy at his mistress's anguish. "It's okay, Pluto. Mommy's okay." She continued toward the door, when suddenly she was grabbed from behind and a bag of some sort was thrown over her head. Pluto was barking up a storm and Adrienne was squirming like a worm on a hook. The man had her arms bent and held in place so tightly that she thought he might break something if she moved too hard, but she still put up a good fight. He had cinched the head covering so tight that she was gagging on the smell of it. She didn't know what it was, but it was taking her breath away. Then she began to feel light headed and she realized the smell might be ether or something else to make her pass out. Then at that very moment, Pluto stopped barking.

"No!" Adrienne gurgled, just as everything became dark.

***

Keeley and Bob got back to their hotel shortly after nine o'clock. The first thing she did after taking off her shoes was head straight to her cell phone, which she realized she'd left behind halfway through the ride to the restaurant. Three missed calls, three voicemails. The first was from Ben, the second from Leah and the third from Detective Dean. She went straight to Dean's call and hit *playback message*. "Keeley, I know you're out of town, but we've got a situation here that we want to advise you of. The woman is only *missing* right now, but it looks like there were minor traces of human blood left behind."

Keeley's knees went weak.

"Harmful intent could be at play. Plus her dog was killed. Not sure if this fits into any of the fictional murder plots you've read or know of. Anyway, call me when you get a sec." She slumped into the couch. Brow creased, she went over in her mind all possible story lines where a pet was harmed during a murder or abduction. Nothing notable came to mind. And she knew . . . she knew *this* guy was going for notable. He wasn't looking for references that people might miss or be unfamiliar with. He was going for renowned plots and using well-known authors - King, Christie, Poe. The piece about the dog wasn't it. The dog must have gotten in the way.

Bob came out of his room wearing drawstring flannel pants and a long sleeve cotton shirt with some sports insignia, which she couldn't place, on the breast pocket. She didn't realize how distraught she must have looked until his face mirrored her feelings.

"What is it?" he asked, growing pale.

Suddenly the surprisingly bearable evening and the sumptuous meal became a dizzying memory. With each victim it became so much more sickeningly real. Losing Jess was, well, a life-altering horrid ordeal; but this was becoming an epidemic. Keeley felt faint. She lay back on the couch. "Don't worry . . . yet. There was a message from Dean and he thinks, even though a body hasn't turned up yet," Keeley forced down the bile rising in her throat, "that this may be connected."

"How? Why?"

"I should probably call him back. He said that they saw . . . human blood. A pet was killed."

"Well was there a book left behind? Why else would . . . " Bob didn't have to finish his sentence. Keeley did so mentally. Why else would they think this was a murder? Because this guy has the market on all recent crime sprees basically? Perhaps the woman fit the bill-- everything to live for, lap of luxury, a loose connection to the cultural scene? She did need to call Dean; but dammit, things were settling down for them, if even for a second. Talk about small victories, but that dinner was a success. She was just about to give Bob a pep talk about how, with one hurdle down, tomorrow would be a piece of cake.

"I need to go find out, Bob. I'll take it in the other room. Why don't you just try and relax." She walked over and patted his shoulder. "You did great tonight by the way."

"You were there. You're always there for me, Kee."

"Of course. I'd do anything for you." *Including mixing myself up with this investigation*, she thought.

"I love you. I'll stay out here for a while. Let me know what they found." She would, but she'd do her best to sugarcoat it. He didn't need this right now. She would never lie to him, but there was nothing that couldn't wait until they were safely at home to hear - hopefully.

She closed the door to her room and dialed Dean's extension. He answered before it even finished the first ring.

"Detective Dean."

"It's Keeley Travis. I just got back from dinner." She winced. Dean was certainly nice enough, but maybe it was the whole policeman thing that made her feel so juvenile. It wasn't like he would reprimand her for not calling sooner. Geeze.

"Thanks for getting back to me. I know I didn't leave much information, but that's because we have very little information to go on. The victim lives alone but she's engaged to a local surgeon and she definitely fits the profile: Successful woman, does volunteer work, well known in her circles, dabbled in the art museum benefits and was on the annual gala guest list . . . that type of thing. There was no book found outside of the book shelves, but there was an extensive book collection in the home.

"The fiancé came home to surprise her. Found the door ajar, the dog was killed -bludgeoned to death – and there was a small amount of blood and a small piece of what looks like nylon. It was on the bottom corner of the door. My guess is she snagged her nylon *and* her skin while she was forced out the door. We have no reason to believe this is the same guy, except that she fits the bill. Now, normally killers don't deviate from their M.O. For example, our guy has yet to do anything but kill on the spot. He sets the stage, leaves a book, moves on. But, since his main focus seems to be setting up these detailed *plots* that he likes to mimic, that leads us to believe that his M.O. isn't set in stone. Meaning, if the book he's picked involves a kidnapping scene, then so be it. A kid-napping it becomes."

Keeley's mind was swirling: Kidnapping. Kidnap-ping. Abduction. She was racking her brain. What books? In what books have the victims taken away from their homes? Her mind was working faster than she could keep up with. Savagely, Keeley scanned the room, zeroing in on the pile of books she had by her bed. And then it hit her. She reached across and swept the pile over with the back of her hand, creating a fan-like array of titles and colorful illustrations. Heart beating, eyes ferociously scanning the pile. "Oh my God!" She picked up the pa-perback. "It might be *Silence of the Lambs*!" she gasped. *And if it is*, she thought, *this is about to get gruesome.*

***

Adrienne awoke, having been floating somewhere in between consciousness and the depths of hell. Of course she was drugged and delirious, but not too far off base. She was manacled, lying in the bottom of a dirt pit, dug so deep that she couldn't see the top. It looked like a rudimentary well once she better accessed the situation. She had only seen her captor once, when she was first placed – no – thrown into the pit. He threw her a sandwich, but then told her it had rat poison in it. Of course the bread and meat scattered when the food landed in the pit. Parts of it were close enough to her face for her to smell it and it smelled like rotting meat. She retched, recoiled, but realized then that her feet were bound. Now she heard footsteps approaching. She got into the sitting position and scootched her way toward the wall farthest from the impending steps. Impulsively she looked up. In the faint light, she saw a man wearing a simple ski mask and holding a lantern.

"Are you hungry?" he asked, with a deep and throaty voice, as though he were trying to disguise his own.

Adrienne couldn't bring herself to respond.

He repeated himself, only shouting this time.

"N-no. I--I just want to go home. I have money if that's what you want." She prayed it was what he wanted.

"Tell me you want food!" he commanded.

"I want food," she whispered, crying.

"Well, you aren't allowed to eat. I'm going to starve you," he simply said before turning and walking away from her.

As much as he terrified her, the idea of being left here was more terrifying. "Please, wait! Don't go!" she wailed. He didn't respond. She cried out again. Still no response. They were somewhere where it didn't matter if she cried for help or not. No one could hear her. She began to wail at that thought.

Finally after her tears had dried, she begin to think more clearly. If she was in the middle of nowhere, she could still try somehow to get out of this place and maybe hide from him. He hadn't been back in a while, it seemed. If he wasn't interested in money, then what did he want? And why starve her? Truthfully she *was* hungry. She'd been hungry since the day she started that damn diet. She kicked at the decaying food he'd thrown down earlier. Adrienne wiped her dirt smeared arms on her pants, then yelped in surprise. Something landed on the ground next to her. She reached for it, against her better judgment and saw that it was a tube of drugstore brand lotion. She pondered over it for a minute, then got a sick feeling in her stomach. She had seen this in a movie once. A woman being held captive was asked to rub lotion on her body. What the hell movie was that? And the song. Tom Petty's catchy tune, *American Girl* floated through her ears. It was also part of the movie. Until she'd seen that movie, she'd loved that song. It was . . . *what*? Is this what he wanted her to do? Rub lotion on herself?

She gagged when she remembered what her mind was avoiding. It was the movie *Silence of the Lambs*, and the psychopath wanted his prisoner to rub lotion on herself because he was planning on using her skin.

***

Keeley and Bob were operating on autopilot for so many reasons: the call last night saying a woman had gone missing, the morose dinner last night kicking off the beginning of the end and the funeral service today. The day wasn't exactly as heart-wrenching as she imagined: tiptoeing around a fragile Bob on the verge of tears, everything shrouded in sadness. No, it was definitely more of a disturbing vibe. She couldn't put her finger on it. The air seemed extra heavy, the early morning view from their room was a lackluster yellowish-gray, and things seemed to be moving in slow motion.

They were both awake long before the wake-up call service had rung the room. Bob ordered morning buns and a pot of coffee. Keeley helped to adjust his tie. They sipped and ate in silence. All the small affects that might normally seem routine. But of course it was not a routine either of them would ever grow accustomed to.

Again she couldn't help but dwell upon the inordinate number of funerals she'd had under her belt for a woman in her mid twenties. Not just the number of funerals. More like the number of family members she watched get buried. The coffee was bitter. It fit the tone of the day so far.

Shortly after their lingering breakfast was finished, the car service had arrived and they were notified by the concierge. They took the elevator down to the ground level and Bob looked at Keeley before letting out a big breath of air. A breath it seemed he had been holding in since the day Keeley arrived. It was as if his heart was saying, "here goes nothing." Keeley held his sturdy hand and they climbed inside the car.

***

Detective Dean was scratching his head when Detective Aerson entered the room. "It's quite literally a head scratcher, eh Dean?" The two men were facing the glass wall where on the other side sat a young man, handcuffed, unable to see them through the two way mirror.

"Funny, but don't quit your day job," sniped Dean.

"If only, Dean-o. If only. So is he the guy?"

"I think it's the guy who stole the books, yeah. I'd be shocked if he was involved in much else." Dean stroked his jaw, his five o'clock shadow taking over. "Then again, I haven't been in to see him yet." He began pacing. "Priors include a bunch of petty theft crap, minor assault, poor conduct, that kind of thing."

"You think there's a chance he's connected to the murderer? A pawn?"

"Could be. Wanna come in there with me? You can be good cop."

"Nah. I'm afraid I'll deck the guy for wasting our time when we could be putting our efforts into catching el jefe."

"I didn't say the guy wasn't connected. On the contrary, we don't know anything about the guy other than his mediocre attempts at a rap sheet and his boyish good looks."

"Ted Bundy was a lady killer too you know."

"This guy's no Ted Bundy," said Dean, "but I am going to find out what I can. Let's go in there, Aerson. And that's not a request."

Dean adjusted the corner of his shirt to expose the grip of his gun. He held the door for Aerson and put on his best intimidation stare. This guy was going to squirm. He looked like he just stepped out of an Abercrombie and Finch ad. He sat up straight when the detectives waltzed inside.

"Good morning," uttered Dean, smugly.

The young man didn't say anything, just sort of grunted and shuffled in his seat. He looked just uncomfortable enough to blow his tough guy routine.

Dean already knew he had him. "Want to tell us why you're in here? It's a beautiful day outside. You certainly could be making better use of everyone's time."

He sat silent for a minute, then let his guard down. "I'm a student. I stole some books, okay? Are the cuffs really necessary?" He relaxed his stiff body and laughed quietly. "I mean . . . since you're so interested in people's time being wasted and all." The young man smiled, like he had just scored a point.

"Listen you little bastard!" shouted Aerson, about two inches from the kid's face. He recoiled and swallowed hard, shifting in his seat. Aerson laughed. "Did you just tinkle? Hey Dean, I think the kid needs some toilet paper!" Aerson was hysterical.

Dean liked the guy enough but he hated when he got all cocky. It wasn't by any stretch necessary. This kid would be putty in their hands, guilty or not. Dean was about to tell the kid that the cuffs *weren't* necessary, but now that Aerson decided to showboat, he figured maybe they were.

"Well, stealing books is a crime, in case you are not aware. And if you get booked for it, you'll have more than enough reading time on your hands."

"Two detectives don't visit you for stealing books."

"Are you in school for criminology?" said Aerson, who was slowly getting under Dean's skin. The kid didn't respond. "Because this isn't your first rodeo, right? Ever hear of three strikes? We could be seeing a whole lot more of each other," smiled Aerson.

"I just know that after seeing the news, you have bigger fish to fry than a small timer like me."

Dean wanted to shake the guy and tell him they knew he stole *Silence of the Lambs*, the book Keeley sensed was being mimicked with the recent kidnapping. But this kid couldn't be their killer. It was either an amazing coincidence or he was just stupid enough to be contracted by a killer who wanted the police off his trail. He was also too stupid to realize he was being framed if that was the case. Dean wanted to scare the kid into confessing that he was paid to steal. He wanted to tell him that he could throw his ass in jail for suspicion of murder, but he couldn't expose the department by giving away inside info.

"Don't worry about us and our jobs," began Dean. "Cause you're here now and you've committed a crime, son. Matter of fact, we have no reason not to link you to the other crime, the one you saw on the news."

"*What*?! You're trying to pin a *murder* on me? No way!" He was shaking in his boots - Dean was savoring it. "You've got nothing to go on," he stuttered.

"All we need is a person who was in the store to identify you for theft. After that, if we see fit, we can book you for just about anything. You wouldn't want to add suspicion of murder to that record of yours, would you?" Dean knew that if the kid had a brain he wouldn't have buckled so fast. Clearly he knew nothing about the system, because he broke down under Dean's preposterous threat.

"It wasn't me. It was some man I never met. He gave me a stack of bills to crack three bookstores. He even gave me a list of what he wanted. There. Am I off the hook yet?"

"Not yet," said Dean, exiting the interrogation room with Aerson in tow. He slammed the door and once they were on the other side of the mirror he slammed his fist hard on the metal table. "Why would the murderer go to the trouble of having someone *steal* the books? He had to know we could get to him this way."

"Distraction? The hope that we were so incompetent that we might actually pin this kid for murder? And of course don't forgo the fact that he's probably missing a few marbles."

Dean nodded his head. "Let's let this Josh kid sweat a little bit, then we ask him to give up the perp while giving him a good plea bargain. This could be it."

***

The funeral went as well as a funeral for a loved one could go. Bob and Keeley had packed, checked out of their hotel and were waiting to board the plane. Keeley figured there would at least be a sort of forced, if not artificial, closure once they arrived at home, which she anxiously awaited. Bob had already told her that he would return to work the following Monday, knowing it would help him to begin the healing process. She offered to stay with him as long as he wanted, but he told her that she, too, needed to get back to her own life. She argued; then Bob told her he'd like it if things were as close to normal as they could be, so she agreed to leave the same morning he returned to work.

They arrived home early in the evening to find a news van and a mini media frenzy developing on Bob's front lawn. Keeley was livid, using the opportunity to finally unload herself of all of her anguish and frustration. She leapt out of the car and ran up to the oblivious newswoman, who yelled out to her camera man to "roll it," but not before Keeley knocked the camera to the ground. "Get off our property, now, or I call the police!" Bob suppressed a smile as the newswoman nearly fell to the ground in shock. The camera man and two assistants gathered the pieces of equipment while the woman sped away towards the van, fearful and skittish.

"I'll be sure not to mess with you anymore!" gushed Bob, jamming the key in the lock. They entered the house and Keeley fell against the wall laughing. Her adrenaline had never been so high. Bob was laughing too. "I had no idea I had that in me!" The smile washed from her face the moment the phone rang. They eyed each other tentatively. "I'll get it," said Keeley, still feeling empowered. She would deal with whatever news was being thrown their way.

"Hello?"

"It's Dean. I'm glad I caught you. We nabbed the book thief and his name and appearance match your description. He's got a record that includes shoplifting." Keeley's heart sped. "He 'fessed up to taking money from some guy to steal the books. The only thing is he never saw him. He got a note on his motorcycle's windshield asking him to call the number if he wanted to make some fast cash. That tells us the real culprit somehow knew Josh was a smalltime thief. Anyway, Josh contacted the guy. Then he received another note on his bike, this time listing the books to be stolen. After that, Josh dropped the bag of books at some park and the money was delivered - tucked into the fender of his bike the morning after the heist."

"Oh my gosh!" Keeley was shell-shocked remembering Josh's innocent yet vexing flirtations that day at the bookstore. Her skin crawled. She looked up to see Bob staring at her, his brow wrinkling. He had seen her shiver. She covered the phone with her palm. "I'm okay."

"Yeah. So anyway, we're working the angles to get to the big guy." Dean sighed. "Meanwhile, good job on giving us Josh. This may be a huge crack in the case, thanks to you, Keeley."

"Would there still be fingerprints on the motorcycle? Or the money if he still had any of it?"

"The kid had his bike washed and the money was spent. We'll get there though. Don't worry."

"What about anything at my store?" Keeley piped excitedly. "The shelves, the window he slipped out of?!"

"Good job. You're already thinking like a detective. Yes, we scanned for prints at your store. We're waiting on that still." The lilt in his voice made her wonder if he was being condescending, but she couldn't care less. If she had held her tongue about Josh, they wouldn't be so far along. She would do everything she could to help even if she came across as some little girl trying her hand at mystery solving. And the next thing she would do . . . was read *The Silence of the Lambs* . . . as fast as she could. If there was any credence to her kidnapping theory, she needed to be up to speed.

Chapter thirteen

Adrienne was freezing . . . Freezing and starving. The pre-dawn air was visibly damp and the sodden earth below her was hard and cold. Still she had no choice but to lay directly on the dirt. She was in the fetal position, mostly because she was weak and terrified; but also because she was chilled to the bone. She always said she was never cold. She joked that her curves kept her insulated, though she had never been in these conditions, these barbaric conditions. She looked around at the spoiled food that covered the ground. She gagged. She was so dehydrated that she choked. Then she winced. She didn't want to make any noise or cause any reason to grab his attention. She wanted him to go away and never come back. She'd rather die in here than have him pull her out to do who knows what to her. Clearly he was a psychopath. Then she heard him approaching the depths of her confinement.

"No food yet, huh? Oh well. You could stand to lose a few pounds. As a matter of fact, looks like you have." She was wearing only an oversized tee-shirt and underwear at his demand. She began to sob, deliriously. "Don't cry," he said, robotically. "I might keep you around for another day. Unless you're ready to go now." He turned on his heels, leaving the gaping holes ledge.

"No," she wailed. "I'm not! I don't want to go *anywhere*!" Adrienne picked up the bottle of lotion off the ground and threw it as hard as she could toward the spot where *he* had been standing.

* * *

Keeley shot up in bed. Another nightmare. It was so real, though. Of course it was from her satanic choice of bedtime stories. She had gotten through a large chunk of the book, then stopped, only because her eyes were closing. She had also started to consider that the kidnapping victim was not going to fall prey to the gory plotline of *The Silence of the Lambs*. For Jess, Harper and Tranise the deaths had all been at the hands of the main antagonist. In *The Silence of the Lambs*, the kidnapping M.O. was that of a secondary antagonist, Buffalo Bill. Hannibal Lecter, who was the chief murderer in the novel. Hannibal committed horrible crimes of course, but he didn't go through the charade of kidnapping. Jess's killer seemed to stick to the main plot, not any secondary plots. And mimicking the kidnapping aspect of the book would mean he was following a subplot. She hoped she was right. And if she was right, then maybe it was a different book altogether. A book where the killer(s) didn't turn human skin into clothing. She picked up the paperback and chucked it against the wall. She winced at the noise it made and hoped she didn't chip the wall paint. Freeing herself of the wadded up covers, she walked over and peeked at the wall, rubbing her finger along the spot where the corner of the book made contact. No scratch. She let out a breath. *Calm, girl*, she warned herself. She wasn't sure what was coming over her. First attacking and berating a newscaster, now throwing things in sheer anger. This wasn't like her. Then again, none of this was like her: frantically scanning the top horror novels in an effort to find her sister-in-law's *killer*, having minimal contact with Ben, while temporarily living with her widowed brother and cavorting around town with a crime scene detective. What next? Sickeningly, she knew what was next. News that Adrienne, the kidnapped woman, would be dead.

And Keeley, who was supposed to be helping, had no idea what novel they should be looking to. And on top of that, identifying the novel wouldn't do much. It wasn't as if the killer was mimicking locations. Edgar Allen Poe's Telltale Heart didn't take place in a cabin in the woods. He just needed a removable floorboard to prove his point. And in regards to Jess's murder, Pennywise the Clown didn't dismember the little boy in an office suite, it was on the streets of Derry, Maine. In the rain. So in reality, she could do all the homework she wanted, but nothing would really help. This guy didn't want to be caught, of course. He just wanted to play his sick little game.

Keeley began flipping through the pages of the book. She flipped forward, then back, finding the scene with the secondary killer, Buffalo Bill. He kidnapped overweight women, starved them for a few days in a ditch, then killed and skinned them before dumping their bodies in a river. She leapt up. She needed to ask Dean for Adrienne's physical description. If the killer was actually acting on Buffalo Bill's murdering technique from the book, how much of it would he recreate? The kidnapping, then what else? Recklessly, she shuffled through her purse.

She dialed Dean's direct line. If Adrienne fit the body type and the killer kept to the plot, they might be able to find a locale with a ditch or a well or something in time to save Adrienne. The line rang. *Please pick up, please pick up.* Keeley hoped she wasn't being too hasty. The settings, as of yet, were never true to the novels. Harper was killed in her own condominium, for crying out loud.

"Detective Dean."

"It's Keeley Travis."

"Hi Keeley."

"I'm calling because I thought of something that might help."

She told Dean everything she had mentally established and he didn't seem exasperated in the least. On the contrary, he thanked her and told her to keep up the good work, and that the prints at her store did match those of Josh. She smiled with satisfaction as she hung up the phone. She determined that she would relay the hopeful info to Bob, pick up breakfast and make the most of their last days together under Bob's roof. If there was any spare time before tonight, she'd read over the remaining novels. And if there wasn't any spare time, tonight would be a long night.

***

"These bagels are really good, Kee." Bob's color and appetite had returned. The burial proved to be cathartic after all. Keeley had just returned home with a whopping dozen bagels (she told Bob he could freeze them for an easy on-the-go breakfast when work resumed on Monday), three tubs of flavored spreads, plus lox. They ate voraciously, while sipping iced lattes. The morning was off to a good start. She had given her brother the PG-13 version of the whole *Lambs* theory, leaving him optimistic rather than distraught. Bob suggested they actually leave the house today, which certainly peaked Keeley's interest.

"Where did you have in mind?"

"I was thinking it might be a nice idea to swing by the art museum today." He smiled at his sister. "She loved to go. Anytime we both had time off that's what Jess would suggest, anyway. Plus, I received quite a few calls after . . . " he trailed off. "And I never returned any of them." Bob let out a deep breath. "The people there loved Jess like we did, Kee. I think I owe it to them and to her." She was reveling in his epiphany. It was wonderful to see the old Bob again. His face was lit up. He was smiling and talking, no longer a taciturn emblem of disappointment. He was actually excited about something.

They were dressed in warm clothes and out the door half hour later. It was a true fall day. Leaves swirled at their feet and the wind was biting and crisp. Keeley loved this type of weather. Scarves, warming your feet by the fire, lingering steamy showers, seasonal soups. She'd have to remember to help make this transition easier for Bob by doing frequent museum trips, or whatever else he felt like doing, especially during the holiday season. And she would have extra time with Ben being abroad.

She jumped into the passenger seat and removed her coat. Bob did the same, then turned on the radio. It was a talk channel, something Keeley always found herself zoning out to. Dad had always listened to talk radio. It didn't matter if it was sports, or politics or the news. It all sounded like incessant jibber jabber to her ears. It used to drive her nuts. She smiled that her brother and father were so alike in the most commonplace ways. Suddenly, though, the commentator did get her attention. *And it seems, Don, that bad news does come in threes. We've just heard that the body of Adrienne Torero has been discovered in the Chesapeake River Bay just outside of the Chapin and Drakesborough County lines. The woman was reported missing just days ago, and it did not end well for her. She shares the ill-fated spotlight with Jess Auberdine Travis of Drakesborough County and Harper Middleton of Dover County. These three women are all victims of wrongful murder."*

The male commentator interjected. *"Are the cases related Ann?"*

"Your guess is as good as mine, Don. A word of advice: Don't drink the water, ladies. . . ."

Bob angrily clicked the stereo off, cursing under his breath. He looked like he'd been punched in the gut. Keeley was numb. Adrienne, the woman she thought she was helping with her stupid little hole in the ground theory just an hour ago, was dead, just like Jess. Yet another family had just learned about their loved one. She felt as if she might shatter to a million pieces. Her stunned existence was interrupted as her cell phone began to vibrate in her pocket.

"Hello?" she answered, her mouth running dry.

It was Detective Dean. "Bad news." He sounded genuinely defeated.

"We just heard it over the car radio. I can't believe . . ."

"But you called it, young lady. We found the book by the edge of the river. *The Silence of the Lambs.* For whatever it's worth, we're one step behind him." *It's not worth anything*, she thought, morosely.

"I might be on to something, but when it keeps happening too little too late, I feel just as guilty as the murderer."

Bob reached across the seat toward her. Instinctively she jumped.

"Sorry," she mouthed to him, taking his hand.

"Spoken like a true cop, Keeley. We all feel that way. Don't beat yourself up, just keep doing what you're doing." He cleared his throat, then lowered his voice. "You knew more than our top staff who have been doing this since you were in diapers. Don't lose sight of how helpful you've been. Please."

The man was good. Like always, he seemed to know just what to say. Keeley sighed. "Okay. I won't. I'm . . . I'm sorry." And she was sorry. Not just about not solving the sicko's little puzzle in time, but about the lives lost, the horrid place their world had become, Dean's terrifically unpleasant and thankless job, her brother being a widower, and her seemingly perfect life crumbling all around her in record time. *Perfect life.* The words stuck in her chest like glue. That was one of the prerequisites for this psychopath, according to the composite victim profile. Taking away a seemingly perfect life from seemingly perfect people. Was Jess a perfect person? It could be argued that she was. She was kind to others, a natural nurturer, never jealous or catty or mean. She took pleasure in the success and well-being of others. Keeley didn't know everything that went on behind closed doors, but her brother never complained. They were in love. And because of that, because of all those wonderful things, Jess had to die. Who in the hell thought that it was their job to play God? To decide who lived and who died? Keeley swallowed a mouthful of bile.

"Can we go in?" she asked Bob, who was staring lifelessly out the car window.

"Please."

Chapter fourteen

Keeley had her bags packed. She and Bob ate re-heated Chinese food and did their best to pay attention to a classic episode of Cheers. After hearing about Adrienne, Bob's weekend consisted of napping and obsessive clean-ing. She knew that was his roundabout way of coping, but it was a far cry from taking in the museums and working toward acceptance. Keeley, on the other hand, compul-sively poured over the stack of horror novels, becoming more and more possessed by the case. She had notebooks full of plots and motives and characters that she had jotted down. By the end of the weekend she gasped when she looked in the mirror, surprised by her own appearance. She had traded ghoulish and gory research for sleep and the ability to properly deal with the matters at hand. Her skin looked pale and the dark pits underneath her eyes betrayed her age. She was giving this task of hers a life of its own, and she didn't like where it was taking her. The little sleep she was getting was tarnished with blood. It was like they had both regressed a few steps.

"Is there any moo shu left?" asked Bob. Keeley snapped to life.

"Yes, here," she said handing him the carton, "but I think it's cold. Let me reheat it." Keeley half-stood, but he was already serving some from the carton onto his plate.

"It's okay, thanks." He haphazardly dumped some predictably cold fried rice on top of the moo shu.

They were both operating on autopilot, once again. They ate in silence, while on TV, Sam and Diane danced around their inevitable love affair. That was kind of how life felt right then, Keeley realized. It was going on, beyond their control, kind of like a syndicated plot on television. Everyone had a pretty good idea of what would happen next, but there was this unspoken possibility . . . hope, in this case. The hope that maybe things would take a different route this time. That there wouldn't be another murder.

Minutes later they both stood and began gathering empty cartons of food and carrying them to the kitchen. After washing the dishes and discarding the picked over cartons, Keeley noticed that once again Bob had poured some type of straight hard alcohol into a glass. She watched as he savored a sip . . . watched as the pain left his eyes and was replaced with a sort of relief. She couldn't let him go down this road, not with her leaving first thing tomorrow morning. "Are you sure that's a great idea?" She gestured toward the glass. "With work tomorrow and everything?"

"I know you mean well, Kee, but let me deal with things my way. It won't become a problem, I promise."

That was all she needed to hear. His word. His promise. "Okay." And that was that.

They separated, going to their respective quarters. Keeley had made a promise to herself that she too would take a break from her own demons - no reading tonight. She needed a clear head and a good night's sleep. It was back to *her* normal routine tomorrow, also.

Keeley washed her face, opting to take her shower in the morning. Along with tons of caffeine, she would rely on a shower to wake her up tomorrow. If everything went well, though, she'd get a full night's sleep. She tied back her hair and changed into pajamas. After taking out her contacts, she crawled into bed. Her cell phone began to vibrate on the bedside table, just as she got comfortable. She winced, then brightened up as soon as she saw Ben's name emblazed on the screen. It felt like an eternity since he'd wrapped her in his arms.

"Ben! Hi!"

"Hey, Honey. You sound good."

"Glad that it's you calling. But otherwise we're drowning here." She hadn't gotten a chance to tell Ben the latest on Adrienne; but unless he was living under a rock, he'd already found out.

"Babe, hang in there. I wish so much I that I was able to be there. But you're coming tomorrow, right? I can see you then."

"Yes. I can't wait, Ben. It just hasn't been the same. I'm not as strong as I thought I was. I wanted to be more of a support for Bob, but . . . "

"Are you crazy? You're a rock. You're the strongest woman I know, Keeley."

"Then you don't really know me either, I guess." The minute the words escaped her mouth, she regretted them. She didn't want to lash out at him or hash out all her insecurities. She loved him and she just wanted to be with him. She wanted him to take all the pain away. To take her away from the dark space she had created.

"Keeley – are you okay?"

"Not really, but I will be. It's just been nightmare after nightmare."

"You've been through a tremendous amount of strife lately. Jess, your brother, the store, the investigation." There was an exaggerated pause. Then, "Keeley, I want you to back off the case. I think it's too much."

"And leave all those people who need help? Ben, I..."

"Keeley, I think you're doing a great thing, but I'm pretty sure the police can take it from here."

Her jaw dropped. How dare he imply that she considered herself the case-cracking element? And how dare he belittle the blood, sweat and tears she put into trying to help find Jess's killer. She felt herself first blush, then fill with anger. Her first inclination was to hang up on him. When had she and Ben lost touch and become hostile with one another? He had never done anything but support her every decision. She didn't want to sink to his level of cruelty, but she also found herself at a loss for words. Since the case began, she had only spoken with Ben a handful of times. How could this possibly be *his* cross to bear? Or his *decision* to make? Yet she feared that if she spoke her mind, she would alienate the one person who she needed so badly right now.

"Keeley, I'm sorry. I certainly didn't mean to . . . I - I've lost so much sleep. Not nearly as much as you have I'm sure, but I'm scared. I don't like the idea of you being so close to this. And with me getting ready to leave . . . I'll be so far away."

"I can handle it, Ben. I want to."

"This is real life, Keeley. What if things don't come together as easy as they do in one of your novels? Think of what this could do to you." She couldn't tell if he was being patronizing or constructive.

"I know, but think of what this could do to me if I don't get involved. I know what I'm doing here, Ben. Please trust me."

"I'd trust you with my life. Okay, then. I'm here for you, Kee. Well, as *here* as I can be when I'm oceans away from you."

There we go, she thought. The old Ben is back.

"That's okay," she said warming up to him. "I'll just have to make the most out of the next two weeks. I can't wait to see you tomorrow."

"I can't wait either, but . . . it's not two weeks any-more." Keeley felt her stomach drop. "I need to leave on Wednesday now."

"This Wednesday?!"

"I know. Keeley I'm so sorry. I found out yesterday, but I was going to wait to tell you, with everything going on. There's nothing I can do. I absolutely have to do this trip."

She could sense his remorse. She felt for him. She took a breath. Of course he had to go. It was his *future* in the making. An opportunity he couldn't pass up. And she certainly wouldn't stand in his way. This was *their* future in the making. "I know there's nothing you can do, I'll just . . . I'll miss you so much." She bit back the tears, but they began to flow anyway.

"You are the most important thing in my life, Keeley. You think I don't regret this? I think of you every minute. That's why I'm being so overbearing about the police work." He laughed quietly. A self-deprecating laugh that fit him so well. That was one of the many things that she loved about him. "I just hate the fact that I can't really be there for you, Kee, but we'll talk every night!"

"I know." She sniffed. "It'll all work itself out, Ben. It's going to be okay."

"And then before you know it, I'll be back and we'll be planning our wedding. Then we won't have to be apart ever again."

***

Dean was finally winding down. He was off duty for the night, but for some lurking reason, he didn't think it was a good idea to get too comfortable. He was eating a late dinner with Terry and Zoey was studying with a friend down the street. Maybe it was the foreboding feeling he was harboring, but he pushed his hand in front of the tilted wine bottle that Terry had poised over his glass. One drink was enough. "No refill for me," he smiled. If there was one thing the force had taught him, it was that you should never let yourself get too comfortable. *Never let your guard down.* That mantra had kept him sleeping with one eye opened for a great chunk of his adult life. It had also kept him from ever completely unwinding – a something that bothered Terry more than it bothered him.

They retreated to the sitting room after taking on the dishes together. Terry ended up with an accidental smudge of bubbles on her sweater after Dean reached across her, declaring an all-out bubble war. They were damp and giggling by the time they got to the couch. Terry immediately reached for her knitting, while Dean opted for the remote.

"This is nice," said Terry, setting the mess of yarn in her lap. "Hardly ever do I get you all to myself like this."

"And no angst-ridden teen to boot." Dean lowered the volume to silence and set the remote aside after settling on a sports update. He scooted closer to Terry and put his arm around her. They sat, enjoying the blazing fire in the fireplace. With the thermostat turned up it didn't feel at all like the coolest day so far this fall. It was cozy and peaceful. Even though Dean was actually quite good at shutting off his job life from his real life, he never took anything for granted. He knew this was the stuff. His family was safe and for just a moment, the whole world felt safe. And he allowed himself to believe that. But, like all good things, it had to come to an end. His work phone began to buzz. Terry was so accustomed to the forsaken interruptions that she didn't even react anymore. "Go ahead," she smiled, removing his arm from around her shoulders, knitting resumed.

"I'll be just a minute." He strode over to his phone and answered curtly. "Dean."

Terry glanced up from her knitting to see a look of worry pass over her husband's face. She would never get used to that. She hated it. "I see. Any other details? Okay. I'll pop in," he glanced at his watch, "in about an hour."

He hung up and turned to face his high school sweetheart. "It's unavoidable, Hon. That kid Josh, who worked as the patsy, stealing those books. He was killed at his apartment. And the sad thing – I figured this kid might be in danger. Yet I didn't even think to place security on the damn kid." Again that stark look of worry and sadness passed over his hardened face.

Terry hated this the most.

***

Exactly an hour later, Dean stood in a small, but to his surprise, tastefully decorated apartment. Lining the walls were several bookshelves, but the books were not thriller novels. They were all historical non-fiction. So Josh was a history buff. Sadly, the poor kid did make history, but not the good kind. He was an unsuspecting punk of a pawn for a serial killer, then a victim of a serial killer, who would also go down in history, hopefully while serving a life sentence.

The place had been swept clean – dusted for prints, fibers collected, notes and phone messages surveyed, drawers searched. If there was a story to tell, it would be told. For now there wasn't much Dean could do, other than make his presence known and nod in disapproval. He did a cursory lap, discovering pictures of Josh and either his elderly parents or his grandparents. There was picture of a pretty young woman, who could have been a girlfriend or a sister. His contact list on his cell phone was limited and it didn't have any familial titles, such as mom or dad or sister or grandma. Only names. The names of those recently called were documented and being checked for relevance, right then and there by a young and befuddled officer. He looked like he was about twenty years old with dark hair and a baby face. Dean knew his type. He was new and eager but couldn't be trusted with more than a menial task in such a big case. Dean approached the young officer during a pause in his calling.

"Anything good?"

"Not yet sir. There were only three numbers that were dialed within the last three days. My first two calls went to voicemail – male voices - and the third call was answered by a female. She said she barely knew Josh, but had gone out with him a of couple times."

"Was she a co-worker? Girlfriend? Fellow student?" Dean began to feel cross, thinking this kid might have blown even the most basic task. If you called someone on a victim call list a second time that gave them more time to think.

"No sir. She said they met through the museum. Said Josh was their research historian."

Dean kneaded his brow. "Ah, shoot." The Goddamn museum again. Was it possible he had underestimated Josh? But if he had, then Josh wouldn't be dead now.

***

Tranise was busying herself with an overflowing basket of fresh laundry while Jeff was finally getting the girls to bed. It was the third night in a row that they were still awake at nine o'clock. Waking them up for school in the morning would be like pulling teeth. But, like most activities these days, it would serve as a distraction from life as she knew it. She was having such a hard time coping that Jeff suggested she go talk to someone about it. At first she felt that was out of the question, but the hard reality was that she was warming up to the idea. She now knew that asking for help in dealing with this was not a weakness. She needed to do it for the sake of her whole family. She needed to be whole again.

The towels were folded and piled high, then replaced in the wicker basket, while small piles of socks and underwear lay in small heaps across the edge of the master bed. She would distribute them to their respective drawers, then settle in in front of the fireplace with a television show. She spun on her heels, screeching, then dropping the armload of the children's undergarments.

"I'm sorry, honey. I didn't mean to scare you," said Jeff with anguish in his eyes.

"It's not you, it's me," she whispered, sitting on the edge of the bed. "I'm still afraid I'll see him behind every corner, Jeff. I'm not healing, I'm getting worse." She stood, sinking into him, allowing him to support her.

"You got away from this guy. You are a thousand times stronger than you know." He grabbed her shoulders and stared into her hazel eyes. "You escaped death, for God's sake."

"And who's to say death won't track me down until it gets its way?" This wasn't the first time she'd voiced this theory, to Jeff or to the police department. They insisted that she would be safe, saying that the killer wouldn't want her any other way since his initial attempt had been compromised. Jeff nearly threatened them into adding their street into the local police drive by route. So occasionally, when Tranise would get the mail or take a glimpse out the window, she would see a police vehicle cruising the streets of upper-middle class suburbia. It did nothing to settle her nerves. Nothing worked, yet.

"He's not coming for you. You are safe," he asserted. Jeff had installed a top of the line security system the day after the dust settled. It made him feel safe, as well as the girls, but she felt like she was being trapped. She sighed.

"I'm going to call someone tomorrow who I can talk to about this." She kissed his cheek. He raised his eyebrows. "Really? What caused the change of heart?"

"Nothing else seems to be working. I don't want to give up. I'm sick and tired of being scared. Is that a long enough list of reasons?" She smiled, wrapping her arms around him.

"Whatever you want, Hon. I'll do whatever it takes to get you feeling well."

"Can you put that lunatic behind bars? Better yet in the electric chair?" She hated being so grim.

"Let's try." He kissed her this time. "Which reminds me, we're supposed to meet up with Detective Dean and Keeley again soon. A meeting of the brain trust." He smiled at her. That nickname was his attempt at making it all seem lighthearted. A meeting of the brain trust. Actually, that could be just what she needed right about now. She felt an undeniable kinship with Keeley Travis. Tranise wished for a moment that Keeley could be the one she could talk to, instead of a stuffy psychiatrist who she didn't know.

"What is it?" asked Jeff.

"I was just thinking about how much I liked Keeley. And I was thinking that maybe we could kill two birds with one stone if I was able to talk things through with her. We might be able to brainstorm about the case *and* it could be therapeutic?" She looked into his eyes, hoping he wouldn't deny her idea.

"Like I said, I'll try whatever it takes. Call her up and ask her if she can lend an ear. I'm sure she'd like to vent too."

"Maybe I'll call her tomorrow." Tranise already felt a bit of relief course through her. The idea of showing up at a shrink's office, bearing her soul all over again . . . how she hated rehashing her horrible saga. Telling a person who was paid to talk to her all about her most raw emotions. The whole idea made her feel so darn vulnerable, as if it were even *possible* for her to feel more vulnerable than she already did. But talking it over with a trusted person who had some idea of what horrors she'd been through? Someone personally connected to the case? That felt therapeutic. "I know that she has her own life, though. And I wouldn't even suggest it, knowing it could put her own healing process on hold, except that she's already engaged in the case." Tranise looked up to meet Jeff's gaze.

"All you can do is ask. Do yourself a favor and give it a try. The worst she can say is no, though I doubt she will. She's got a kind heart. Smart too. Between the two of you, you might just catch a killer." His eyes crinkled at the corners as he gave her his famous smile.

Chapter fifteen

Over leftover bagels, Keeley realized how much she was going to miss staying with her brother, despite the circumstances. She was happy to see that he had decided, on his own, to get back to a normal routine. Clearly that was the best thing for Bob. And it's not like she was here for a vacation. It was just that due to their age differences they never had time together under one roof, so to speak. Decidedly, Keeley came to the conclusion that weekend sleepovers might have to become one of their new traditions to keep Bob's spirits up.

"I was thinking maybe I could come stay the weekend in a couple of weeks. Maybe we could do the museum then. Check out a few of the restaurants that you guys . . . enjoyed." *Darn!* She'd been tiptoeing around even the slightest mention of anything related to Jess or the case. Now in the bittersweet final moments together she blew it. Bob smiled, sympathetically.

"Keeley, it's fine. Don't beat yourself up. There's nothing wrong with mentioning Jess. She was my wife. In fact I challenge you to use more than a few sentences without her name coming up." He smiled again. Good ole Bob. "I don't want to live a life where my beautiful Jess just becomes . . . erased. Okay?"

"Okay," she said, settling next to him on the couch. "You're right."

After they carried her bags to the car, Keeley kissed her brother on the cheek and promised to call him tonight. It was early still, and the air was heavy. Dew clung to the trees and the windshields. Her breath was visible as she hopped inside her car. What an impact the weather has on a situation, she thought. Things might seem easier, less somber somehow if the sun was out and the birds were chirping. Instead it was a biting, lonely, cold morning. Her steering wheel was ice cold. She decided that stopping for a warm coffee on the way outside of town before entering the highway might raise her spirits. She needed to warm her seemingly defeated spirit. Anything to cheer her up. She thought of returning to her store, which filled her with pride; of seeing Ben, who would envelope her in his protective embrace, of being in her own home and her own bed. Those things gave her a sense of comfort, to some degree. When she envisioned her store, though, a sensation of trepidation swept over her. She knew it was because of the burglary and that that was irrational because Josh was dead.

Dead.

The words rang in her ear. But Josh was a thief. Of course he didn't deserve to die just because he was a thief, but Jess, Harper, Tranise and Adrienne? They were a group of people known for their kindness and their blissful lives. It just wasn't fair. How was she supposed to find solace sleeping in her own bed when someone was out there doing horrible things to people? She knew the answer to that. She could make peace with her life if she could help nab this lunatic. And if she didn't? Well then maybe Ben was right. Maybe this would take too much of a toll on her. Maybe assisting on the case was the quickest route to diminishing what was left of her own sanity.

She turned off the main road into the neighborhood Starbucks. She was wishing it was a drive-thru when her phone began to buzz. She pulled into a parking spot just outside of the store and secured the emergency break before answering the call. Knowing it would go straight to voicemail if she wasn't fast enough, she neglected to even glance at the caller ID.

"Hello?"

"Is this Keeley?"

"Yes. Who's calling?" she asked, guardedly.

"I'm terribly sorry to bother you, Keeley, but it's Tranise Gray."

"Hi, Tranise." Keeley felt a mixture of pleasant surprise and that sick feeling that came over her every time anything associated with the case came up. Then her stomach tightened. Had something else happened? Was there another murder? An update? She braced herself, then realized that of course Detective Dean would be the one calling with that type of information.

"Is everything okay?"

"Yes." Tranise cleared her throat. "Yes, everything's great. I . . ." Tranise was surprised at how nervous she was. "I mean . . . things are . . . *okay*. I'm having a little trouble with anxiety and Jeff and I were thinking it would probably be a good idea for me to talk to someone about . . . everything."

"I think that's a wonderful idea. You've been through a horrendous ordeal. I couldn't even imagine coping with something like that." Keeley posed the phone on her shoulder and leapt out of the car. She clicked the alarm and headed toward the Starbucks. A man opened the door for her on his way out. She nodded a thank you and savored the warmth of the store and the rich aroma that came with it.

"It is a good idea, only . . . I'm not in love with the idea of pouring my saga out to a total stranger. I feel kind of awkward about this, but I wonder if maybe I would be able to talk to you about things . . . just to kind of vent. I mean I know you're busy and you'd like to bounce back from this as quickly as possible too, but . . ."

"Tranise, I'd like to help. I would, but I just think maybe I'm getting too involved." It was like Ben's words were taking over her thoughts. Did she actually just tell Tranise *no*? Is that how she felt, or how *Ben* felt? Dammit.

There was silence on the other end. Then, "Oh, okay. I totally understand, Keeley. I just had to ask. There's something about you that's so soothing. I just . . . "

"I'll do it. I'll meet with you, Tranise. I'm sorry. I guess I'm just scared too. But - I'm already invested in this thing and I'd love to help out. When can you get together?"

Keeley felt a little relieved after agreeing to her proposal. Afraid, but secure with her choice. Ben would flat out hate it, but it wasn't up to Ben to decide. She needed to heal too and this would be good for her as well. She liked Tranise. Tranise had confided in Keeley and trusted her. It would be good for them both.

You are now leaving Drakesborough. The sign just about summed it up. Only Keeley read it as: you're now abandoning Bob; leaving the house of the woman who you'll never see again; and escaping responsibility, even though it's totally out of your hands. Yup, that was just about it. Good bye for now, Drakesborough.

***

Ben was standing there, right on time, holding a bouquet of flowers that nearly obstructed Keeley's peep-hole view of him. She couldn't help but feel a lilt in her heart, though she was still feeling an unwanted touch of bitterness toward him. She willed herself to let the feeling go, and opened the door, pasting a smile on her face.

"For you, my dear," he said, walking past her into the room. He gave the obligatory kiss and hug.

"They're beautiful."

"Something beautiful for my beauty." Ben walked over to the spotless kitchen and located the vase Keeley's mother had left her. Expertly, he chopped the ends off the flowers and arranged them in a vase for her. He was a truly good man. Keeley admonished herself for thinking anything negative about him. Ben frequently gave her flowers and he knew how she loved the appearance and fragrance, but had confided in him that she hated preparing them and tending to them to the point of not wanting to fuss with them at all. So with his gift of beautiful plant life came the added job of maintenance. She loved how he felt as at home here as she did. Her life would really be missing something if there were no Ben. Now, with Bob's tremendous loss, was the time to appreciate him.

She gave him a giant hug from behind as he finished up with the bouquet and said, "I have the ingredients for chicken carbonara. We could just stay in and keep each other warm?"

Ben had mentioned dinner at Bully's but she wasn't sure if he had his heart set on it or not.

"Oohhh," he cooed, "that sounds nice. It is pretty cold out there." He turned to face her embrace. They kissed, passionately, dispelling all of her misgivings from earlier today. Ben didn't try to control her or speak conde-scendingly to her for that matter. It was just that they were both enduring an undue amount of stress right now. He was worried about her. That was all. Plus, she had heard a million times that just being engaged put a lot of pressure on thriving relationships. And here they were going through a death in the family, a soon-to-be long-distance relationship and a murder investigation that neither of them was adjusting to very well. Things would be fine. She knew this was normal and it would simply be a tem-porary bump in the road, something to make them even stronger as a unit.

But she wasn't too confidant. Not when she remem-bered the call from Tranise today. She knew she had to tell Ben, but maybe not right away. After all, they were having such a good moment. For the first time since the murder, in fact, things felt natural and she was optimistic. *But not telling him was lying by omission.* She promised to tell him first thing tomorrow morning. Tonight they would simply enjoy their precious and dwindling time together.

Keeley pulled out a package of fresh chicken, an onion, a tray of bacon, a carton of cream and a bag of spinach for the salad. From the pantry she chose a box of angel hair pasta, a bag of croutons and an unopened jar of minced garlic. Just being in her own element gave her a feeling of insatiable hunger. She had logged in a few hours at the store, took a long lunch where she shopped for fresh groceries and tidied up the house, then returned to work to finalize a few tasks and close up shop. She didn't feel ill at ease there, as she had anticipated she would. There was too much catch up work to keep her busy. Plus business was booming, and she knew that in part, morbid curiosity was the catalyst. Nonetheless, she deemed today a successful transition. Once dinner was underway she would call Bob and just check in. Right now she was busy cooking up a scrumptious storm, pleasantly oblivious, while Ben poured two glasses of Merlot.

***

Josh's body had been discovered nearly twenty-four hours ago, netting four victims and one near-victim for this creep. *A total serial*, thought Dean. The new knowledge regarding Josh's part-time job as the museum historian was a leap in the right direction. Bob Travis said he knew of the kid, but had never been formerly introduced. Said he was a wallflower who was disinterested in the social aspects of the art world – a total spin from Keeley Travis's description of the guy. She, along with Summer from the bookstore, made Josh sound like a Lothario of sorts. So when exactly was Josh playing a role? Was he fooling the world as the noble and quiet historian or as the student turned shop-lifter? Didn't much matter, thought Dean, now that the guy was dead. Harper Middleton's fiancé, Carson, didn't have clue number one about anyone associated with the museum named Josh. He even refuted knowledge of him after being shown a photograph.

Adrienne's fiancé, Peter, sang the same song as Bob. Josh was a background fixture, modest and dedicated, but no one really knew him beyond that. It would be up to Tranise to hopefully provide any solid information about Josh.

Dean turned onto Tranise's street and saw the porch light flick on just as he pulled up alongside the curb. They were expecting him. They said that his drop in would be okay because they had put the kids to bed early, but they wanted to make it a quick visit. He could empathize. The poor woman had been through hell and back they weren't letting her repair herself. Not yet anyway, and there was no way around it. In all his years on the job, he'd dealt with only one survivor before and he learned a valuable lesson from her – if you didn't make peace with the fact that escaping death was now a part of your life, you were done for.

That little tidbit wouldn't be something he'd share with Tranise tonight, of course, but at some point. The survivor often thought that the aftermath was a *phase* of sorts. It wasn't. Survivors rarely ever found peace. They would still be alive, but a part of them was dead. Real nice reward for what Tranise endured, huh? But, she was upbeat and tough and smart. She had a lot to live for - a possible motive for someone wanting her dead. Well now it could be her reason to carry on.

Dean shivered slightly when he stepped out of the car. The fall weather was starting to feel like winter weather. Boy, were they in for it this year; summer had been unseasonably cool. The frigid air suited his mood. Hopefully they'd catch this bastard before the holidays. His breath came out in visible plumes. Tightening his collar, he knocked softly on the door. It was opened before Dean had a chance to stuff his cold fist into his jacket pocket.

"Hello. Mr. Gray."

"Please – call me Jeff. Come in. It's freezing out there."

Dean followed him into the cozy and well lit home. It smelled like home cooking.

"Can we get you some coffee or tea? Tranise is just finishing up in the kitchen."

"Either would be fantastic. Thanks."

Jeff led Dean to the living room and Tranise arrived drying her hands on a small plaid towel. "Hello, Detective."

Dean nodded.

"I'll get some decaf brewing," said Jeff, excusing himself. Tranise passed the towel to him as he left the room.

She was a strikingly beautiful woman. She didn't have a hint of makeup on, yet she was breath-taking. Below her hazel, exotic eyes there was a hallow affect that didn't suit her. He wondered if she'd ever lose that out-of-place pallor.

"How are you holding up?"

"I'm hanging in there. Is there new news? Is that why you came?" Dean noticed that she was trembling. He wouldn't leave her wondering any longer.

"Yeah, we got some news on Josh, the one who stole the books. He was the historian at the Museum of Art. Do you know him?" Dean pulled out a photograph and held it up. He noted, not for the first time, that Josh looked handsome and friendly, reminiscent of a model's headshot. Tranise leaned in and took the snapshot from his hand. She didn't have to answer. Her reaction was enough.

***

It was a bright and sunny morning. The haze had finally dissipated, though the morning was still new. And after last night's glimpse of winter, it was a welcome switch for Laney Brooks. She had been in such a funk lately, and it wasn't just because of the three deaths to rock Drakesborough and its neighboring areas. Clearly Laney couldn't help but compare herself to the victims - all successful women, all involved in charity work *and* the City Walk cultural scene. It was more than that, though. Her entire life, Laney was always the one who could predict rain when it came out of nowhere; the one who had the dream about Pops dying when he was healthy as a bird, only for it to come true the very next night; the one who felt an odd little inkling of a change whenever there was something life altering about to happen. And lately, she'd felt that change. It was similar to when someone was staring at you across the room, or when you walked up to a group of people talking and you were certain they were talking about you. Whatever it was, she couldn't shake it, and typically "the feelings," only lasted a day at best before something came to fruition.

She unzipped her jacket and tied it around her waist. She was almost done with her walk. Two and a half miles, thank you very much. She had worked her way up to that distance and was prouder than proud. She had been cancer free for five years, after being told she wasn't going to make it to her forty-fifth birthday, and she'd never been healthier. So on a day like today, she couldn't help but smile, despite her uncertainties. The dew was still heavy on the grass, so she cut through the tunnel in West Harbor Park. It was certainly more chilly in the tunnel where shade presided and the cold walls never saw any sunlight. The tunnel bended around, creating a beautiful ess-shaped bridging path for those above ground. She tightened her collar with her fist to fight the cold, noting how much of an echo her running shoes created in the empty hallow. She half-paused for a moment, straining to make sense of the form that lay at the end of the tunnel. She was always warned by her husband to appear self assured in this type of situation, even if she wasn't. Walk with your shoulders straight and your head up high. She picked up the pace to a brisk speed. *Self-assured, self-assured*. Laney kept her pace. You didn't get much riffraff here in Drakesborough. The occasional homeless person toting a sign stationed at the intersection before the freeway, some hoodlum kids on their skateboards doing ollies over the *No Skateboarding* signs. Nothing much . . . until lately. Laney swallowed hard. Maybe the tunnel was a stupid idea. She moved to the far left of the tunnel, averting her eyes from the figure on the right side. At the moment where light finally crossed the threshold, the literal light at the end of the tunnel, the figure began to move in on Laney. She gave a cartoon-like squeal and backed herself into the cold cement wall.

"Spare some change?" asked a toothless, haggard old lady, rattling her can of change for effect. Laney couldn't even respond she was so flustered. *So much for self-assured*. She stood motionless long enough for the woman to back off, muttering something about Laney being crazy. She stepped out into the safety of the sun, still a bit breathless. She burst into a sprint and decided that until anyone was put behind bars for the murders, her walks might have to be put on hold.

Almost ten minutes later, Laney was inside the house. She locked both the regular lock and the deadbolt. She set the coffee maker to brew and went upstairs to shower and change. She wondered for a moment if maybe the scary scene in the tunnel could have been what her mental "feeling" had been about. It was no catastrophic event, but it had certainly freaked her out as well as knocked some sense into her. She remembered that one could never be too careful. *Maybe that was all it was this time*. Her mind having settled, she decided to push past the event.

Stripped down, she stepped inside the shower. It was a semi-new addition to the bathroom. It had two shower heads and one overhead feature that mimicked rain. It also had a sauna setting. She loved a good shower, but this one would be quick. She reveled in the warm water as it caressed her cold skin and bitter psyche. Yup, she already felt better. Dismayed at the idea of having to be cold again, even if just for an instant, she turned off the shower. She grabbed her towel and let it envelop her body. *Better*. She heard a click and figured it to be the coffee maker ending its cycle. A nice cup of warm coffee sounded perfect. After she was dry and wearing a comfortable outfit, she heard another noise, this one closer and louder than the last. Haden rarely came home during the work week, but if he did it wouldn't be completely far-fetched.

"Haden, Honey? That you?" When there was no response, Laney went back to brushing her hair and applying face cream. Dressed and ready, she took the stairs two at a time, while affixing her diamond stud earrings. "Honey? You home?" No response. She figured she was just hearing things or it was normal house noises. Or maybe she was just so freaked out from the tunnel and the premonition that she was being oversensitive. Whatever it was, it was over now and the aroma of French roast took precedence. She doctored up her black coffee and took a seat at one of the bar stools. She was working on a list for the charity ball at Haden's company. She was their unofficial event planner. She loved setting up the annual affair, but suddenly they were using her expertise for the opening of an envelope. But who didn't like feeling needed? Again, came the noise. She knew just where it was coming from now. Downstairs. The family game room turned man cave. Years ago when the kids were younger they had a billiard table and a foosball table and a few old school stand-up arcade machines put in. Over the years they added a gorgeous sunken bar, a mini theater, and countless neon brew pub signs, making it officially, Haden's Pub.

Laney set down her mug and walked toward the door that lead to the man cave staircase. What could be causing that commotion? A raccoon had once climbed through a window that was left open, back before the game room was even complete, but nothing since. Plus since then they never left the windows open, especially in the fall. She climbed down the staircase, ears ready. No sound. She turned the knob slowly, in case there was a wild animal down there. She did a complete scan upon opening the door. There was nothing awry. The only segment of the room out of her line of vision was the tiny half bath, tucked off in the corner. She was tempted to just turn around and close the door. One dose of fear was enough for one day. *The feeling.* She suddenly had goose bumps. *Damn feeling.* Now she wouldn't be able to relax until something justified the damn feeling. *Just go into the bathroom, see that there's nothing there, and live your life.* She started toward the bathroom, though her better judgment was screaming "no!" She wondered if she should have some sort of a makeshift weapon in case their furry friend had in fact returned. *Perfect!* She saw Jimmy's baseball bat leaned against the other corner of the room. She hustled toward it then heard the noise again.

She cursed under her breath and held the bat, poised high above her shoulder.

She took soft, short steps toward the bathroom. She willed herself to remember that this could make a great story. She could see herself regaling Haden with it tonight over dinner--*I was so amped up about the old lady from the tunnel that I used all my pent up adrenaline to beat the stuffing out of a defenseless critter!* The thought made her smile, but she kept her game face on. She got to the bathroom, where the door was ajar. She could see almost the entire bathroom between the mirror view and her own perspective. She began to relax her arm when suddenly, to her horror, she saw the image of a man in the mirror. His lips curled in a smile and she saw that in place of teeth he had shiny white fangs. She let out a blood-curdling scream, then dropped the bat and turned to run, but he was already on her. He grabbed her by the arm and she was yanked to the floor. Face down she couldn't see what came next, but the next thing she felt was a warm pain at the side of her neck. The room began to wiggle slightly, then sway, then spin, then she slipped out of reality all together. She was nearly dead before he siphoned the blood from her body by way of the puncture wounds he'd made in her jugular vein. Laney's *feeling* had come to prophecy.

Chapter sixteen

The blare of the neon St. Pauli Girl sign was distracting. "Can we get someone to unplug the beer signs, please?" asked a disgruntled Dean. Much like the blinking sign, every murder was like a blazing reminder of the level of incompetence the force was exhibiting on this case. This woman, the newest victim, Laney Brooks, totally fit the bill. She was living a life others would envy, had the same interests as the others, yada, yada, yada. This was a full blown serial and the media would get wind whether or not he agreed to the press conference scheduled for tonight or not. At least things could be controlled, or more like manipulated, if it came from the horse's mouth, Dean being the metaphorical horse.

He finished scrutinizing the body and immediate crime scene, dealt with the grieving husband, and spoke with the others on site. They were dusting for prints at that very moment. It looked like things were moving in the right direction, but appearances could be deceiving. Dean audibly sighed. There was one thing that stood out though – something the husband had said. Laney was a cancer survivor. She really did have everything to live for. She'd cheated death once before, a rare form of the disease with a dire prognosis, then went on to die anyway. No, to be *murdered*. He would have to look into the other women's backgrounds to see if they had been through any health ordeals. He knew he was grabbing at straws, and that they had enough similarities between the women already, but he was fresh out of ideas and people were dying. Matter of fact, things were spiraling out of control. He wanted to punch a hole in the wall. Instead he put in a call to Keeley Travis, the resident book expert. It went straight to her voicemail. He told her he needed her to read off the list of stolen books and that was all; he didn't want to scare her away. Even though they had nothing solid to go on, she had been a big help. He was still reeling from Tranise's feedback on Josh. He'd have to run that by Keeley as well.

In a perfect world he could speak to his *girl Friday*, as Keeley had been teasingly dubbed around the office, before the press conference. He would need to work up a good statement that would quell hysteria, yet get the community thinking vigilantly. He wanted to come across as being in control of the situation while letting individuals know that they needed to do their part too – stay safe, keep eyes opened, report anything harry and bring back the neighborhood watch campaign. He'd done countless statements before the press and knew that sometimes even the wrong word choice could screw things right up. Plus he had to be prepared for questions. His favorite come back was, "There will be no further questions at this point." He'd keep that one in his back pocket in case things went out of control. Additionally, he should be hearing from the FBI profiler, who would hopefully provide a little more insight, allowing Dean to take the murders apart piece by piece. He was having a hard time with the levels of consistency when it came to carrying out the murders. Why was Jess killed in her office, where she would normally be at that hour, making only the detached arm the reason her murder matched a novel? On the other hand, Adrienne was kidnapped, taken to an actual hole in the ground where she was starved, skinned and placed in a river bed? The sicko responsible took painstaking measures – risky measures – to replicate almost the entire murder. "A" for authenticity there, whereas Harper and Laney were both killed at their respective homes and only the method of murder was replicated. Minimal effort there, in contrast to the murders of Adrienne and even Tranise to some degree. But these jobs were clearly the handiwork of a total nut job and he basically replicated whatever parts got him off.

Dean removed his gloves and disposable shoe covers. "Call me when you get the results, Joe," he called over his shoulder to the medical examiner.

"You too, Dano."

His phone rang as if on cue. "Dean here."

"Detective, it's Keeley. I just got your message. Busy day at the store. Anything new?" She realized she hadn't taken a breath since dialing his number.

"Yeah, new stuff. Where are you?"

"Just left my store and I'm about to stop in at the drug store by my house for a few things."

"Well I'm afraid I have some bad news." She unconsciously gripped the steering wheel. Her mouth became dry.

"What?" she begged.

He hated to freak her out more than he already had. She was a sweet girl and he knew this was wearing on her terribly. "First off I talked to Tranise about our boy Josh." He decided he'd ease her into the hellacious nightmare that was his world. "She saw the picture of him and she had a lot more to say than that he was just a background fixture. She says she'd never known him as the museum historian. She says the guy used to date her old sorority sister. She'd met him at a gathering or two and wasn't even entirely sure they were still an item. He'd even been at her house one time. But for whatever reason, Tranise is the only one who knew him outside of the museum. Haven't shed any light on that one yet." He wanted her to first digest this piece of news.

"That is weird. It would make better sense if they had each had a non-museum run-in with him. Maybe like he was researching them or something."

"Yup." Dean suddenly sounded side-tracked. "But... uh... we found another." He cleared his throat.

"Another ...?" she asked tentatively. She had known it would be too good to be true that the first information was the *bad* news he had called her about.

"Another body." *Why sugarcoat it?* "A woman on the upper east side of Townsend, outside of Drakesborough, was found this afternoon. And it didn't take a brainiac bookworm like you to know that this time the book was *Dracula*. Poor lady had her jugular pierced and she was drained of her blood. Plus the copy of the book turned up on the wall shelf. We'll run prints, but this'll turn up like all the others. Like no one had ever been here."

Keeley fought to keep her mid-day croissant down. "I'm . . . I'm so sorry." She didn't know why she said those words, but she didn't know what else to say. It was too much. Ben was right. It was consuming her. It was getting to where she was nervous every time the phone rang, every time she went to the bathroom, every moment she was alone. She still didn't know what to say, but the silence was deafening. "What next, Detective?" She didn't even recognize the sound of her own voice.

"Good question, but there is a next. We've got a profiler on this. He can help figure why the victims were chosen, or at least expand upon that. He can try and figure who the guy might be, and he can provide a better insight on the link between the killer and the victims with Josh. We'll do a press conference tonight, which will cause a bunch of community members, typically all the loons, to come out with any information they may have. And sometimes this actually helps. So we have a few fountains to tap yet."

"How's Tranise's doing?"

"Seems to be holding up. It's a tough set of shoes to fill. She'll make it."

"She asked to meet with me. She thinks talking it out with someone who's kind of in the loop will help. I think it's a great idea," she asserted. It was like she was practicing what to say to Ben. Or, maybe, she realized, she didn't think it was such a hot idea after all and she wanted Dean's take on it.

"Sounds smart to me. The more we can hash this out the better. For Tranise and for the case. And probably even for you too, Keeley. We appreciate everything everyone is doing."

"Thanks."

Keeley got off the phone and had an overwhelming desire to speak with Ben. She got out of the car and headed into the drug store while the phone began to ring. He answered on the third ring.

"Hey, Hon."

"Hi." She was suddenly very aware of the shoppers around her. Why was she doing this in the store? She was trying to hurry home so she could lock herself in before dark, that's why. She snuck off to a desolate aisle of the store that housed wheelchairs and furniture for people who needed physical assistance. Currently the store was bustling with hurried shoppers, ready to get home and start dinner.

"Ben, there was another murder. And it was based on a book." She felt the barrier rise through the phone. Ben was upset. But it was for her own good. Who would want their loved one dragged through a murder case? Especially one where her own store was more or less involved.

"Keeley, are you okay? Where are you?" The response was typical doting Ben, but not what she expected. She expected him to tell her that the detective had no business calling her about it, and that she needed to back out before she got in even deeper.

"I--I'm at Carver's Pharmacy. I needed a few things on the way home."

"Let me just tie up a few things. Fifteen minutes tops, then I'll come over."

"Okay." She was a little blind-sided. But thrilled that she wouldn't have to be alone. Keeley hadn't expected Ben to show up until closer to eight o'clock tonight, and it was barely a quarter passed five.

"I can grab something to eat. What sounds good?"

"Anything." She realized that except for the croissant she scarfed down about an hour ago, she hadn't eaten much today.

"List a couple places and I'll get your usual. I'm shutting down my computer right now. I'll have to work a little from the couch tonight."

Keeley felt guilty for portraying Ben as the bad guy earlier. He was a wonderful person with her heart at interest. She couldn't help but smile, despite the dire circumstances. "Um, how 'bout Mackenzie's, Giotto's or Buffalo Joes?" She began perusing the hair care items.

"Great. They all sound good. I'll surprise you?" he asked. *You already did*, she thought. *Pleasantly*.

After hanging up she took her handle basket up to the cashier for check out. The Goth-looking young woman at the register was busy reading the paper and didn't look up until Keeley's items were all on the counter. "Sorry. I was totally engrossed in this article about the slayings. Have you heard?"

More than you know, thought Keeley. She figured she'd better at least nod or Sunday Adams would give her an unsolicited earful.

"These women probably asked for it. Shaking their rich bitch asses around town, acting all high and mighty." She set the paper down and grabbed the bottle of lotion to scan it.

Keeley's jaw dropped. Then she took a deep breath, fighting every urge to punch this girl right in her pierced lip.

"Besides," the cashier went on, "who the hell...

Keeley was willing her to shut up, staring at the thick black makeup lining her eyes, and the black and purple hair, which slowly transformed into muddled dark spots. The next thing she knew, she was surrounded by a group of gawking strangers and a tall man in glasses was pulling her to a sitting position.

"I'm a doctor, Doctor Feldman. You've were unconscious. Do you know your name?"

I fainted? "Yes. I - I'm fine, really," she said, rubbing the back of her head where it hit the stiff, tiled floor. She tried to stand, then thought better of it. "If you can just help me to the bench, Doctor." She pointed in the vague direction of a wooden park bench near the newspaper stands – and away from the three ring circus she had just created.

"Of course. Come on." The doctor supported her shoulder and held her other arm, leading her to the bench. "You okay?"

"Yes, I think it's that I haven't had enough to eat today," she half-lied.

"Do you have someone who can come pick you up? You really shouldn't be driving after that."

"I do. I'll call him. And thank you."

He took the hint that she had it from here. "I'm still shopping. I have a long honey-do list," he smiled. "So I'll check back in a minute?"

"Thank you. I'm fine, really." She reached into her purse and called Ben.

***

"Keeley," Ben began as he rushed through the automatic doors and knelt beside her at the bench. "Thank God you're okay!"

She'd had her elbows on her knees and her face buried in her palms. The doctor refused to leave her side and shoppers-slash-onlookers were still eagerly staring at her, as if she were a celebrity.

"Let's just get out of here." Her head felt like a balloon, and the dizziness was increasing. She wanted to get out from under the blaring fluorescent lighting and the heavy gaze of the drama thirsty shoppers.

"Thank you, Doctor." Ben shook his hand, then whisked Keeley out of the lime light.

"Oh!" she sighed. "Thank you so much. That was awful."

"So you fainted?"

"The clerk was reading an article about the murders and she started badmouthing the victims. My blood was boiling, Ben." She rested her head on his shoulder while they walked to the car. She looked up at him. "I got this unbelievable feeling, like I was going to do something drastic, but instead I fainted." She burst into easy laughter.

"My poor girl!" Ben tightened his grip around her shoulder. "But you're okay now?"

"A little shell-shocked. I've never fainted before. And I feel a little blah."

"So for the record, what does 'something drastic' mean?"

She let out a little laugh. "I can't explain. I thought for a minute I might knock her out."

Ben went around to the passenger side of the car and opened her door for her. He eased her into the car, before closing the door. Instantaneously he was sitting beside her. "I don't buy it for a second."

"Buy what?" she asked, genuinely surprised.

"That you could punch someone. You don't have a malicious bone in your body."

"You better not try and find out," she joked. "But seriously, Ben. She was saying awful things, like that the victims were asking for it." The smile had vanished from her lips.

Ben glanced across the shadowy interior of the car. "People are *going* to talk, Keeley. Let them. But we know the truth." He squeezed her knee, eliciting a forced smile from her. "Hey, I never picked up any dinner. Should I take you home or are you well enough to endure the drive thru with me?"

***

The press release went off without a hitch. The slimy media tried their damndest to get a rise out of Dean and his team, but that didn't work out. Dean delivered his spiel, sounding like he had some clue of what was going on, and then basically told the piranhas to go shove off. Translation: he informed the cameras that they had several promising leads (lie) and that they were in the process of waiting for the information to make its way back to headquarters (lie). He reminded everyone to use extra precautions and to remain vigilant on the streets and within their communities. When Dean was done, instead of taking the usual easy way out by saying, "There will be no questions at this point," he simply allowed one particularly annoying reporter, Luna Truss, to expose herself as the bottom feeder she is. Luna leaned in and yelled, in her exasperating voice, "These women are all pillars in the community. You can only cast your bait for so long!" Still unsure about what her idiotic fishing analogy even meant, Dean waved his hand at Luna and the masses in general. Satisfied that this was enough for now, he reached for his cell.

***

Keeley and Ben ate pasta and garlic bread from circular foil containers while watching Dean manage what must have been a complete nightmare for him. She had developed such an extreme level of respect for the man over the short duration of their relationship. This ordeal had taken so much out of Keeley in a matter of days; she could only imagine how it would feel to make dealing with crime a lifestyle.

She set her empty container on the coffee table and pushed it out of reach, still feeling off- kilter after her little episode. She stifled a yawn, deciding she had to power through and utilize every second she had with her knight in shining armor. Instinctively, Ben reached over for a blanket and scooted closer to Keeley. He could read her like a book. She leaned into him.

Neither of them had said anything at the close of the press conference. This time, however, it wasn't because it was depressing, awkward or because it was a bone of contention. It was simply that neither of them wanted to talk about it any longer. She vowed she wouldn't say a thing about it and that she'd stay in the moment. Tomorrow, on the other hand she'd mention her plans to indulge Tranise. She realized that if Ben was the kind, caring man she knew him to be, being afraid to confide in him should be a non-issue. He'd have to respect her decisions, and she'd have to give him a little more credit.

***

Waking, Keeley's head was pounding and her breath was tarnished with garlic. She looked up to find that she had fallen asleep in Ben's arms on the couch. A glimpse at the wall clock told her it was past midnight. Their evening together had been spent napping. Keeley softly rubbed Ben's arm until she elicited a reaction. He jumped at her touch and loudly mumbled, "No!" His eyes were wild and he was breathless. It was then that she realized she wasn't the only one having nightmares.

The tumultuous evening turned into a fitful night. If one was tossing and turning, the other was awake; neither slept for more than half an hour at a time. Keeley finally threw in the towel at quarter til six, an hour before her alarm would sound. Ben rolled over, made some more inaudible utterances and then settled in. Keeley figured he might actually get some rest if she got up.

Setting the pot to brew, Keeley walked over to her book collection in the spare room she liked to call the library. She plucked the worn copy of Dracula from the shelf and sighed. Willing herself to open it. She hadn't done any reading of the "chosen" novels since returning home. She pretended that it was because she was preoccupied, but the reality was that she wanted to keep her home a sanctuary for as long as possible. But heck, things back here at home were already growing complicated so she decided to make use of her time. She settled into a chair and picked up right where she left off.

***

Keeley jumped when Ben shadowed the doorway.

"Sorry. I startled you?" He looked as though he was daring her to say otherwise, as if to show that his hunches and theories about her getting lost in the case had come to fruition.

Refusing to indulge him, she smiled and shut the book. "Not unless you're here to suck my blood," she said jokingly in her best Transylvanian accent. But her joking manor betrayed her emotion, and she felt bothered at her competitive nature. She had never felt like she was on the other side of any issue with Ben. Nonetheless, she stuck to her guns, carrying on as if nothing was wrong. "Want breakfast?"

"No time. I want to hop in the shower and head out in the next few minutes." He winked at her before turning and leaving. Then he called after her, "Care to join?"

And for the first time ever, she didn't.

***

Tranise was too restless to sleep and too tired to do anything more productive than sit on the couch and fidget. There was a sink full of dirty dishes calling her name but she didn't want to wake the others. The girls had a full thirty minutes left of precious sleep, although luckily, sleep seemed to come easily to them. Thankfully the girls seemed fully adjusted and accepting of everything. She knew it was due to her stoic behavior and wouldn't allow them to see her breakdown or panic or act anything other than brave and self-assured. Surely the girls were frightened when they received the downplayed, PG version of her nightmare. But not once did they say anything alluding to the fact that this might not be over. And she certainly wouldn't ever imply that in so many words. She wanted them to be vigilant, although they were never out of her sight, except while at school. She told them that it was a good lesson that people could never be too careful, to never talk to strangers and blah, blah, blah. She was putting up a good front and she wouldn't let it fall; that was one thing she could be sure of. She also knew that, if it weren't for her daughters and her need to protect them, she would crumble to the ground.

She willed herself to stand up and go make a cup of coffee. Quietly she grabbed herself a mug then flinched when it clanked against another mug. She cursed under her breath, then listened as the floorboards above creaked. She must have awakened someone, despite her attempts to stay alone in her sleepless misery. Jeff was her best guess.

And sure enough, he was in the kitchen minutes later.

He smiled warmly and hugged her.

Tranise found herself actually wishing he'd acted even the slightest bit irritated that he was awoken early. Of course he wouldn't though. He would never reprimand his fragile little wife who was seemingly on the verge of a full mental implosion. He would probably never complain to her about anything again. Things would never be the same and she would never be treated like a normal person; and dammit, that was scaring her more than anything else right now.

Chapter seventeen

After Ben was showered and out the door, Keeley decided to call Bob and say a quick hello before he too was off to the grind. He typically got to the office at a modest hour, meaning she should have been able to reach him, but no one picked up. Instead the answering machine picked up. It appeared that no one had thought to change the outgoing message, recorded by Jess. Surprised, Keeley slammed the phone down without leaving a message. She hoped that Bob wouldn't have to hear Jess's greeting in case anyone did leave a message. Since she knew that on her own answering machine, whenever she played back any messages, her greeting played first, she'd have to remind Bob to change the message next time they spoke, and decided to call him during her lunch break.

After the spook of hearing Jess's voice, Keeley found herself once again on high alert as she showered and finished up her morning routine. She kept straining to hear noises that weren't there; realized she had shut the bathroom door to shower, which she never did; and was twice covered in goose bumps. She reprimanded herself for being so silly, but thoughts of Count Dracula were twirling through her mind. She was practically giddy as she stepped outside onto her porch and into the sanctity of daylight. When had her house become so ominous?

***

Dean was feeling about as well as could be expected after the last bloodbath. He was optimistic because the profiler assigned to the case was an old friend. They were recruits together in the academy. He knew his old buddy, Tobias, would come through and spare him no details unlike some of these other guys often do. It was as if some profilers were possessive of the powerful information they held and rationed it out at their discretion. Stupid. But with Tobias on the job. . . Dean practically had a fricken spring in his step.

"Why are you so damned happy? Reyes said there was another corpse," said a fellow detective, butting into Dean's thoughts.

Dean grabbed a donut. "Can't a guy be happy?" He pulled off a chunk of fried sugar, then sighed. "I think we're about to get some good news here; does that work for you?"

The other officer didn't pick up on Dean's sarcasm, just smiled and told him congrats.

Dean never liked the guy. He was an odd ball to say the least: His name was Robin and he had red hair. Some of the others called him *Red Robin*, making it almost completely impossible for Dean to take him seriously. But that wasn't all. *Anyway, it takes all kinds*, Dean thought, tossing away the second half of his donut.

Once back in his office, he beamed when his personal extension began to ring. *Please be Toby, please be Toby.*

"Dean, here."

"Hey Deano! It's Tobias, your old buddy!"

"You don't know how happy I was to see you were my man on the job. Feed me some good news, old buddy."

"First, I'll give you the no-brainers. Our guy is in his mid-thirties. He's socially cooperative, attractive, intelligent. Possibly has a background in literature. A teacher, librarian, professor . . . someone like that."

Dean interjected, "Journalist perhaps? That way he's got an in with the local news?"

Tobias laughed. "Now you're thinking like a profiler. Maybe those aren't his careers, but his hobbies. He could be a doctor, a lawyer or a garbage man with a love of reading for all we know. Now for some more evaluative stuff. Because of his connection with the Harvard kid-turned-petty theft, we think he could be a former trouble maker who was cautious enough to not get caught or end up with a rap sheet. Two friends of his lackey, Josh, had heard of the guy but never met him. They just heard Josh was doing an under-the-table gig to make some fast cash. No one knew his name; no one saw the guy. They knew he was handing out a bankroll. So since he had funds to pay out to Josh, he has some dough. Demographically and by association, that puts him in with the well-to-do. The whole cluster of museum-supporting rich people. He may even live in Drakesborough or the other more affluent areas where our victims hail from. Much like Josh the museum curator, he may be a major cog in this whole thing. I'd bet the victims' families know him. He probably blends right in. He's got himself a front row seat to the slaughter-fest. I'll also bet he's got connections higher than we'd like, who would keep his dirty little secret safe. Bad news is that none of this explains motive. We're looking at the victims as those who had everything to live for, is that right?"

"That's our guess. Yes."

"Well then what would a country-club-going middle-aged man want with these local 'America's sweethearts?'"

"If you're thinking affairs with the women, you're way off. These ladies didn't have it in them to stray. On the contrary, they were all seemingly part of the greatest love stories ever written."

"Stories? Written? Maybe this guys a deranged author who wants to turn promising happy endings into horror stories," Tobias smirked.

"You're smooth, my friend. Some sort of vengeance-driven psycho who must have been burned along the way. If he can't be happy no one can type of thing?"

"Not bad, Dean. We've also looked into the possibility of "it" being a her. Doesn't fit with the fact that Josh referred to the killer as a him, but he said he had no real basis as to why he thought that. So . . . you start looking into everyone attached to that world – art, museums, upper-crust culture. Figure out who has no solid vouchers. No solid public life. That's where you start."

"Better than nothing."

"You don't sound impressed."

"Oh I'm impressed alright, Toby. I just hate the idea of this sonofabitch is all. Anyway, if it was a woman? What would we be looking for?"

"She'd be very similar to the victims – at least she'd appear that way. She'd be someone mourning the fact that her love story was over or coming to an end."

***

When Keeley finally reached Bob he sounded out of breath. He told Keeley he was tired because he pulled an all-nighter trying to crack an over-seas deal. He also said that, overall, things were going well. He said he was adjusting. She knew his cover, his outer-self, was adjusting. He was doing a great job with his charade, but he just didn't sound like himself. She couldn't be angry. She basically told him a bunch of half-truths too: things with Ben were fine, she was fine, and everything was fine. Once they cut through surface-level pleasantries, Keeley decided it was time she dug deeper, but not deep enough to let him know about Laney Brooks . . . yet.

"When can I come over? I miss being around you."

"Any time, Kee. I miss you too."

"Maybe in a couple of days? Ben is leaving for business . . . sooner than we thought." She swallowed over the lump in her throat.

"What a shame! Come over once he's gone. You can catch me up on the case."

"That'd be good." *Thank God!* She was hoping he wouldn't ask, so she wouldn't have to tell. But if she didn't, he'd find out on the evening news, if not sooner. She wasn't sure which method would be easier for Bob – no, that wasn't true at all. Of course it would be easier for Bob to hear it from her than on the news or in a paper. It would be harder on her, yes. She was being selfish. She needed to tell him.

"Listen, I have a call to make before my meeting that starts in five minutes. I'm so glad you called, Kee."

"Okay, I . . ."

"We'll make plans to get together for sure. I'll call you tonight."

"Okay." She felt deflated when she heard the click on the other line. It wasn't enough that Jess had to die, or even be murdered? Isn't losing a spouse hard enough when it isn't being morbidly drawn out and replayed every waking second? She could feel her stomach roiling. It was such a travesty. And here she was being unappreciative, even irritated with Ben . . . over what? She needed to take a step back from the anger that was clouding her mind. She had everything a person could want and she was looking for holes in it. On some underlying level was she trying to punish herself for having what her brother lost? Was she trying to sabotage the one good thing in her life? What was the matter with her? Maybe Ben was right. For her own health's sake, maybe she should get out before it's too late. Maybe she should walk away from the case.

***

Regina looked like hell. Her normal olive glow had turned to a yellow pallor. Her eyes were bloodshot and she looked like she was going to be sick.

"Are you okay?" asked Keeley upon entering her store.

"I think I might be coming down with something. I didn't realize I looked as bad as I felt."

"Regina, you need to go home. I can do inventory another day."

"Normally I would never bail on you, but I think you're right; I need to leave. I feel awful." Regina was already gathering her purse and coat from beneath the register.

"You're not bailing on anyone. You really helped out by putting in those extra hours when I needed you. Go home and get some rest."

"Thanks, Keeley." She shuffled out the door just as a customer came in.

"Welcome to 'Buy the Book'."

"Good morning," said the woman, apprehensively. She looked like she had just seen a ghost. Keeley fought back the urge to ask her if she was alright. She looked worse than Regina, who was clearly coming down with something. "Can I help you find something?"

She stammered. "I was looking for . . . yes, I . . ." The woman dropped a slip of paper and fell immediately to the ground, scrambling, as if she had just lost a precious gem. Keeley rounded the checkout desk and the troubled woman looked up and stared into her eyes. "My sister is the woman who was just murdered."

***

It was just a dream. She stood, breathless, her forehead beaded in sweat. It was only a dream. No, it was only a nightmare. The things that had just felt so real it was like they were actually happening to her . . . those were not the things dreams were made of. There was no disputing that those were nightmares. More accurately, night terrors. Or maybe that wasn't the proper term. Lucid dreaming. That was what she had just experienced. It was so real that . . . her hand grazed her tender collar bone. To her surprise, the skin was textured, and achy. She ran to the bathroom mirror and saw the network of small lacerations running the length of her shoulder and chest. It was the same spot where . . . but it couldn't be. She must have subconsciously scraped at it during her imagined attack. Her fingers traced the scrape and produced a tiny smearing of blood.

"Ouch! Hope I didn't do that last night," purred Drake, standing behind her and enveloping her in his embrace. His lips slowly trailed down toward the scrapes.

"Stop!" she yelled, surprising both of them. "I mean . . . it hurts. I think I did it in my sleep."

"Okay," slurred Drake, defensively. "I've gotta get going anyway." She hated when he acted like that. He was too sensitive. Too much of a wounded puppy for a girl like Zane. And it wasn't the first time she had felt this way. Deciding to push the horrid dream, and subsequent injury out of her mind, Zane hopped in the shower. Tonight she would try the Melatonin her coworker had suggested. Maybe that would stop the dreams.

She reached for her razor and placed her toes on the rim of the tub. When she looked down, she let out a bloodcurdling scream.

***

Dream Catcher read like a modern day *Nightmare on Elm Street.* Maybe that was where Keeley Travis got the idea for the book. He closed the hardback copy and placed it back on the shelf with the thrillers. He'd already secured a copy of her other novel, *He Knows You're Alone*, but he couldn't resist sneaking a peek in public. It felt good, all the little dangerous preludes to murder. It was almost as exciting as the main event, though nothing could really compare.

He walked past the security guard stationed in the center of the major chain bookstore and smiled. Once again, no one was the wiser.

***

Keeley sat across from the woman who was Laney Brook's older sister. Her name was Rose. She sipped the tea that Keeley offered her and stared into space.

"I'm terribly sorry for your loss, Rose."

"Thank you. I'm so sorry for your loss too. I'm not gonna feed you some lie about how I got your name from a list of victims or something like that." Rose stopped to take another sip.

"Then where did you? Get my name, I mean."

"Reporter. Told me that you were the sister of a victim and that you were somehow involved in the case. That you had some run-in with the guy even."

"A reporter?" Keeley wasn't sure whether to be irate that a reporter knew who she was and was spouting off information, however scrambled, or shocked that whoever Rose's source was, they were pretty close. "Which reporter?"

"They're harmless. Can't say much. I called in a favor. But look, I'm here now. I want to know if you have any information about the other victims. My sister . . . she was the best person I knew. She didn't have a selfish bone in her body. And especially after she got sick. Once she was through with her treatment, she spent so much time and energy at that damn hospital trying to cheer up perfect strangers. She wasn't someone anyone would want dead, let alone tortured." Rose touched the corner of her napkin to her eyes.

"That's exactly how Jess was. She was my brother's wife, but she felt like a sister to me. And that's how all the others were, Rose."

"Then you agree. It's like it's a hit list of the All-American girls."

"Yes. I'd agree. The police are already working that angle. They have it all under control, Rose. They're really doing the best . . ."

"Then tell me what they have!" Rose leaned in, a menacing look in her eyes. "If they're doing their best, what is it? Because I don't see a darn thing being done." She leaned back in her chair, the threat still present.

"We're about to see changes. They have a profiler now!" Keeley felt like she was in a pressure cooker, fumbling for examples to provide this poor, angst-ridden woman. "They just had a press conference. I promise you that things are getting done. Be patient." The minute the last words left her mouth, Keeley regretted them. *Be patient?* Who says that to a grieving person? Would Bob be okay with someone telling him to be patient in the wake of his precious wife's murder? Would she? No.

Before she could open her mouth to defend her hurtful and stupid statement, Rose stood up. She leaned in and pointed a finger at Keeley. "Mark my words! This joke of an investigation had better show more promise than a . . . young punk book store owner, who in my opinion, is in way over her head!" And with that, she stormed out of the store.

Keeley didn't know whether to be sorry or infuriated. Clearly the woman was acting out of major grief. Those wounds didn't heal easy. She still ached for Jess who was not even her own flesh and blood, or someone she'd created a lifetime of memoires with. Sad. She should feel sad. Yes, that woman lashed out at her wrongfully and had no right to come barging in here spewing hate and dragging the police department through the mud. But Keeley needed to remember how she felt as soon as she'd heard the news. This woman had clearly not even begun to deal with accepting what had happened. Would she ever, though? Bob popped into her cluttered thoughts. He was doing a little better. And Rose would soon have her answers and could begin to heal. This couldn't go on forever. Keeley shivered and went back behind the counter.

She decided to call Tranise. The case was taking on a much bigger role in her life than she could tolerate right now. She reached into her purse for her cellphone, but it wasn't tucked in the side pouch where she always left it. Then she remembered she had used her phone earlier and set it underneath the cash register next to her own novel which she was reading for the umpteenth time. She was her own worst critic and with the recent rise in her popularity after hitting the best seller list, she knew more eyes would be scrutinizing her novel than ever before. She had a personal tradition of re-reading her own books whenever she heard a friend or acquaintance had read one of them. She wanted to try and see the stories through their eyes. She sighed. It was silly, she knew. She also thought it might be "healthy" to read something other than the grim fodder for Mr. Murderer. Then it hit her. She was so befuddled over the case, Jess's murder, Bob's emotional stability, and even her misgivings about Ben that she forgot that one of her own novels had been selected by the evil hands of Josh. *Dream Catcher* had been in that group of stolen books, too. She shivered at the thought. *Dream Catcher* wasn't exactly something that could be replicated. The premise was that people were tormented in their sleep by a dream villain only to find that he was very real. The murders were completely incapable of replication . . . or were they? They were pure fantasy. Preposterous murder plots. The very thing that made it easy for Keeley to spend endless nights typing into the wee hours without terrifying herself.

Breathe. Breathe and call Tranise. Initially she was going to call her new friend to back out, but now she needed to call for moral support just as poor Tranise had done with her. How could Keeley back out on her? That would not resolve her problems. Breaking their grim and unavoidable bond was the last thing she should be doing right now. And feeling that Ben wasn't going to be supportive made the situation more difficult, but Keeley was now more than ever determined to contact Tranise.

She dialed the number and waited while it rang several times. Her gut twisted, which was stupid, she knew. Just because Tranise doesn't answer her phone on the first ring doesn't mean she's in danger. The phone continued to ring, but instead of being answered by a family recorded answering machine greeting, there was the sound of silence, then a click. The call disconnected. She felt lightheaded, but that didn't stop her from grabbing her bag and her keys. She flipped the door sign from opened to closed and locked the store behind her.

***

Twenty five minutes later Keeley was pulling up alongside Tranise's gorgeous little piece of suburbia. The home was both grandiose and modest. It had a welcoming feel to it . . . typically. But right now, Keeley wasn't sure what to expect. On her way over, she convinced herself that she was definitely over reacting, but kept her pace well above the posted speed limit. And now here she sat, staring at the house from the safety of her car. It didn't look menacing or as if anything was out of order. The door wasn't forced open, the blinds were raised low and parted as would be the norm for this time of day. No, nothing was awry. And there was probably nothing wrong. *Probably.* She forced herself out of the car and walked up the winding entry way. She rang the doorbell and waited. She didn't have to wait long. Tranise opened the door, a look of shock replacing her pretty smile.

"Keeley? Is everything okay?" *Oh God, she feels afraid every time she sees me,* thought Keeley. *I'm a negative association for her.* At that moment she realized that dumping any more drama onto this women would be a really big mistake. Tranise didn't want to hear about Rose, the grieving sibling, and how she had negatively impacted Keeley's day. And she certainly didn't need to hear about Keeley's excruciating fear of her nightmarishly scary book becoming the next mode of operation for her former tormentor's next victims.

"Sorry for just dropping in. I . . . I was thinking of you. And then I called . . ." Keeley faltered. "The phone rang several times, then when someone picked up, it disconnected." She felt about as foolish as they came. *Basically I rushed over here because someone accidentally hung up the phone when I called and I wanted to remind you that I, and everyone else, considers you a sitting duck for a second murder attempt.* "I guess I was . . ."

Tranise jumped in, saving her any further embarrassment. "Come in! I was thinking of you too and I appreciate your concern." Tranise opened the door all the way and gestured for Keeley to enter. "That was my fault. I had two telemarketers in a row call me this morning. The calls from the darn newspaper crew and reporters have finally died down. Today was the first time I actually picked up that darn phone and it was two ads in a row. The call you made must have been the time I was taking my anger out on the telemarketers. And after that, I even took the phone off the hook."

The two sat down in the living room and Tranise flipped off the news channel she was presumably watching before Keeley decided to pop in. "The news replayed the press conference. I'm not sure why I watch it."

"Same here. It feels like some sick obligation or something."

"Exactly," laughed Tranise. "That feels good," she said. "Laughing is hard to come by lately. When the girls are around I play as if everything's fine. When it's just me and Jeff I feel like I'm torn between having to act strong for him and wanting to take advantage of my opportunity to be vulnerable and be nurtured. And when I'm alone . . . well, I feel scared. And I guess that could be my real reason for taking the phone off the hook. Every time I hear the shrill ring, I jump out of my skin."

Keeley wanted to curl up into a ball and disappear. She had both called Tranise and rang her doorbell. This woman who is barely hanging on, although her exterior would never betray that, was being tested at every juncture, by normal everyday occurrences. And who would ever blame her? The maniac who tried to hurt her – to take her life – is still out there somewhere.

"I'm sorry, Tranise. And I certainly didn't mean to frighten you by showing up here today."

"You actually helped me. I need to stop living like this. I need to go forward from here."

"Don't beat yourself up. You are in a really hard spot right now. Once the investigation is finished and this sicko is behind bars you will be able to live again, Tranise."

"Even then, Keeley, I can't imagine waking up in the middle of the night, NOT feeling too afraid to go to the bathroom. I can't imagine for one second not feeling my heart drop whenever the floorboards creak. I just think that it might always be like this. Like a little part of me did die that day. Like maybe the murderer did get me."

"Tranise, you have your life ahead of you. For the victims, and especially for you and your family, you have to remind yourself that you survived that day. I promise you that things will get better."

"Of course you're right. It's weird. I feel like I've known you for more than just a short time. Like we're kindred spirits."

"I do too." Keeley flashed a big and sincere smile. "And, I guess that's why support groups work so well. People bond over life-altering events they share."

"I know, but . . . it's more than that. I think we're very alike, you and me. I know our back-story is grim," Tranise smiled, "but I'm glad we got the chance to meet."

"I second that."

Tranise stood, smoothing out her sundress. "Like the inscription you wrote me." She walked over to the oaken bookshelf behind her. Keeley was puzzled, but continued to watch as Tranise plucked a copy of Keeley's book from the shelf and lifted the book's cover. " 'Burning souls together for eternity. Without the flames to stoke our life fire, we will burn out and exist no more.' Is that a poet? Or are you just good with words in general?"

"I didn't write that." Keeley stood, baffled. "Where did you get that?"

Tranise looked just as befuddled as Keeley felt. "It came in the mail. Wrapped in brown paper and the return address was your shop. Of course it's from you." Tranise's eyes were brimming with tears.

"It's not."

Chapter eighteen

Dean arrived at Tranise's roughly twenty-five minutes later with an oversized fountain drink and blood-shot eyes. The poor guy obviously hadn't had adequate sleep or nourishment since the press conference. He walked through the door and got straight to brass tacks.

"Let's see the book, please."

Tranise had replaced it on the bookshelf for what-ever reason, and now, she pulled it down again and hand-ed it to the detective. He read the inscription aloud. "Since you thought this was from Keeley, it reads like a friend-ship vow. Together bonded and having to deal with life's ups and downs, right? Makes perfect sense that you would believe the book was from Keeley." He jotted the words from the cover onto a notebook, then stuffed the book in-side a plastic bag and handed it off to the young woman who accompanied him. "But now that we know the book didn't come from Keeley, the note becomes a little more cryptic and even menacing. Like the killer is aligning himself with you, Tranise. And without . . . who the hell knows what, death will ensue. Any insight from the pro-fessional writer?" Dean turned to face Keeley, who was hunched in despair on the love seat.

She sat up straight and began picking at a hangnail, and said, "I agree with the first meaning. If it were sent from one friend to another it would interpret like that. But as far as the other option . . ." Keeley couldn't bring herself to say the word murderer. "He's definitely linking himself to the victims, by saying 'burning souls together for eternity." Keeley leaned in close to read the words scrawled on Dean's notebook. "The next part is unclear. 'Without the flames to stoke our fire, we will burn out . . .'" Keeley repeated the line again. "What about this? Without the flames we will burn out – what if this ties in to the whole thing about his motive being that the women lived perfect lives? What if he is assuming that without *flames*, or problems or speed bumps along the road of life, people just sort of fizzle out? What if maybe he was implying that he was somehow . . . *saving* these victims? Giving their lives a little bit more . . . what? I don't even know what I'm saying anymore. And does this connect to the other novels?"

"No, this is good. Better than I would have come up with," encouraged Tranise. Dean nodded in agreement, taking notes.

"It's certainly out of character," said Dean, looking up from his notes. "I mean up until now, we've had to go off someone else's written word. But then again, a survivor is an anomaly for the killer. Tranise's survival stumped the bastard. Maybe he'll end up giving himself away yet."

Keeley reached for her purse and wrangled out her phone. "I'll type in the inscription and see if it's a real poem or quote. Maybe it'll produce a clue. And if it's not an original, we already know the guy likes literature, so maybe he's a fellow writer." Keeley finally felt less impotent. She realized this could really be useful if it popped up as an existing quote. She typed in the first line: Burning souls together for eternity. Nothing solid, just clips with any of the words tossed in. But something did catch her eye. A blurb. "Souls are in an eternal state of torture for not understanding or accepting a certain earthly dogma." Okay, so it was definitely something about teaching a lesson. But why was it being done through renowned horror novels? Keeley shared her findings.

Tranise and Dean continued brainstorming for the next few minutes, while Keeley became lost in thought. *What did any of this have to do with everything they had already determined? What lesson did these woman, these victims, need to learn? They had gotten to their stations in life based on their own merits, kindness, ethics, business smarts. And why would Laney Brooks need to learn a lesson in human suffering or humility or whatever the hell it was? She had already suffered her own ailments. None of this made any sense at all!* Keeley wanted to scream. Instead she returned to the hangnail.

Dean was explaining that the book would be checked for prints and that was a good thing, even if the inscription was ambiguous and frustrating.

Tranise was clearly still shaken, her cocoa skin looked waxen, yellow even.

After another few minutes of hopeful, yet pointless, brainstorming, Dean departed, glad to have some prints to run.

***

Ben was there, like she asked him to be, waiting for her at her shop. The place felt violated, like her own personal crime scene. Keeley wasn't sure why. She was less fearful after the whole Josh theft thing. Was it due to Rose's hysterical ranting from this morning? Or the fact that her book once more came into play? Neither, of course had anything to do with the store. She couldn't pin point what it was, but all her jumbled thoughts subsided when she came face to face with Ben. "Thank you so much! I know you're busy." The two embraced. Keeley produced her key and let them into the shop, turning the closed sign over to open.

"Of course I came, babe. Want me to go look around?" *Just like a parent does with their toddler's closet.*

"Sure. Thank you." Keeley placed her items under the cash register where they had been this morning, checked the answering machine, then set a pot of coffee to brew. She felt silly having her fiancé "check under the bed for monsters," so to speak, but she didn't really care. She needed all the reassurance she could get. *Ben will be leaving soon, then what? Who will help to lick my wounds then?*

"All clear," announced Ben, descending the vast staircase two steps at a time. He glanced at his watch. "I smell coffee. I have time for a quick cup."

Keeley's smile faded. Of course she knew he needed to go back to work at some point, but just not so soon.

She felt her hand shaking as she poured the hot coffee into two mugs. All she could do was hope that the lunatic was caught before he left for Australia. Of course she had other sources of moral support. She had Bob, she had close friends, co-workers and her most recent go-to clique: Detective Dean and Tranise. But the sad reality was that she wasn't going to call on them for the things she would ask Ben to do.

"You okay?" asked Ben with that gorgeous smile of his. Even now, it lit up the room, the room that once signified a dream come true and now was foggy with fear and apprehension. How would she do it without the light of her life? Not only would he not be in the same room with her during the remainder of all this, he wouldn't even be in the same country. And Keeley had been stupid enough to distance herself from him lately. Had Ben even noticed? And maybe on some level she had been doing it, distancing herself, as a preparatory measure because she knew she couldn't become too reliant with his departure on the horizon.

"Keeley?"

She realized she hadn't answered him. She didn't even know what he'd asked.

"Sorry. What?"

"I asked if you were okay," repeated Ben with a look of concern in his eyes.

"No. Truthfully I'm not okay." Keeley surprised herself with her sudden candor, then realized it was something she should have done a long time ago. "I'm terrified to be alone in my store. You're about to leave the country and people are dropping like flies." She began sobbing. Ben stepped in and gave her a hug, while she went on and on, wailing about everything that was falling apart around her. Ten minutes later, their coffee was reheated in the microwave and Keeley was semi pulled together. Ben was the typical rock that he always was and she felt as safe and secure as could be expected. For now at least.

***

Dean was savoring a rare few moments with the loves of his life. He was content, somewhat at least, with having fingerprints submitted. This was their big chance to get the solid leap this case so badly needed. Zoe and Terry were discussing the upcoming school formal, but

Dean couldn't focus. Every time he looked at his loving wife, a woman he had been with well over half his lifetime, he saw Tranise, someone else's loving wife and mother. The fear in that woman's eyes was eerily visible. If anything ever happened to his Terry, or Zoe, he didn't know what he'd do. He'd end up in prison, that's what he would do. That is, if he could find the perpetrator. He sure as hell wasn't doing a good job of that now. If it was his wife or daughter, would he be more effective? Of course not. He shook the thought before it had time to blossom into full blown guilt. He'd been through similar situations many times before, so he wasn't sure why this time was so difficult. Probably because so many women were being murdered.

Dean was a mama's boy. He had a wife that seemed like she was made to be his other half and a daughter he would go to the ends of the earth for. That's why. This was hitting too close to home. These poor women were assets to society. Not that anyone else's life didn't have the same value. Another moral dilemma faced by people in his occupation.

Ah hell. He willed himself to stop being a detective, then tried to join the conversation. As soon as he did, though, he wished he was still day dreaming. Zoe had just asked if she could stay at the Johnston's guest house with the kids after the dance, meaning the Walton kid would be there too. *Boys* would be there too.

"No way, outta the question," he broke in.

"Honey," began Terry - forever a softie-, "you remember being young once. The kids are all staying there together."

"Yeah, Dad. It's not like we're pairing off and sleeping in rooms or anything." Dean covered his ears, semi-jokingly. "We're all bringing sleeping bags and camping out on the floor." Dean winced at the thought of the killer, hallowing out the wooden floor of Tranise's cabin in preparations of stashing her body there. "No parents, no way!"

"But Dad!"

"Honey . . . let's not be rash."

"No! I said no. You're not going to spend the night with boys on the floor or anywhere else for that matter." His first inclination was to storm out of the room for effect and because he was flat out ticked off and worn out. Though after another few minutes of Terry's soothing and typically very practical rhetoric, he had somehow agreed to host a chaperoned sleepover at his house. On his floor. He somehow managed to be a force to be reckoned with while at work, and a pussycat at home with his girls. Feeling once more defeated, Dean cleaned up the lunch mess he'd made at the grill, knowing he had to head back to the station soon. At least Zoe and the kids would be safe under his roof. The idea of her being out at some sleepover with no adults while there was a maniac on the loose wasn't even an option. Even if Zoe didn't fit the profile.

***

"Consider for a moment the juxtaposition of the main character and his new love interest. Would this pairing take place in the *real* world? The non-fiction world? Or is this just a play by the author to show us Jonas's true character? His soul, if you will. I'd like you all to write a minimum of two hundred words discussing the reasons Georgina serves as a perfect *or imperfect* character in regards to exposing Jonas for who he truly is." In unison, half of Professor Michael's class groaned. "Make that two-hundred and fifty words," he smiled.

"Bastard," whispered Summer, smiling at her classmate, Lori. "These people are a bunch of whiners. Two-hundred and fifty words in an upper-division lit class is something they should be able to do in their sleep."

"Yup, I've already got mine up here," she teased, pointing at her head." The two packed their bags and headed down the stadium style stairs toward the door. "Hey, how's your boss and everything at the book store?" asked Lori

"It's okay. As well as could be expected." Summer suddenly became tight lipped. "I don't know everything and what I do know is private information. I'm not allowed to share anything."

"Okay, okay. I'm not pumping you for information, I'm just wondering how it's going over there."

"Sorry. It's alright I guess. I don't really like being there alone; the whole thing is pretty scary, especially working evenings."

"I know," said Lori sympathetically. "Hey, we should host a study group there again; it's been a while. That way you'd have some company."

"Sure, okay." Summer smiled. That was a nice gesture from Lori who's no nonsense attitude often got the best of her compassion.

"Summer? If I could have a word with you." Summer turned, surprised to find Professor Michaels standing there with a stern look on his face. Had he heard her call him a bastard? She blushed at the thought, but gave a tight lipped smile and a slight wave to Lori.

"Sure, Professor."

"I wanted to talk to you about something."

"Okay," she said tentatively. "What is it?"

"I was hearing rumors around campus that you have some inside information about the Drakesborough murders?"

Summer was surprised. Speechless. "No, I . . . my boss and friend lost her sister-in-law. She was murdered. That's all."

He studied her, closely.

"And that's all? Because I heard there is a component about the murders being from horror novels."

Summer was racking her brain trying to remember if that information had made its way public. She hadn't thought so. She instantly put her guard up. This man was not going to use his position to intimidate her into saying anything. She had made a promise to Keeley and the policeman she had spoken with.

"I don't know anything. I need to catch up with my friend."

Summer ran out the door, suddenly afraid about more than just having to close up shop tonight.

***

"Urchins. That's all. These people get a piece of information from their journalist brother or reporter neighbor. Don't let it bother you, Summer, but thank you for doing the right thing." Of course Keeley would be kind and serve as the voice of reason. Keeley would probably be glad she was able to use her as a sounding board after class and before her night shift. Neither of them needed anything else to worry about.

"I won't let it get to me, but honestly, I expected more of Professor Michaels."

"Professor Michaels? As in Len Michaels?"

"The one and only."

"He's a close friend of Ben. And me. Well, actually, he was my professor. I took one course at Fairview during my undergrad. He's actually the reason Ben and I met. Did he mention my name when he asked about the case?"

"No. He didn't say a word. He knows where I work though. That's odd."

"It is odd. Anyway, don't let anyone get to you." Keeley's thoughts went straight to Rose, grieving sister, and then scolded herself for being a giant hypocrite. Here she went running straight to Tranise when she was prodded by the inquisitive public. "Summer, I really need to go. I'm meeting Ben for an early dinner. It's one of our last chances to see each other before he leaves."

Summer looked uncharacteristically stoic.

"Will you be okay here?"

"Yes. Of course. Go see your fiancé. I'm just tired."

Keeley looked hesitant.

"It's just for a few hours. *Go!*" urged Summer.

***

Thirty minutes later, and no more at ease than she had been when she left Summer alone, Keeley arrived at The Lighthouse, a trendy new bistro on Main Avenue. She felt guilty. She didn't even want to be there alone and it was *her* store. But it's not like Summer, or anyone in the store for that matter, was in danger. It was just becoming too much with the media and the fact that the case had been inactive . . . until now, hopefully since the fingerprints could provide answers to all of their problems. *The fingerprints*. She knew she absolutely had to discuss the fingerprints and the Professor Michaels incident with Ben, but she really just wanted to focus on Keeley and Ben for the evening. She also knew the case was a sensitive topic for them and the last thing she wanted to do was widen the gap between home and Australia. Keeley entered the restaurant and greeted the host. Ben stood up from a seat at the bar and smiled his famous smile. She would miss him so much. She walked over to where he stood and hugged him. He smelled like soap, shaving cream and fresh air. She loved that about him; it was his own unique aura.

"Hi, beautiful."

"You don't look so bad yourself. As a matter of fact, you're a sight for sore eyes."

"You too, babe. I was thinking of ordering a drink here, but we can go straight to our table if you'd like." Keeley scanned the dimly lit and heavily populated bar.

Too cozy for everything this meal entailed: a chance to share sensitive and private information about the case and an opportunity to pour out all the love she held in her heavy heart before saying sayonara to her future husband.

Agreeing, the two walked up to the host and told him they were ready to be seated. They sat in a private booth, much to Keeley's pleasure, and the ambiance was perfectly soothing and even romantic. They snacked on oysters and fried calamari and sipped dirty martinis, which neither of them had had in ages. It was like old times: not a care in the world, no pending months - long separation, no murderer on the loose.

"How was work today?" asked Ben matter of factly. The perfect segue to everything she had considered ignoring all together.

"It was interesting. Actually strange is a better word." She went on to detail the sad, but unconventional meet up with Rose; her desperate, though rushed decision to go see Tranise; and finally the inscribed copy of her novel that was mailed to Tranise. Ben tensed up, balling his fists. "Dammit, Keeley, this is getting way too close to you!" A few scattered patrons at booths across the main dining area glanced in their direction.

"Ben, please. I know this makes you uncomfortable and that you don't completely agree with what I'm doing, but the alternative is lying to you and not telling you anything at all."

"You're right, I'm sorry. You're a grown adult and it's your decision."

Good ole Ben – back.

"But you have to admit. You're very close to this *very* dangerous case."

New, agitated Ben – back.

"No matter how you justify it, Kee, the killer has taken your brother's wife and has now selected one of *your* books and targeted *your* bookstore. Let's get real. This is . . ." he leaned in, making sure to whisper this time. "This is getting way too close to you!"

Everything he listed was right. Everything. But she was already deeply into this. It wasn't exactly a choice she made. Maybe helping with the investigation had been by choice, but otherwise, her involvement seemed to be beyond her control. And that was one thing she wanted back, control.

"Ben, please understand that I was selected by this psycho, not the other way around. You're right that I am in this too deep, but now I can either help to end it, or become a sitting duck letting everyone else fail at catching this guy without me."

"Is that an option? Letting others do it without you?" Ben clasped her hands in his. "I won't be there to protect you, Keeley." So this wasn't some attempt to control her. He was genuinely scared about leaving her, maybe more than she was.

"I'll take a step back, Ben, but that's only because I think things are wrapping up. There are going to be prints on the book from Tranise's house, hopefully. And then they'll nail this sonofabitch. Okay?"

"Okay. I just hope they do catch him soon."

The two separated and acted as if they weren't just hashing out a major drama as the waiter brought their main courses, lobster scampi for Keeley and seafood bisque for Ben. They tasted the food, and Keeley decided to broach the last topic on her list.

"So apparently Summer was sort of bombarded by a media-hungry mutual friend. It left her pretty shaken."

"Who's that?" asked Ben between bites.

"Len Michaels."

Ben nearly choked on his soup. "What's he doing bugging his students? That's pretty inappropriate, not to mention out of character for Len."

"I know, I thought the same thing but at the end of the day; he teaches Literature and probably wanted a good lead for his next lecture. It just shook her, that's all. And quite honestly it was the last thing any of us needed. The poor thing was shaking like a leaf as she recounted the story." Keeley pierced a giant piece of lobster with her fork.

"That doesn't sound like our old buddy, but I guess the intrigue was a driving force. And I'm sorry to say that this just strengthens my case, babe. This type of thing brings out the worst in everyone. It' a dangerous game. But for Len I'd say again that it's because it's hit on something he's interested in. He's a big book worm like you are." The phrase resonated, as Ben kept on talking.

A big book worm like me. That was the same conclusion I came to when I read that elegant inscription, that our guy might be a part of the book world.

She felt chills run down her spine. It couldn't actually be Michaels. That hadn't been her point just then, but actually – who knew? Why else would he sink to the level of badgering one of his best students? Maybe Ben was right and the good teacher was simply captivated by the topic; or maybe her gut was trying to tell her something and the killer could be someone ordinary, like Len Michaels, who just happened to know his books. Perhaps it wouldn't hurt to visit one of her old haunts.

She decided to worry about all that tomorrow night, when Ben was gone. For now, she would focus on the one thing she *was* sure of in her life.

***

Amy Walker was preparing for the challenge of a life time - dropping her nineteen year-old daughter off at the airport where she would leave for Paris, France, to pursue her dream of becoming a famed photographer. Chelsea was a good daughter and even better photographer, but Amy knew becoming famous was a pipe dream as well as a long shot. Chelsea had all the makings of a grade-A student, but a college education wasn't what she wanted. After much convincing, Amy jumped on the bandwagon, well aware that Chelsea refused to be "confined by the system." Photography was her daughter's number one passion, so why not allow her to spread her wings and follow her dreams? They had the means to make it happen after all.

The drive to the airport was light-hearted. The two joked and made small talk and even sang along to the *Grease* soundtrack – a shared guilty pleasure. But as soon as the airport signs started popping up, Amy began to feel the lump in her throat. Chelsea had been living in a small bohemian apartment with her childhood friend since graduation last year, but the mother-daughter duo stayed in frequent touch with shopping, lunch, and painting class every Tuesday. Things would definitely never be the same. Amy knew this the minute she finally accepted her daughter's plan. But what could she do? Her baby had grown up. And she wouldn't dream of standing in the way of her only child's dream.

Amy parked the car and helped Chelsea with her luggage – a small amount. Chelsea was very sensible. Something Amy always admired in her daughter who could have instead simply embraced the comfort of her privileged upbringing. Amy was the same way. She was raised with a golden spoon shoved down her throat. She rebelled at every opportunity, but ended up marrying a wealthy man after all. The heart can't help who it falls in love with.

"I think I've got it all, Mom," sighed Chelsea, once her luggage was tagged. She was standing a few feet away from the sanctioned-off area for passengers only. This was the moment Amy had tearfully been envisioning for weeks.

"Okay." Amy couldn't hold it in any more. A tear escaped, causing the damn to burst.

"Oh Mom, don't cry," said Chelsea, who now too was sobbing like a baby. They hugged, creating a total spectacle for the next five minutes. Finally, Amy let her daughter loose. She put on her oversized black sunglasses and waved, laughing through the tears as Chelsea disappeared into the masses.

The ride home was devastating but oddly a little bit comforting. The worst was over; she had survived Chelsea's departure. She grabbed her blue tooth and dialed Matt at the office. He wanted so badly to be there to see their daughter off, but today was a meeting that would impact the rest of his thriving career. He was being considered as the new C.E.O. The family of three had celebrated Chelsea's new adventure over dinner last night, and Matt and Amy had decided to visit by the beginning of next month. Everything would turn out okay.

Amy slowed as she reached the turnpike. It would be nice to pick up a coffee. It was something she had normally only indulged in with Chelsea. Their special thing . . . coffee. Amy sighed and dealt with a fresh wave of tears. *Definitely leaving my sunglasses on for getting coffee,* she thought to herself. She ordered a huge dessert-type calorie extravaganza, then headed home. It was exactly what she needed right now.

The drink was halfway gone by the time she arrived home. Her stomach was full and the dose of sugar was practically causing the jitters. Maybe it wasn't exactly what the doctor ordered after all. She would use the excess energy to her advantage and finish up her work on the garden. They had two new garden boxes. She had anticipated her first week without Chelsea being extremely difficult so she had armed herself with plenty to do. First she would fill the garden boxes with soil, then plant a variety of seasonal produce and flowers. Once that was done, she was going to paint the boxes. She had stepping stones to set out and plants to be repotted. In the end, she'd have her own little relaxation spot to sit and read - a way, she speculated, to keep herself busy. The garden, as she called the yard, was already quite beautiful with a white wooden fence and landscaping that was full and green. It was situated on a huge plot of land, and neighbors were far enough away so that there was plenty of privacy, but not so far that you wouldn't be able to borrow a cup of sugar if you needed to.

After changing into more comfortable clothes, Amy went to her secluded yard. Her thoughts were heavy, but she had finally stopped crying. Gardening would definitely do her some good. She had enough to keep her busy for at least the next few days. As soon as she opened the door she could smell her magnolias. She closed her eyes, remembering the day she planted them. And of course, as in all of her memories, Chelsea was there. She sighed, picking up the small shovel and soiled gardening gloves that sat on the stoop. She rounded the corner, feeling the tears well once again, when she stopped dead in her tracks. "What the . . .?" She smiled, though, once she realized what it was that caught her eye. It was a child's kite, with a happy face on it that must have lost its way in the recent windy weather. She bent, reaching for the kite, when she was startled a second time. There was a sound behind her. She turned in time to see the sun's reflection on the enormous knife. Her last thought was *Thank God Chelsea isn't here.*

Chapter nineteen

It was the biggest bloodbath, including those stupid films they show you in basic training where some rookie always throws up, that Dean had seen in his career. The victim, Amy Walker, was beheaded; and her insides were on her outsides. She was ravaged head to toe; and it looked, quite literally, like a monster had done it. Even Dean was green around the gills over this scene.

It was a total nightmare; and it came on the heels of the fingerprints, which once again turned up as belonging to some kid patsy. A college boy who needed some cash was instructed to purchase the novel, write the inscription and mail it to Tranise. Dean came to the conclusion that the killer was, in fact, well respected – as the profile had stated – and probably a mentor of sorts, who would have plenty of young pawns at his disposal. Dean decided he would call Keeley as soon as he did the precursory tour of the crime scene, but he was well aware of the fact that he knew jack about literature. And where the hell did the killer leave the book this time? Keeley would probably know right away what a headless, torn-open body left in the backyard meant to symbolize. And Dean was pretty sure the kite was a prop as well. Since the woman, Amy, had no little kids, it was about as out of place in her picturesque garden as was the shredded cadaver. *Dammit!* Dean started to turn his back on the grisly scene when something caught his eye. He felt his throat tighten. It was the novel, a paperback titled *The Cycle of the Werewolf.* But there was something else, and it was what sent chills down the seasoned detective's spine.

***

Keeley was planning to meet Ben at his place after he got home from work, which would be later than usual. He was finalizing loose ends before heading abroad and was leaving on a red-eye tonight. She planned to help him pack, and of course savor their last moments together. Then she would drop him off at the airport before squeezing in a few hours of shut eye. Suddenly, her phone vibrated, and, for some odd reason, she knew the phone call was bad news. First of all, it had startled the heck out of her when it went off. She must have accidentally set it to vibrate, and it was also in her pocket, where it rarely is stored. She leaped and a small shriek escaped her lips. Then, once she saw who the call was coming from, she winced. Her stomach began to turn almost immediately. Sure, Detective Dean had called her at times without bad news, but not often. With foreboding, she sensed it was time, time again for the dark cloud to return. So when Dean briefly mentioned the weather after Keeley had asked how he was, she jumped in.

"Something's wrong. It is, isn't it?"

"You sound like a true detective, Keeley." She heard him sigh, but he said nothing else just then.

"I just have a bad feeling. Am I right?"

"Something is wrong. Very wrong. There's been another one. Can you come by? Please." "

Sure . . . I mean, of course." There was her gut instinct again. Something told her there was more going on than Dean let on.

"You can come to the crime scene, but I'll meet you out front."

"What was it? The book I mean?"

"Stephen King. Again. *Cycle of the Werewolf*, but that's no big surprise. It was on our reading list. But, um . . . there was something else that our guy left behind. I'll show you once you're here. 8371 Carmichael Street. By the pier."

"I know where that is. I know someone on that street." Keeley's voice raised several octaves. "Who was the victim?"

"Her name is – *was* Amy Walker."

"Oh my God!" Keeley nearly dropped the phone. She knew Amy and her daughter Chelsea from her book club. And they were also friends with Jess and Bob, through the museum of art. She had been to their home. Ben was right. This was getting much too close to Keeley.

"Keeley, you there?"

"Yes. I knew the victim. Amy Walker was both a friend of mine and my late sister-in-law's." She wasn't sure why she didn't use Jess's name. Perhaps because that would be the last straw. Things were fast growing out of hand. Keeley's head was spinning. Ben was leaving tonight. Maybe he wouldn't go. Maybe the fact that Amy Walker had died would be enough to keep her man by her side. But that was stupid, a stupid thought. This was Ben's career. Her own family member had been killed and he was, of course, still planning to go. So why would things be different now? She wasn't thinking clearly.

"Keeley? You there?" Dean asked again.

"Yes." She kept her answer short. She was afraid she might throw up if she opened her mouth for too long.

"I'm sending a car over to get you. Where are you?"

"No, that's not necessary. I'll be fine to drive." She wasn't so sure of that, though. What turn could the case possibly take now? And what did Dean have to show her? She felt like her heart might burst. Should she call Ben? Her first inclination was to call Bob, but why put him through any more of this? Come to think of it, why put Ben through any of this? It would just give him more fuel for his fire. She could already hear his response – "You're too close to the case, Keeley. It's dangerous." And he would, of course, be right. Then again, if she told him, maybe he wouldn't leave. She cursed herself for being so selfish. That wasn't the type of fiancé or wife that she wanted to be. Ben needed to go and the whole idea of her manipulating him into giving up his dreams was so not like her.

Keeley almost forgot Dean was still on the line. "I'll be right over."

"Wait, Keeley. I think since you knew Amy that maybe it isn't such a great idea that I haul you over here."

"No. I really want to come." The last thing Keeley wanted to do was show up at the crime scene of a friend, but she felt that if she didn't she'd be somehow letting her down. The same thing happened with Jess. Walking into Auberdine Designs that day was a nightmare, but she had to get Jess's address book. And come to think of it, if Keeley hadn't gone that day, she would never have found the copy of *IT*, not that the book clue has been so helpful in catching the murderer, but still, it was something. And something was better than nothing. While there was a slight chance that her going there might uncover another clue, she had no choice. "Dean, I have to come. I'll be there in fifteen minutes." She hung up, not giving him a chance to argue with her. She needed to be there; it was unavoidable.

***

Dean was waiting by the front door of Amy Walker's house. Her husband had been called and was being debriefed in the kitchen. The poor guy was completely distraught. He told them his daughter was unreachable for the next few hours because she was on a plane to Europe. Apparently Amy had dropped her off at the airport in the morning while he was in a mandatory business meeting. Dean sighed. Again his thoughts went to Terry and Zoe. He would never ever find telling a family member that they had lost a loved one to be commonplace, or just part of the job. As a matter of fact, if that ever did happen, he promised himself he would quit the force.

He realized Keeley would be there any minute and decided that, despite her emotional connection to Amy Walker, it would be valuable to get her take on the situation. He would detail the murder case, figure out the connection to the novel, show her the additional item that was left behind and then discuss the fingerprint findings on her novel. He laughed aloud at the faith he was instilling in the young woman, who had no more experience in the criminal world than having written a couple of scary books. But nonetheless, she was an asset, and he would have to be sure and compensate her for the emotional turmoil the case was undoubtedly causing her. He would give recognition where recognition was due. He recalled that two years back a woman claiming to have psychic abilities had helped nab a serial rapist, and she had been given an honorary detective's badge and a fruit basket.

Dean kicked at a loose stone and then smiled when he saw Keeley pull up at the curb. She was really growing on him. She was successful, dedicated, selfless and kind. Who wouldn't like the girl? Then the smile left Dean's face and he felt his throat tighten . . . Keeley was a woman who had everything to live for.

***

Being at Amy's house was surreal. The place felt desolate, despite being cluttered with police officers and various officials. Keeley caught a glimpse of Amy's husband, Matt, hunched over the kitchen table. Her heart went out to him. Another grieving husband. She thought of Bob, and then she pictured Ben in their positions. It was too much to bear. Keeley nearly fainted as a team of young men walked passed with a stretcher holding a black, zipped bag. She had never seen a dead body before. But the clincher was what Dean had found partially hidden near the copy of the book . . . a newspaper clipping announcing that Keeley's book had hit best seller status. It was a human interest piece in the local section of the newspaper detailing her specialty book store and her rise to the top. Three-fourths of the article was dedicated to the story and one-fourth displayed a closely shot photograph of Keeley.

It was one thing when her book store was chosen as a playground for the murderer's henchmen, and another thing when her *own* novel was added to the list, but this? Why was she playing such a starring role in this sicko's story? Story. Was this someone else's horror manuscript come true? She began to describe all of her recent concerns to Dean, who looked like he might lose it at any minute. His eyes were underscored by black circles and he looked like he had aged about ten years, things Keeley had noticed in herself when she looked in the mirror last. She went on to tell him all about her various theories and even mentioned the odd scenario with the professor. Dean reassured her once again that any theory was a helpful one and that she should keep them coming. Then Keeley asked if he thought it would be reasonable for her to pay a visit to Professor Michaels.

***

Matt Walker was beside himself, naturally. Behaving just as anyone would expect a newly christened widower to act. It was apparent that Amy's death was too much for him to handle. The room was dimly lit and there were close friends and family and a spread of food, varying from store-bought fare to home-baked casseroles. Anyone taking in the scene from the outside would see a small group of concerned individuals banning together over a tragic, tragic event. Some were feeling genuine anguish for the family and others were concealing concern for their own well-being; there was after all a serial killer out there. A spectator of the gathering would also have no idea that the very person who committed the crime was mingling among the mourners, for that person was a master of disguise, a well-respected community member and a stellar performer. Blended in just as well there as everywhere else. And hopefully, the charade would hold on until the game was finished.

After sharing a few shared condolences and finishing a plate of food, he slipped out the door. His other life was calling.

***

Keeley had some time to kill yet before meeting Ben and strongly considered showing up on campus to confront the fruit of her wild imagination. Driving to Fairview's campus would take about twenty minutes, and evening classes would probably still be in session. Was she out of her mind? She couldn't just ambush the guy. This was a totally far-fetched idea since she didn't actually believe Michaels could be the killer. She didn't even hope he was, although the idea of getting a killer off the streets was comforting. She figured she might get a better handle on her feelings after talking to him; that was all. Wasn't it? Was there actually any part of her that believed he could be the one? Maybe. But that would be too easy. As far as Keeley knew, his inappropriate confrontation of Summer was the only thing that connected him to the murders. But he was also a fellow book worm, as Ben had put it, and her next idea hit Keeley like a ton of bricks: The two "helpers" the killer had enlisted to steal and mail books were both college-aged. Perhaps this was like a Manson regime? Realizing she was probably being ridiculous, she leapt over three lanes and took the exit for the college.

***

Keeley parked in the lot she had been familiar with when she had taken a course here herself. The lot was mostly full and there were no students coming or going. She checked her watch. Assuming Michaels was even here now, she would try his office at the Literature department or ask where his class was being held. This whole thing was so utterly insane that she could feel herself blush as she walked through the parking garage. *Oh well*, she thought, *worst case scenario I greet an old friend.* The wind was cool and the sky was diming. She regretted not wearing her jacket that she left in the car.

She exited the garage and descended an attached staircase, noticing how much more fierce the wind was once she left the concrete structure. Jogging down the stairs, she nearly bumped into a young woman heading up the stairs. She apologized and kept going, as if it were just yesterday that she had taken this route to class. A moment later she reached the Lit building. She took a deep breath. What could she say to him to constitute a visit? An unsolicited, unannounced visit to a man she hadn't seen in ages? Was she nuts? And what would Ben say? She toyed for a brief instant with the idea of not even telling Ben. That would be lying by omission though and she didn't lie to Ben. But telling him something that hair brained their last night together, which she'd have to do . . . . that sounded about as appealing as coming face to face with Len Michaels right now. She decided to bite the bullet and go through with it. She would see how it all played out and then deal with what she'd tell Ben. She decided that it would be okay to skip telling Ben if she didn't actually see the professor. That seemed fair. But she knew it was devious and not fair.

Resolutely, she opened the large, heavy door leading to the building. There was a main office in the center, then several corridors leading to small offices for the instructors, other staff members and faculty. The woman manning the desk turned away from a file cabinet to face Keeley.

"May I help you?"

"Yes, I'm hoping to speak with Professor Michaels."

"Let me check his schedule," said the heavyset, pleasant woman, in a sing song voice. She turned back to the desk and flipped some pages. "Michaels. He is teaching a course right now." Keeley felt herself let out the breath she had been holding far too long. She was relieved. He was teaching. End of story, and despite the way she envisioned it, she would not come barging into his class, prepared to indict him of who knows what. The receptionist smiled, then cleared her throat, staring at the wall behind Keeley. Keeley turned to see an oversized clock on the wall behind her, and nothing else. "I stand corrected. His class just got out. He should be here any second for office hours. The time got away from me," she smiled.

Keeley felt beads of sweat glistening on her forehead. She was genuinely panic-stricken, but why? She had every intention of conversing with him. And now she was glad she had missed him, then terrified when she heard he might be here any minute. She realized the receptionist was waiting on her to react.

"Thank you. I'll go wait outside." Keeley slung her bag over her shoulder and hurried toward the door.

"Wait, Miss. You can wait here. Or on the bench outside his office. Much more comfortable." Keeley waved her off and kept walking. She was in such a hurry, that she didn't see Professor Michaels walking toward her. She looked up just before they would have collided and let out a yelp.

"Pardon me," he exclaimed, not realizing it was her. She was getting ready to go along and pretend she didn't recognize him either when he said her name, "Keeley? Is that you?" He used his hand to block the artificial lighting that flooded the entrance to the building.

"Yes. Len. How are you?"

"Great, great. How have you been?"

She didn't answer right away. She felt like a deer in headlights.

"And what are you doing here on campus? Book signing?"

"No. Not a book signing." She didn't know what to do other than lay it all out. Sort of. "I actually came here hoping to talk to you."

"Yeah?" He wrinkled his brow. He looked taller than she remembered. "Well, come on in then." He pushed the door opened and scooted to the side.

What was she doing here? She was wracking her brain trying to come up with what to say. She half smiled at the receptionist on the way to his office.

"What brings you here?" he asked again. She thought he looked bothered. He was probably just as perplexed as she was about why she was popping in.

"It's actually really bizarre, I know. I'm sure you've heard about the serial murders going on lately." She knew she couldn't divulge too much about the case, but it seems like Len at least knew the murders were loosely based on horror novels.

She had no idea where she was going with any of this, it was all off the cuff. "And I was hoping that you might be able to shed some light on the issue." She hoped maybe she could bait him into saying something incriminating, without making a total fool of herself. *What had Summer said?* She told her that Michaels asked about the novels and their relation to the murders. Keeley pursed her lips.

"In what capacity? I'm just an absent-minded professor," he laughed.

Len Michaels was a kindly-looking man who was always nothing but nice to her. She was totally out of her mind. Certifiable. She decided to end this before it started. Here she was trying to pin the crime on anyone so this whole nightmare could be over, at the cost of what? Then she remembered the completely inappropriate manner in which he bothered Summer over the issue.

"I'm not sure. My employee told me you spoke with her about the murders. I was just wondering what you meant when you said the crimes involved horror novels? I ask because I'm close to the case, having lost my brother's wife. And of course you know my writing background." Keeley looked down at his desk. There. She had laid it all out. It seemed like a reasonable reason why she'd come to him. It didn't seem too far-fetched. Hopefully. And it laid the groundwork for him to provide all the details he knew. Perhaps she would also find how and why he knew the details.

"I heard exactly that. That the crimes may somehow involve horror novels. Naturally, like you, I wanted to get more information."

"But where did you hear that? That horror novels might be involved." Darn, the guy wasn't giving any information. She had been totally off base with her silly instincts.

"Hearsay. Word of mouth. I have at least fifty young, busy-bodied media followers in the class I just left." He began organizing his desk. Perhaps to indicate that the meeting was over.

"Of course. But was that really all you heard? Just that one detail?"

"I heard a few different things. You know these kids. But that piece of information caught my interest."

He was now sitting on the edge of his desk, facing Keeley.

"Anything you can tell me would be greatly appreciated, Len. I really value your opinion."

Len got up and shut the door to his office. Keeley felt her stomach tighten.

"One thing I can tell you I've learned from being around kids all the time – the only thing they love more than good gossip is sharing good gossip. I've heard a few pretty preposterous things in my day. Nothing that I've heard in the past week or two was noteworthy until this. You don't want gore-hungry hogwash produced by these entitled brats."

"So you haven't heard anything substantial?"

"If I knew anything I would tell you. I'm very sorry for your loss. You and I share a love of books and I too respect you a great deal. Please tell Ben I said hello." Just then came a knock on his door. "Office hours," he smiled.

"Thank you, Len. I appreciate it." He seemed sincere. Harmless. She was an idiot. But she didn't regret her trip. She had seen a copy of Dracula on the bookshelf behind him. Did it mean he was the killer? Probably not, but their conversation just reminded her that everyone wants a piece of a good mystery. He said his students were sensationalizing the hell out of this case. Everyone with a taste for mystery novels would want a piece of this. And someone with a taste for mystery novels had more than likely caused this; committed the murders. Someone, much like Len Michaels, who had specific knowledge at his disposal. She needed to expound on this train of thought, but right now, she had to decide what to tell Ben when she saw him later.

Chapter twenty

Keeley's phone vibrated and she felt a pang of guilt when she saw Bob's name light up the screen. She had meant to touch base with him. Technically, she should have visited Bob instead of Len in her mission to pass the time. But she decided that even though she couldn't pinpoint what it was, she had a feeling that she might get somewhere with today's meeting with Len.

"Hey, Bobby!"

"Hi Sis. I hope it's a good time. I know you're meeting with Ben."

"We're meeting later on, but that wouldn't matter. I can always talk to you." She loved him with all her heart; the sentiment was true. "How are you doing? How's work?" She tacked on the second sentence to lighten up the conversation.

"Work's work. I'm doing well. I don't want you to worry about me, Kee. I almost didn't call you."

"Why?"

"I hate to appear like I'm bothering you. You have your own life, Kee. I don't want you to feel like you need to babysit me is all."

She smiled. She was feeling the same way about Ben. Like she didn't want to make him feel burdened.

"Let's just get this clear, Mister. There is no part of you that will ever burden *or* bother me. That statement will never change, Bob."

"Okay. That statement goes both ways, you know. Please let me know if you need anything at all while Ben's away."

"Of course I will." She wouldn't let him know how terrified she was becoming with the idea of being alone with everything that was going on.

"I just called to check in and to tell you I'd be glad to come down and meet you for dinner one night this week. If you're feeling like you want some company," Bob said.

Keeley realized that he might be the one needing company, and she knew she would love his company. She agreed whole-heartedly and they got off the phone, with a promise of plans to come.

After plenty of deliberation, Keeley knew what she would say to Ben in regards to her visit to Fairview College and Len Michaels. The simple truth. It would hopefully sound just as innocent as it was. That she was asking him if he had any information on the case. Ben would remember how Len had revealed to Summer that he knew about the horror novel connection. It was simple. It was basically the truth. She would leave out the fact that she wondered, if even for a minute, if Len Michaels was the butcher who was going around murdering innocent women. The idea sounded silly yet again, but it didn't feel too cuckoo anymore. The killer had to be someone. Someone who knew his material, or plots. Someone familiar with the victims, or characters if you will. But what in the world would the motive be? Dean didn't share much about the profiler's report. He did tell her at the time what the results were, but it hadn't been brought up since. She was keeping loose notes of all of their conversations. She would need to glance over those again later.

Keeley pulled up alongside the curb. "Here goes nothing," she said out loud. She gathered her small over-night bag and her purse. Ben was just pulling up. Perfect timing. He parked his car, then came over and embraced her before taking her bags.

"I'm gonna miss this," he said, his eyes moist. "I love that we both have our careers, but can see each other at a moment's notice."

"Me too." She was afraid if she said much more that the damn might break and she'd never stop crying.

"I want to have a set schedule of phone calls, Keeley," he said somberly. He unlocked the door and held it open for her. "I want to pick a time during the day and night where I know I'm going to hear from you or vice versa. A check in." He was scared for her safety. The thought gave her goose bumps.

"That's a good idea. But what about the time change?"

"I don't care. We can leave messages." He looked desperate. Scared. She wanted to yell at him that if he was so worried that he shouldn't go. But again, that's not what she wanted for him.

"Okay." Keeley could barely finishing uttering the word before Ben swooped her up, grabbing her face and kissing her passionately. Luckily for Keeley, she didn't have a chance to tell Ben about Professor Michaels before they fell asleep, bodies entwined.

***

Keeley set down her cup of tea. Bob had of course made some, knowing she might be feeling low since Ben had left. The family cure all. She swallowed hard over the lump in her throat. She had to keep her emotions in check. Ben was on a trip, not dead. There was no way she would allow Bob to see how distraught she was actually feeling. She was struggling with plenty of feelings right now. She was feeling guilty about the fact that she was ever so slightly happy to drop Ben off for his flight without having to divulge her news about Len Michaels. That feeling was gone of course, the second his back turned on her. She walked to the car and nearly crumpled underneath her own weight she was so intensely sad. But now she had had a small amount of time to deal with it and she would persevere. Especially in Bob's presence. The poor guy had been to hell and back.

Her life was far from being over. On the contrary it was getting ready to begin. Ben would return and there would be a wedding. She would get back to writing and ultimately, if things went as hoped, they would start trying for a family. It was what they had always talked about. Keeley hoped to have a child or two. With the age difference between her and Bob, she felt like she knew what it was like to be both a sibling and an only child. She basically grew up alone. As a result she was very close with her parents, but as fate would have it, she lost them far too early. Like Chelsea Fisher. Again, her thoughts went back to death. *Way to stay chipper*.

"So what did you decide?"

Keeley stared into space, realizing she must have ignored whatever Bob just said. "Sorry. Day dreaming I guess."

"That's okay," he smiled his warmest smile.

Keeley was relieved. She was afraid she might never see it again.

"I was just wondering what you decided on to eat. Going out? Or I can throw steaks on the grill."

"Oh, whatever you prefer." Despite feeling like she had to hide her true emotion, she felt a true sense of well-being now that she was here with Bob again. The entire thing had been such a blur. She squeezed the bridge of her nose, realizing a headache was coming on. Bob must have seen her because he suggested then that they stay in. "I have corn on the cob and some baked beans. Why don't you sit here and I'll mix up a pitcher of margaritas. Or mojitos. I have both." Bob was catering to her? She stood up, deciding that her unintentional pity party ended now.

"Don't be silly. I'll start on the sides. And let's definitely have margaritas. That sounds great."

As soon as Bob turned his back to walk toward the kitchen, she reached into her purse for a couple of Aleve. Cooking with her brother and staying in sounded right up her alley. She shuffled through her purse, not finding the very item that she needed, as always. Ben would always tease her about that. She had a hundred things in that bag, but only actually used a few. "You never know what you might need," she would tease back. Finally her hand gripped the bottle of pills. She tipped the bag and her phone slid out of its pouch. She had one text message.

Keeley fought everything within herself to not respond immediately to the text from Dean. Well, it didn't really even require a request. What he wrote to her was a statement and what it required was action. But not right now. Not with Bob and not right now. She was way too focused on her role as playing non-anguished-sister to brother-she-needed-to-babysit. And it wasn't like Dean's news was a matter of life or death. Death, she supposed. Everything about this case revolved around death. Death, escaping death, planned out but not yet executed death.

"Kee? Margs are ready," called Bob from the kitchen. *So much for not brooding.* She stuffed her phone into her jeans pocket and followed Bob's prompt to come and enjoy a margarita. Another minute of pretending none of this had ever happened would do her some good.

"I'm on my way!"

***

Dean was pacing. Keeley usually answered his calls on the first ring. *But you didn't call her, you moron,* he chided himself. *You decided to text her. You never text anyone, but you texted her. You thought texting might seem less . . . intimidating. Less serious? Whatever the reason it was dumb,* he thought. *Because now I can't call her. I guess I can, but the girl needs to breathe.* He went back to pacing. *The poor girl sounded really distraught the last time we spoke. Like she's getting pushed to her limit.*

And it's not like he was calling – no, texting – about any breaking news or really, anything that couldn't wait 'til morning. He decided to text her this evening though because he was feeling that . . . feeling he sometimes got. He couldn't even really make heads or tails of it, but he figured he would run it by his girl Friday. He didn't want to shake the hunch, that was all. If she didn't contact him within the hour he would call her cellphone, like he should have done earlier. The poor girl was either busy with her own life or maybe she was sick and tired of having to be a part of the case. God knew Dean was. Maybe she was dodging his calls, or *texts*, for the night. If that

helped her cope then so be it. He decided to give her the
night off. If she didn't get back to him tonight, then he'd
call her tomorrow. At a decent hour. This wasn't her life's
work. And now that she had known *two* of the victims . . .
it would be a well-deserved break for the poor gal.

Dean continued his brainstorm, but swapped the
pacing for his favorite recliner and a pad and pen. He
would jot down his "feelings" or whatever they were and
see if he could make heads or tails of them. Perhaps he
was becoming too reliant on his author friend. But he
knew it was a coping mechanism; he'd used a zillion
throughout his career. Keeley was safe, non-toxic.

She wasn't an actual part of the case, but she was
close enough to it that she could share the weight of this
burden. A person set so far-back enough so that they too
wouldn't get eaten alive by the job, but with a new set of
ideas. Someone to commiserate with. And at the end of
the day, didn't we all want that? Someone to just share
your most raw emotions with.

Of course in his real life that was his loving wife.
But he wouldn't dare share his work issues with her. She
was pleasantly as far-removed from his horrific career as
possible, just where he wanted her. And every thought he
just had, made him come to the conclusion that he wanted
Keeley as far-removed as possible. *She knew some of the
victims . . . The other day he realized that Keeley also fit
the bill of the perfect woman who had it all. . .* How the
hell had Dean not realized she had gotten too close to the
case?

***

After a whopping three margaritas and the best
steak she had consumed in a while, Keeley was starting to

realize she needed to get to bed. It had been a while since she'd allowed herself to cut loose, but she reminded herself to take a bottle of water to the guest bedroom. She would guzzle the whole thing and cross her fingers that tomorrow wouldn't involve regrets of a carefree night. She had allowed herself to forget about Ben, Len Michaels, Amy Walker, the creepy book at Tranise's, the crazy involvement of her novel, and even Dean and the entire case.

***

The two siblings bonded and engaged in conversation like they hadn't in a long time. It was like old times- Keeley and Bob against the world. Again, she hoped she wouldn't pay for it tomorrow morning, as she hopped into bed. She took out her contact lenses, pulled her hair back into a ponytail and drank her bottle of water. She remembered that she wanted to charge her phone and then remembered that she blatantly ignored Dean. She didn't so much as text one word or allude to when she might. She groaned, then looked at the bedside clock and saw that it was eleven o'clock. Eleven o'clock on a Friday night. The poor man probably never slept, but she decided to send him a quick text and call him first thing in the morning. *Heading to bed. I'm sorry I didn't respond earlier. Let's talk tomorrow morning- Keeley*

***

She woke up, a little groggy, but overall feeling rested and, under the circumstances, relaxed. She heard movement, pulled on her robe and walked out to see if Bob was in the den or the kitchen. She hadn't bothered to put on her contacts or, for that matter, check the clock.

The parted blinds in the front room revealed that it was still a misty gray outside. The sun hadn't fully risen. She pushed open the French doors to the kitchen and of course it was empty. It was far too early for anyone to be up. The noise must have been the house settling. She cinched her robe and headed back to her quarters. She surprised herself when she bolted the door behind her. But who could blame her for having the jitters? She had been through a great ordeal, and sadly, it seemed far from over. She settled back into her bed and saw that the clock read 5:19. Her almost euphoric satisfaction turned to unalloyed exhaustion. She fell back into a fitful sleep and finally had to force herself awake from a horrific nightmare where she was the victim of a masked murderer.

***

Tranise was doing her best to play the role of complacent wife and mother. It was after all, the weekend. Her daughters were there and Jeff was home all day. So she would paste on a smile, laugh and joke whenever necessary and put on the performance of a lifetime. She knew it was unhealthy. And she certainly knew it wasn't who she wanted to be, but for right now, it served a greater purpose. She would keep her family happy, and under the notion that she was fine and that she was, in fact, a survivor. Then once they were okay, she could worry about herself. She had all week long to brood. And she had Keeley. And even Dean. She certainly didn't want to discredit Jeff. He was wonderful. But, as the matriarch that she was, she knew she needed to coddle him to some degree. He and the girls were all that mattered. And if they were happy, she was happy. That and making sure that she stayed alive. She knew it was a long shot that she would be his target again, but still . . . it was a possibility. The fact that she was *chosen* to begin with was still so . . . haunting.

What would stop the guy from coming back to finish his goal? But Dean had said that she would be safe because if there was a second try it might blow the killers' plan. A second time would be too risky, he'd said. But it's not like there was a firing squad standing outside her front porch. The police had come by only a handful of times. Tranise was petrified to be home alone, but she was also afraid of being out and about, for fear that he might find her and follow her back home. After all, the saving grace was that her attack didn't happen at home. She knew there was some degree of safety that would certainly be lacking if she had been attacked here. Her entire home that she had created, her sanctuary, would have been violated. She also felt solace in the notion that maybe he couldn't get to her if he didn't know where her real home was. Yet, he had found her family's cabin. That makes a whole lot of sense. And she wasn't an idiot. She knew that nowadays one could find anyone they wanted through the web. For this minute she was safe, and that was good enough for Tranise. Mostly.

Her thoughts were interrupted by the kids, entering the room, laughing. The sweetest sound, bringing light to her darkness.

"What's so funny?" Tranise asked, slinging the kitchen towel over her shoulder. She opened the dishwasher and stepped to the side to avoid the steam bath from the machine just having finished its cycle.

"Chrissa just told me a joke. It was super corny but not bad," smiled Shanae.

"Do tell," smiled Tranise, leaning her hip against the counter. "I love a good joke."

"How can you tell if a tomato is falling behind?" asked a giggly Chrissa.

"How?"

"He'll try his best to catch-up. Get it? Like ketsup?"

Tranise forced a laugh and noted how sweet and happy her daughters looked. Maybe they wouldn't be ruined by this. And maybe she wouldn't be either. This didn't have to define them. Tranise thought that if anyone looked through the window at this moment, that they would see a group of laughing, happy people. Not a terrified woman who was barely hanging on and two little girls who might have serious psychological issues below the surface. She smiled, then cringed at the image of someone looking through the window. She turned away and went back to drying the dishes.

Minutes later Jeff came in and regaled the girls with his own repertoire of corny jokes. The entire family had heard them all dozens of times, but they all still laughed. Again, Tranise imagined what the four of them might look like from a bystander's point of view. They'd look pretty normal. The thought put her mind at ease. Because for this very moment in time, she wasn't feeling the fear. She was feeling normal again.

***

Over greasy, powdered donuts – what Bob referred to as "brain food," – Keeley regrettably told her brother she would need to basically beat it out of there. Dean responded to her text just before she woke up the second time. He asked if they could meet up. She wasn't sure what to expect. She was going through so many different things right now. She still wanted to help with the case, but she had decided, for Ben's sake (and from the guilt associated with lying by omission) to tell Dean she needed to ease up a bit. It was the right thing to do. Somehow she had become an integral cog in the case and that was the true deciding factor. That and the fact that Ben was near frantic when he was discussing their daily talking schedule on the way to the airport. She figured it was the least she could do. She would give Dean input on the novels, (God forbid there be any more murders) and she would continue her friendship with Tranise. Other than that, she would no longer treat the case as a second career. She was anxious to let Dean in on her thoughts. She was also interested in what his "gut instinct" regarding the case was. That and why he asked to meet up with her in person rather than speak on the phone. Meeting up was for the best, since she had things she wanted to share as well. What didn't sit well with Keeley, who was basically eating and running out on her poor bereaved brother. They were having such a good time. If Dean hadn't reached out, she had envisioned a leisurely morning spent with Bob, then maybe even a little site seeing. Bob did his best to ease her visible guilt, saying he had things he needed to tend to anyway. They would catch up later. He would come down to her neck of the woods.

She pulled on a pair of yoga pants and a knit shirt and gathered her few belongings before kissing Bob on the cheek and wishing him well. She couldn't believe how well he appeared to be handling everything. And if he was belying his true emotion, and he was still painfully grieving, he was an excellent actor. She hopped into the car and turned it to her go to station - all 80s all the time. Widows lowered and *Dexy's Midnight Runners* belting out their famous ballad to Eileen, it felt like almost any other beautiful Saturday morning. She would of course not be rushing away from her newly-widowed brother to talk to a police detective about the murders of several people in her personal or physical proximity. And of course her knight in shining armor wouldn't be time zones away. She lowered the volume and raised the windows when she reached Main Street. Dean had asked to meet at Keeley's shop. She agreed to it. The scene of the crime – that's what her store was last time Dean had been there. But it was perfect. Keeley was prepared to tell Dean about her decision to slow down on the case, plus her findings about the professor, which were really, nothing. She would hear what he was coming up with and hopefully that would sum things up. Then she could tend to business of her own.

He was there waiting, perusing the book stacks when Keeley breezed through the door. He smiled and approached her, still holding a book in his hand.

"You like Tolstoy?" she asked, a perplexed look on her face. "I didn't peg you for a fan."

"The wifesaid something about his book one time recently. Me, I'm not much of reader, unless you count the Sunday paper."

"Well, the book's on me. And you really should start reading more." She bit her tongue on that last sentence. Was she insinuating that he should be reading to keep up with the killer? What a horrible way to lead their casual conversation. She felt herself blushing.

"Well, I figure soon I'll have a little more free time on my hands and I'll pick up a Keeley Travis book."

"You feel pretty confident about your hunch then?" Good. The relaxed banter was back.

He smiled. "I think so. Where can we go?"

"Follow me back to my office." Keeley led the way. Her office was basically a room with a desk and a computer. Most of her work was done at the check-out counter. She had a few files in the desk cabinet, but everything important was stored at home. Keeley scooted a rolling chair across the desk from her own.

"I'd like to start off again by thanking you for everything you've done for the case." She felt the guilt slipping in. "We really have gotten so much farther along because of you and I know it's not your job and you have to be freaking about the news clipping found at the Walker residence." It was like he was reading her mind. "Anyway, you've gone above and beyond. We like to recognize that in our business. So don't think anyone on the force is feeling anything but praise and gratitude toward you."

"Am I getting a get-out-of-jail-free pass?" He didn't do much more than curl up one side of his mouth. "Sorry. Played a lot of Monopoly as a kid."

He did allow a full smile for that comment. "Anyway, you've been invaluable. On that note, I think maybe we were barking down the wrong tree when we were using the museum as the common thread for the victims." He cleared his throat, and for the first time she realized, he looked nervous. "This comes on the heels of Tranise receiving a copy of your book and Amy Walker's crime scene containing an excerpt on you." He stayed deliberately silent. Waiting for Keeley to say something, but what?

"What are you saying?"

"What I'm saying, Keeley, is that I think *you're* the common thread." She felt her head spinning.

"But . . . With Jess and Amy, sure, but . . . I didn't know the others."

"I think maybe you do, if we really looked into it. Maybe they were fans, readers, acquaintances. Anyway, like I said, it's just a hunch. I've got photos and summaries about the victims, including hobbies, backgrounds, home towns, etc. I'd appreciate if you can go over those at some point." Dean slapped a manila folder beside her on her desk. Simple enough request. But the fact that was hard to swallow was that he believed this sick murderer on the loose was spurred by her? She thought she might vomit.

"You look pale, Keeley. Don't panic."

"Don't panic? I came to this meeting today, prepared to tell you I was feeling 'a little too close to this,' now you're telling me you think I'm the driving force! How can I stay calm?!"

He touched her hand across the desk. "Keeley, let's hope I'm wrong. Sadly it's happened more times than not. I just want to see if there is an ounce of credence to this. And to make you feel better, we can have men watching your store and house. I'll do all I can to ensure that until my hunch is shot. Which I'm praying it isn't."

She took a deep breath. Her mind was swimming. What else was she planning to talk with Dean about? She had no clue. Her mind was an empty slate. Her stomach roiling, she slid the file towards her. She opened it. "Should I do this now?"

"When you can," smiled Dean. "The sooner the better."

Keeley glanced at the wall clock, tentatively fingering the papers. "The store's gonna open any minute, but Summer is . . . well she's not here yet I guess, but she's supposed to be. Keeley suddenly felt worried. About Summer. About everything. Where was Summer? It was one minute until ten. Summer was known for being over the top early. Keeley recalled how Professor Michaels had harassed her that day on campus. *What if* . . . then came the sound of the key in the lock, the opening door and signal bell. Thank God! Keeley hopped up. Summer was safe and sound. But why had her thoughts gone straight to the professor again? She made a mental note to mention that to Dean. She had almost forgotten. But she would do that after rushing up front to see her friend. "That's Summer. I don't want to frighten her. She didn't know we'd be here.

Summer also had a case of the jitters, apparently, because when Keeley rounded the corner, Summer squealed. Keeley apologized, explained why she was here and unconsciously searched her employee's eyes. She was unnerved by the fact that Summer was "late." She would never dream to ask her about it. They were good friends, but that would seem rude. And of course, Summer seemed fine after being frightened to see another person in the store. Keeley returned to Dean, sitting solemn at his desk. He was tough to read sometimes. But she knew he had to be a tortured soul with a job like his. She could hardly even stand being on the side-lines of it for just a matter of weeks.

"I wanted to tell you something too." Suddenly she wondered if she wasn't breaking a law or something by chasing her own whim. "I mentioned to you about the professor at Fairview. He was questioning Summer and seemed to know about the horror novel piece."

"I remember."

"Well I went to see him at his office." Keeley cleared her throat. "He basically said that there's a lot of hearsay floating through campus and that he had just picked up that knowledge along the way somewhere." She felt embarrassed. This didn't sound like much. At the time she thought it was breaking news. What else was there to say? *Think!* "I guess I'm not a very good interviewer. I was actually scared. Because when I was there with him . . . I thought it could have *been* him. Or someone like him." Now she was making some sense. This was what she had been thinking all along. "He has the knowledge of books, he's an upstanding member of society, he has young people at his disposal, like Josh for example."

"These are all great observations, Keeley. Good job. Do you still feel like we need to look into the guy?"

Keeley was astounded he was giving her theory life! She was also happy to have his approval. She knew she was always subconsciously looking to people as father figures, having lost her own so early on.

"Not really. I mean I don't think so. But on the heels of what you said today, he does have a connection to me."

"I can look into it. It wouldn't hurt."

"I don't think it was that I thought it was *him*, per se. It was more like the idea that it could be someone like him. Someone, anyone – "

"I like how you think." He winked at her and stood, indicating that the meeting was over. She felt a little better than she had when the bomb was dropped, but she was desperate to share the news with someone. Who was the question. Bob would panic and he didn't need another thing to upset him right now. Ben would absolutely flip out and that would be selfish to tell him because there would be nothing he could do. He would feel helpless being so far away. Plus he was adjusting to a lot right now with his new surroundings and huge responsibilities with work. This was just a hunch. No reason to overreact – Dean said so himself. She didn't want to burden Summer or Regina or even Leah, who she considered her best friend, but hadn't talked to since before Jess died. They had sent some texts back and forth, but it hardly seemed appropriate to bombard her with this. She had her own things going on.

Keeley felt suddenly lost and alone. She really didn't have a ton of people she could rely on. No one could possibly relate to what was happening in her life right now, except of course – one woman.

***

Tranise nearly jumped at the chance to get out of the house. Keeley's call came at just the right time. Tranise's feelings of well-being were short–lived. And her foreboding thoughts of someone looking in the window were dead on. A tabloid reporter, found by poor Chrissa, had hopped the fence and was camped out in the side yard. Jeff chased the guy, but restrained himself at Tranise's urgings once the guy made it to the street. He was caught by a police officer at the end of the street who was following up on a possible car theft. Anyway, she decided to take Keeley up on her offer to come to her bookstore because she knew she couldn't keep the happy-go-lucky façade up much longer. It would be nice to get out and be with someone, the only one, who could really understand her right now. And she was also hoping to pick out a good book. It would help to keep her mind off of reality.

She pulled up to the store, admiring the exterior. Tranise had seen the shop before but had never been inside. She drove only one block before finding a spot on the bustling Saturday morning. She passed a couple eating at a bistro table outside of the local deli. Not a care in the world. Then a male on a bike peddled passed, craning his neck to leer at her. Her stomach turned. In general that sort of thing made her skin crawl, but lately, everyone was a potential threat. The biker could have been her attacker for all she knew. He could be anywhere. She could have passed him on the street or even known him for that matter. That creepy fact was not lost on her. The fact of the matter was, not that many people knew the location of her family cabin. Clearly, she had been watched, selected. She shook the thought as she approached the door. The signal bell even startled her to her dismay. She saw Keeley immediately at the counter, chatting with a pretty college aged gal. She stopped talking and came quickly to Tranise's side to give her a hug.

"Thank you so much for coming. Tranise, this is Summer. Summer, Tranise." The two women each politely greeted one another, commenting that they had heard good things. After small talk about the weather, Keeley escorted Tranise back to her small office and offered her coffee.

Minutes later they were both seated with warm hazelnut lattes.

"I called you, Tranise, because like you, I feel like I'm at a breaking point. I know I told you Ben was getting ready to leave and he just did."

"Oh, I'm so sorry. I can't imagine being alone through all this. You're welcome over any time. Our house is a three ring circus most of the time."

"Thank you. I might take you up on that." Keeley quickly imagined of having her own little circus with Ben one day. The thought soothed her. "Detective Dean came by today. Since the arrival of your little "gift" I have been feeling a little freaked out. Then Dean mentioned that he thinks the case has something more to do with me."

"What do you mean?" asked Tranise, brow wrinkled.

"He said he thinks I'm the common thread." Keeley felt the familiar wave of nausea.

"As in . . .?"

"As in, he thinks the women might have had more than just the museum and the whole perfect life thing in common. But I told Dean that was silly because I only knew Jess and Amy." Keeley clamped her jaw, realizing she was beginning to ramble. "He gave me these," she said, sliding the case file across the table. "It has a brief rundown of the women's hobbies and likes and other specs."

Tranise simply stared at the papers, afraid that if she opened them she might never return. "Have you looked at them?" she asked, pain in her beautiful eyes.

"Only glanced."

"Are you going to . . . look at them? I mean, I guess you have to. Sorry. I wouldn't be able to."

"I know. I wouldn't expect you to. I, on the other hand, have no choice. But I'm also afraid. I'm afraid of what I might find. I'm afraid of humanizing the women I didn't know. I'm afraid this nightmare might never end."

"Keeley, you don't *have* to do anything, but I know you will."

"It might help. And it might be that the angle has changed. But I really hope not." She paused and stared at Tranise. Her eyes looked glossy. Keeley knew that feeling all too well. If she so much as blinked, the damn would break. "I'll look through them later today. Didn't you say you were hoping to find a book?"

"Yes!" Tranise seemed appreciative for the change in topic. They stood up and exited the little office space. Keeley led the way. Summer smiled as they passed the counter.

"What type of books do you usually read?" asked Keeley, genuinely interested. She was after all, in her element.

"Mostly fiction. I like mysteries, but not for now. I also like biographies."

"Then follow me," smiled Keeley.

After about ten minutes, Tranise had three books in her arms. Keeley promised she'd love them all. They were light and fun reads. Nothing whatsoever having to do with either of their real lives. Perfect. Tranise left after paying for her books, then Keeley headed to her office to go over the dreaded files.

***

Keeley had taken over for Summer who had an emergency study session, talked with Ben and done the order for the week. Basically anything to avoid going over Dean's files. By the time she was done with everything else it was forty five minutes until closing and dusk had fallen. A customer, a man, had entered the store and Keeley felt her stomach flutter. Whether it was the fact that night had begun to fall, that she was alone in the store, or the files describing the dead women, she wasn't sure; but she was instantly on high alert. Wanting to rule out her worst fears, she left the safety of the counter and approached the man. Her heart lifted when she got a closer look at him and he appeared to be a kind-hearted man in his late fifties. She asked if he needed any help and she pointed him in the right direction. *Phew! Safe . . . for now.* She went back to the case files and finished up the first one – poor Harper Middleton. She had a fiancé. She liked to volunteer. She was young! She was beautiful. She had a sister, a mother, a father and several friends. She was a socialite if Keeley had ever seen one. Nothing about her interests struck a chord. At least there was nothing that tied her to Keeley. The next page read like a resume – her schooling and jobs. The page after that was a list of her close friends and contacts. Keeley was intently reading the second page when the man approached the counter. She closed the folder immediately, realizing it was probably not a good idea to have this top secret information lying open on her counter. He purchased a book and left. He was not a threat, despite her nagging gut feeling that every male at night was a danger. Actually, it didn't have to be at night and it didn't necessarily have to be a male. She was always skeptical nowadays. She went back to her reading after glancing at the clock. Twenty minutes left.

Harper was an intern for a well-known PR company, went to a private and pricy high school, did her undergrad at Washington State and took several upper division courses at Fairview in an effort to achieve her Master's degree, which she apparently never will. Keeley wasn't feeling so well. This was too upsetting. Forcing herself to focus, she glanced at the timeframe during which Harper was at Fairview and Keeley realized that they had been there at the same time when Keeley was gathering missing units. She wondered if she would be able to track down her schedule. Could that be the connecting piece? Between Keeley and the first victim she was studying? Keeley stared at the picture of Harper. She was not particularly familiar, but she looked like many of the pretty coeds who graced the halls of her college. She had the appearance of a well-bred Ivy League type: beautiful, blonde, tall. *Dead.*

Keeley shut the files. She was scaring herself too much. She would finish this up at home. Alone and terrified, but on her own turf. She was itching to text Dean about retrieving Harper's old course schedule, but she knew she had to finish reading everything before leaping to conclusions. Fairview was a big campus. The fact that the two went their – briefly – was hardly the missing link. Keeley's thoughts immediately flitted back to the distinguished professor.

Chapter twenty-one

It was nine thirty and Bob had just finished eating reheated leftovers. He had stayed late at the office then stopped by the market for a bottle of mouthwash and a few impulse buys on the way out. He stacked his rinsed dishes in the sink and washed his hands. He sure missed Jess. And after last night, he missed his sister. She wasn't acting herself though. He knew she had to be bothered by the fact that Ben was gone, but wouldn't dare make that known. She was like an opened book with her emotions, bless her heart. He also knew the case was taking its toll on her and couldn't help but feel guilty about that. He should be the one pouring over Jess's murder and others like hers. But Keeley was the one with the eye for mysteries. He sighed. It was wonderful that she was helping so much, but she was too pure for this. She was an optimistic, happy-go-lucky type who wasn't the slightest bit jaded by the world. He had already lost Jess, and the last thing he wanted was to lose his sister, or at least her sense of wonder and thirst for life.

He dried his hands and went upstairs, stopping at the bottom step to grab his grocery bag containing the mouthwash. He was getting the hang of things, slowly but surely. Jess ran the household, did the cooking, kept track of dwindling mouthwash and therefore replenished it. He would miss so much about her and the little things, like shopping for himself, would be a constant reminder that his love was gone.

Bob placed his purchase in the medicine cabinet, then went into the master bedroom, where he had not slept since Jess died. He had stumbled upon a ritual of sorts over the last week. He would sit on Jess's side of the bed and look at and hold her bedside items. A sachet of lavender that she got at a bed and breakfast in Long Horn, a picture of her dear Granny Auberdine, a picture of the two of them in a beautiful Tiffany's silver frame and a small copy of the bible she bought in Vatican City. She was not exactly religious, but she appreciated how special the item was. These were small tokens, but she cherished them enough to have them resting on her nightstand.

After sniffing the lavender, which Jess always said helped her fall to sleep, Bob walked to her vanity in the bathroom and rubbed his fingers along her silver hand mirror, brush and comb. He would picture his beautiful wife, sitting there grooming for some such occasion. She was always smiling. That smile was what first caught his eye. That and her huge personality lit up any room. *Ah Jess. Did you know how much you meant to me?* He knew she did. She was his world. He set down her mirror and retreated toward the guest room. He paused at the bedroom door, wondering if he could ever bring himself to sleep in here again. He didn't think so. Throughout their marriage, they had spent only two nights apart due to business travel. It was so hard to be away from he that he vowed he would never sleep without her by his side again, and since he was the boss, he didn't have to. Turning off the light he remembered something else he wanted to look into.

He wanted to get himself a copy of the book Keeley had found in Jess's office. The horror novel. He was ready now to read it.

***

Keeley sat pouring over the case files, while some such syndicated CSI show was unraveling, unwatched in the background. Ever since her first night alone since everything began, she used the television as constant background noise. It was soothing. But maybe the show wasn't the most appropriate. She winced when she looked up to see a body bag being raised onto a stretcher. She grabbed the remote and flipped the channel to a game show she had never seen before.

She was a little startled to find more than a few slight comparisons between all the women's files she'd read so far. Dean's theory may have been right, however subtle the commonalities. So far she had a small chart going. She was surprised to see that there was another Fairview alum on the list: Adrienne Torero took a few refresher courses and it specified that she was a Lit major at San Diego State University in her youth. Again her thoughts ran to Len Michaels.

As they already surmised , everyone had some connection to the museum of art and friends could be found that connected the group together. Obviously Keeley had a familial connection to Jess. Harper was at Fairview with her (she noted again to ask Dean for her course schedule). Laney was a cancer patient at the specialty center at the university – where Keeley had once donated a sizable amount of money after her book made it big and she had also donated stacks of books to the waiting and treatment rooms. It seemed like a stretch, but it *was* a connection to Keeley. Amy was in the book club with her and Adrienne had actually done PR for Ben's company last year when Ben had just signed on. Again, a stretch, but it was something. With night falling, Keeley was glad to see Dean's theory might be losing steam, but he was correct in that there *were* connections between her and all the victims, with the exception of Tranise. Keeley was still working on that one. Then again, what was it they said? Eight degrees of separation? It was probably easy to find a link between *several* people in this city. Or was it?

Keeley shut the files. Gladly. It was easy to see both sides. Either Keeley was the common link, albeit a weak one, or it was mere coincidence. Time to switch gears. She walked down the hall into the kitchen, turning lights on as she walked. She would have one hell of an electric bill these next few months that was for sure. With the constant lighting and television . . . it was the price she had to pay for a long distance relationship (coinciding with a killer on the loose).

She opened the freezer and took out a pint of Ben & Jerry's and set it on the counter to defrost. Ice cream helped everything. She set a spoon next to the pint on the counter, deciding not to even bother with the bowl. Since the television was already on, she decided to channel surf. *What program went best with ice cream and a broken spirit?* She settled on an old favorite: *Remember the Titans*. Not much of a sports fan, the movie still topped her list of tear-jerking, heart-warming and all around great movies.

Once the ice cream was softened to her liking she brought that to the couch and snuggled up with the blanket that she had already determined smelled like Ben's after shave. She missed him. Things were harder than she had imagined. For starters she hadn't spoken with him, by text or anything, much at all. He told her he would be busy settling in the first few days, which he undoubtedly would be. A new country, new position, new living quarters. She couldn't imagine. She just hoped that they weren't creating a pattern. What if once he was settled in, then he became too bombarded with the workload that was certain to follow his acclimation? She now began to regret not being totally forthright with him about the case. In her defense he was already gone when Dean sprung her with the fact that she might be ground zero. But it suddenly seemed very unnerving that he was a million miles away and had little idea of her potential involvement. Of course God forbid anything happen to her, Dean knows everything. And Tranise. She has been very open and truthful with Tranise.

Bob was given a victim-friendly description of practically everything. It was getting to where she wasn't sure of whom she told what to. It was becoming one big blur. She pushed her spoon into the soft ice cream with too much gusto, causing some of it to spew out the side of the carton. Distraught, she stood up and walked over to the kitchen sink. With a wet paper towel she removed the chocolaty blob from her shirt. Just as she was leaving the kitchen she saw her phone, which was plugged into the charging unit, light up, indicating a text. Her heart sped up whenever her phone did anything these days. When she leaned over and saw that it was from Tranise her adrenaline began to skyrocket. A quick glance at the words on the screen told her she was right to panic.

***

Dean took in the scene, feeling nostalgic for his days as a criminology scholar. The campus was nearly empty at this hour, except for a handful of early birds and a few tardy students rushing to their morning early classes. Dean contained his laughter as a young girl wearing some God-awful high heels balanced a stack of books, a gourmet coffee and a too-tiny purse. Two young punks riding skateboards were eating bagels on the go and an elderly woman sat reading from a text book at a café table. He realized that he didn't stand out as much as he thought he might. Nowadays a student came in all shapes and sizes… and ages. He walked a few more feet to the directory and searched by department. He was following up on Keeley's hunch. Things were slow and there was no new information to keep him busy so he went with it. He had also received a text from Keeley saying that it seemed coincidental that both Harper Middleton and Adrienne Torero went to Fairview. He would have the perfect excuse to grill the guy. Two students went to his college and after some research, it turns out both of them had a class with Professor Michaels. It wasn't such a long shot after all. Plus, if a detective wasn't chasing every lead, he wasn't doing his job. There would be no rock unturned as far as Dean was concerned. This killer wasn't going to win.

With only the elderly woman in his vicinity, Dean turned from the directory with the information he needed. He smiled at her and she smiled back. "Are you a student here?" he asked.

"Yes," she replied, closing her book. So she was in the mood to chat . . . "I'm no spring chicken, but I finally have the money I didn't have the first time around," she chuckled. "How about you?"

"Me? Yeah. I'm no spring chicken either," he joked.

"I mean are you a student here?"

"That too," Dean lied.

"What are you studying?" she asked with genuine interest.

"History," he lied again. "You?"

"English."

Dean's brow raised. This might be more fruitful than he figured. He was just planning to ask her if she had heard about the murders, but she might actually be one of Michaels' students.

"Sounds like lots of reading and writing. Not my forte." Not a lie.

"Yeah, well, I love to read. Figured I might as well come out with a degree I had fun earning." She glanced at her watch. "I'm sorry to say I have to run off. I'm meeting a couple of youngsters for a study session."

Damn. She was so loose-lipped and clearly wanted to talk.

"Oh, okay. Hey, can you recommend any of the English department teachers? Just in case I get the writing itch?"

"They're all real good. Actually, there's one right there." She gestured toward a tall attractive man dressed in casual business attire.

He nodded in her direction.

Dean thought he looked smug. Smug and heady. He knew even before she said it who he was looking at. "That's Professor Michaels."

***

Tranise had received a little gift. Another novel actually, but this one was *undoubtedly* ominous. She didn't think it was a gift from a friend this time. She knew exactly who it was from. The text she sent to Keeley simply said: "A copy of Poe's *Tell Tale Heart* was on my front porch." They both knew what that meant. It was from him. No one apart from the case knew for sure the books were a gimmick in the murderer's game. And if word had somehow leaked, it would be impossible that anyone knew which books and which victims. Then again, Josh, the unsuspecting patsy knew the book list. He was the one who procured them for the killer. And somehow Professor Michaels knew there were calling-card novels left behind. Or what about the one of many policemen on the scenes? Whoever left it didn't have good intentions… just the opposite. It was a malicious act and right now, Keeley and Tranise were convinced that Tranise was in major danger.

After reading Tranise's text last night, Keeley picked up the landline and called Tranise at home. Tranise explained that the book had a handwritten inscription on the inside cover. It read: "Now I know where to find you." Understandably shaken, she called Detective Dean and Keeley had to wait to hear his take. Luckily Jeff and the kids were all safely at home with Tranise. Keeley was glad about that, but couldn't help but make a parallel comparison. She was alone. And if the killer was in a gift-giving mood . . . She'd had nothing to do but wait. Eventually she passed out from sheer exhaustion on the couch and woke up before dawn. After a shower and a cup of coffee she didn't feel any less unsettled than she did the night before. Dean had bagged the Poe book as evidence and told Tranise to be careful and to rest assure that squad cars were driving by both women's houses.

***

Dean was waiting on the prints, but knew there was no way the cretin would leave evidence now. He was a ghost so far and he wasn't going to suddenly start getting messy, that was for sure. Dean wondered if his trip to the university had been in vain. The professor gave a few alibis that Dean needed to check on, but all in all the only thing the guy seemed guilty of was being an ass. He was cocky, argumentative and seemed to have a grudge against the world at large. But Keeley had a good idea to look into the guy. As a matter of fact, Dean wouldn't be at all surprised if the guy had done something shady with a student at some point or another. He acted very inappropriately when an attractive young coed popped her head in at his office during their meeting and he didn't even bother trying to hide it from Dean. Dean decided to follow up on the professor's alibis as soon as he got back to his desk. Just to rule everything out. Other than that, he was also waiting on Keeley to finish going over the women's files. Hopefully, something productive would come of that. Until then, he would have not much more to do then wait.

He was scheduling second interviews with the spouses, significant others and fiancés in the next day or two. None of them seemed "of interest," but it was procedural. And again, anything was better than nothing. This case was bringing new meaning to the term, 'no rock left unturned'. It reminded him of Seamus McIntyre, the Vineyard Strangler from his second year on the force. Same scenario, where the perp literally left no tracks. Another ghost. Until at last McIntyre finally got sloppy. If a certifiable lunatic goes on a long enough spree, it's bound to happen. The screw up is inevitable. But how many more victims would he claim before the sloppiness hit?

Hopefully it wouldn't take another life to get their info. The three outstanding items were probably not Dean's ace in the hole, but a guy could hope, right? And hope he would. He was preparing to host Zoey's sleepover. He knew he wouldn't be sleeping that night, but he could at least rest a little easier if one of their tasks helped to turn over a new leaf in the case.

***

Keeley arrived at the store and was doing another inventory when the signs of a migraine struck. She knew she was due for one with all the stress she had endured. She took her prescription at the immediate onset and knew it would take at least a half hour to work. Until then she would just have to endure the pain and hopefully minimal side effects. Both Summer and Regina were unavailable, but hopefully it wouldn't come down to her needing a replacement. The last migraine she'd had was brutal. She didn't have her prescription on her so she had to wait to take the pill. As a result she had suffered nausea, tunnel vision and numb extremities until it finally began to wear off an hour and a half later. She crossed her fingers and sat at the desk. She opened her laptop and opened up her latest document, *Untitled.* She was working on another book. Actually it was her first attempt at writing that never made it off the ground. With everything going on Keeley wasn't ready to start a new book, but she had the itch. She decided to spend a little of her free time playing around with this manuscript. It would keep her busy. Although it was another murder mystery, it was easier to deal with fiction than the real thing, hands down. She read the last paragraph she had written. This wasn't the first time she'd revisited this unfinished – nearly un-started – manuscript. She had always thought this one would be her masterpiece, but she had no end prepared. It was a modest one hundred pages, but with no plans on where to take it, it was over before it began.

She rubbed her temples, realizing she was no worse off than she was ten minutes ago. That was a good sign. Maybe this *headache* would be over before it began. One could only hope. She winced recalling how painful the last one was. Thankfully Ben was there to help. He left her in her dimly lit room, having drawn the blinds and turned off all the lights, brought her a heating pad and eventually some soup. He was also the one to pick her up from work when it had already gotten so bad that she knew she couldn't drive. Who would be there to nurse her back to health this time? Of course Bob would drop anything to help her, but it wasn't like he lived around the corner. Keeley hated feeling so reliant on another person. She did perfectly fine by herself before Ben came along. But now that she knew what she was missing . . . plus, it was times like this that she really felt the deep loss of her parents. Any kind of tragedy was so much easier with her mommy and daddy around to make everything feel all right. She sighed. No more self-pity. There were families mourning loved ones all around her, including her brother. A headache and a temporary break from her loving soon-to-be spouse were hardly things to cry over.

She was beginning to feel the tension alleviate just a bit. Her headache was going away. She would be okay, for now, in regards to her fears of not having a nurse nightingale waiting in the wings. But what about everything else? What about her relationship to the case? Actually, she was planning to call Dean this morning and share with him her chart of commonalities with the victims. She was praying he would tell her that his idea was debunked. That it was just the eight degrees of separation – nothing substantial enough to keep his theory going. After all . . . who wanted to be the star of a murder investigation? Not Keeley. She wanted to be as uninvolved as possible. It felt like just yesterday that she wanted to leisurely back out, and stop being so invested in things. Now she might be the catalyst? It couldn't be. It was a preposterous idea and Dean would confirm that as soon as she called him. And since her headache was going away, that call would be soon. She picked up her phone and saw a smiling emoticon from Ben.

Earlier the two had been texting. Due to the time difference, they would often engage in conversations that would take a full twenty-four hours to conclude. But she was thankful for any type of communication. She was glad to hear that he was happily busy. He voiced his concern about Keeley being alone and had asked several questions pertaining to the case. He also told her he would be too busy to engage in the webcam they had planned when they last spoke. It was good to hear from him, and yet there was that familiar guilt because she didn't divulge everything. She wouldn't dare. With him so far across the globe it didn't seem fair. She did however ask him if he remembered working with Adrienne Torero when she did PR for his company. He wrote that the name definitely sounded familiar and was shocked to learn she was one of the victims. He hadn't put two and two together. Plus he was a newbie, busy clinging onto the bottom rung of the ladder. She wasn't sure what she was hoping to glean in asking Ben, but it was worth a shot. Keeley sent back her own emoticon – a kissy face with hearts.

She quickly left the front and ran to the restroom. The day's business had been slow, so it would be poor timing if someone actually came in during the three minutes she would be gone. The bell would sound though. She reprimanded herself for suddenly making a federal case of everything, but then again, who would blame her? Her life had turned into a perpetual ping pong game. One minute she felt one way, the next, the complete opposite. Like with Dean's theory. It seemed preposterous, yet possible. She finished up by washing her hands and since she hadn't heard the bell, she stocked the toilet paper and paper towel cupboards, cleaned the water spots off the mirror and added a new scent to her plug in. With her headache a mere memory, she reentered the main area of the shop and was totally baffled when she saw the front door perched open on its hinges. The bell, or what remained of it, had been torn from the upper region of the door frame. Exposed wires hung mockingly. Her eyes darted to the counter, zeroing in on its empty surface. Her laptop was gone.

Chapter twenty-two

"Clearly this is personal, whether it has been from the beginning or not," began Dean. In his hands he was holding the chart Keeley had prepared, as well as the sheet they had filled out just moments ago to document her stolen laptop. Her head throbbed, but it wasn't from a migraine this time. It was from pure exhaustion and adrenaline. Another emotional dichotomy. Dean then went on to tell her it wasn't necessarily indicative of the murderer. He said it could have just been some poor bum of the street who was possibly spying on her from the street in waiting. A high quality laptop like hers could do good resale on the street, he'd told her. But his face said different. She was sure it was a tactic to keep her from totally losing it. He had said before he had a daughter. He was probably afraid to tell Keeley the hard truth and his fatherly kindness was trying to protect her. But she knew; she wasn't just close to this case. She was someone's fixation. She wondered if maybe it wasn't just her book that was going to star in the next murder. She wondered if it was going to be her.

Reading the fear in her eyes he went against his last statement. "We have nothing to indicate foul play here. Without the bell the murderer could have had a field day with you alone in here. Why disable the bell and not take full advantage unless it was totally unrelated? Someone wanted to make some cool cash by stealing a computer. Until we learn otherwise," he began, "*that* is what you need to believe."

The officer who had dusted for prints was just packing up his belongings. He patted Dean on the back as he left through the still perched open door.

"What's the alarm situation here?" asked Dean.

"It's over on the wall. On the way to the back office." Dean went to the system. They both knew it was in vain. The store was not in jeopardy, she was. The alarm was not the issue. Including Josh, this was the second robbery while the store was attended! No one would need wait for night to break in. After looking at the alarm, Dean turned to her, giving a sympathetic look. "The prints off Poe were unintelligible. That's what we suspected of course. He wouldn't give himself up by leaving his prints all over a book that he voluntarily provided." Dean realized that was one hope down. After reading Keeley's list of her similarities to the other women, he was somewhat disappointed. In some way, minus Tranise as of yet, they did have little things in common. And quite often in these situations that was all it took. In the killer's sick mind it was possible that he wanted to target women who had it all, and for whatever reason, Keeley Travis; and this was how it played out. The connections were loose, but they were connections. After all, not that many women out there "had it all." Finally, the alibis for Len Michaels weren't exactly airtight, but without major evidence they were good enough for now. So therefore, here he was again without a damn lead. And once again he was facing the sweet young woman whose eyes reminded him so much of his Zoey. They had a determined set to them, but there was kindness and compassion there. Dean knew it sounded silly. Heck, even Terry teased him over it, but he knew how to read a face. And it had gotten him pretty far in his career. His instinct and his ability to read a person. He used it in his everyday life without actually meaning to. He could tell almost anything by looking at a person's eyes. If they were lying, suffering, elated. It was a blessing and a curse. Especially when it came to that punk Ryan Walton, who Zoey liked so much. *Damn!* Ryan Walton, Zoey. Tonight was supposed to be the big after party once the dance ended. Dean would want to oversee everything with the case, but there was no way he'd give up overseeing Ryan with his daughter under his roof. His protective side kicked in immediately. "Do you like pizza?"

"Yes," Keeley answered, looking a little confused.

"Would you like to come over tonight? I mean . . . Zoey, my daughter is having a few kids over for pizza. Then they go dance at the school, then they come back to our house. I'm in for the night, so I thought maybe you'd like to have some company, meet my wife."

"That sounds good." She said tentatively.

"Except what?" smiled Dean.

"My fear of coming home to a dark house. Lately at least."

"Let's do this. You think about it and if you decide to come out, I'll personally pick you up, then escort you home while the kids are at the school."

"Thank you, Dean. I appreciate it." And she did. She didn't like being home alone, dwelling on *everything*. Another thing she didn't like was appearing so vulnerable, or maybe just pathetic, that an unlikely friend felt the need to bail her out on a Friday night. Or worse, a police detective felt the need to protect her from a prospective prowler. Whatever the case, she would take him up on it. He'd been nothing but kind to her and had become a friend. Besides having nothing else to do, this would make her feel safe to be in his presence, occupy some time and save her the trouble of going to the market. She had little left in the fridge, let alone the combination to make an actual meal. This would be good for her. A family settling was just what she had been craving.

After taking Summer up on her offer to let her close up shop (she was meeting a study group there tonight), Keeley did end up stopping at the market. She bought a bouquet of flowers and a bottle of sparkling wine. She wasn't sure what type of wine Dean and his wife drank, if they even did drink. This felt like a safe bet. She drove the remaining few miles home. She put the wine in the fridge and rested the flowers on the counter top. She had time to freshen up and unwind a little before her police escort would arrive. The thought made her giggle, but it was mostly because of the safety the situation would provide. She was such a wimp! Granted, there were supposedly police cars cruising her street off and on, but she had yet to see that. And after today's violation, she was reaching a whole new level of fear and concern. Spending time with Dean and his wife and a room full of young, energetic people felt warm and safe. Yup, she was looking forward to it.

She took off her wedged shoes and set the pile of mail on the counter top. Perception was everything, she noted. Here she was waist-deep in a murder investigation, her laptop had just been stolen – containing a solid book in the making – and her fiancé was not there to see her through everything, yet she was going to a teen pizza party of a virtual stranger and it sounded wonderful. She would make lemonade from her lemons. After all, her migraine had ceased before it started and she would be under the protective arm of the law for the evening. Come to think of it, she had her novel on an old disc drive. But the idea of it being in the hands of a total stranger? Prospectively the hands of a killer . . . she willed herself to keep the glass half full. Things would be fine. She would change clothes, then send a text to Ben. If there was time, she might also call Tranise just to see how she was feeling. Maybe some of this windfall of positivity would rub off on another poor soul who could use some cheer.

Walking down the hall, something felt a little askew, but she couldn't pinpoint it. Just nerves, she thought. But there it was again. She stopped in her tracks. She knew what it was. It was the fact that she seldom came home at this hour of the day since her shift didn't typically end at this time. The lighting in the hall was a meld of late day sun and shifting shadows from the nearby foliage. She could see the particles floating in the shaft of light – something she used to call pixie dust as a child until Bob pointed out that it was everything from dead skin cells to dust . . . not magical fairy dust. She took the remaining steps to her bedroom and stopped again just inside the door. Yes, it was definitely a different time of day. It was warm and musty. A hot day in the middle of a cool week. She wouldn't of course open any windows because she was too petrified, and also because she was leaving soon. Cautious still, she retreated to the bathroom. Her heart leapt into her throat when she saw that a candle was burning on the ledge beside the tub. She clutched her chest, then remembered. She had been burning a candle this morning. She laughed in relief. It wasn't an intruder who had lit the candle, it was her. And here she irresponsibly left it burning all day. Her house could have caught on fire. She was obviously not thinking clearly lately. She needed to get it together. Giggling at her relief, and stupidity, she blew out the dwindling candle, then jumped again when she saw something move in the bathroom mirror. She was almost completely sure that something had moved. Yes, something had moved in her bedroom and was reflected in her bathroom mirror. Then again it could have been a trick of the light. Or a certain way she had tilted her head. She and Ben had just recently watched some show about the tricks your mind can play on you. It even demonstrated how your eyes will adjust to fill in objects that aren't really there as a means of identification, based solely on past experiences. And sometimes people see things, or blurs, that the eyes create as a method of self-awareness. She was over-stressed, over-tired and her medication sometimes made her slightly drowsy. This was just a figment of her over-active imagination. Wishing she believed herself, she walked into the master. She would just have to take a cursory look around to assure herself that everything was fine. She was letting herself get all worked up over nothing. But why wouldn't there be anything to worry over? Women were being targeted and killed. And she was definitely on his radar, Dean even thought so. So why wouldn't she need to worry right now? The room was small enough that a lingering glance showed her there was no one . . . in plain sight. She had a walk in closet and what mystery author would discredit the beauty of hiding under the bed? She braced herself before opening the closet door. She opened it slowly and let out a sigh of relief as she took in every square inch of the interior. Next she went over to the bed and knelt down. The area concealed by her ruffled bed skirt was cluttered with scrapbooking supplies and photo boxes. She should have known that no one would be able to hide under there. But again, she wasn't thinking straight. She was under an insane amount of stress. She was just scared, there was nothing awry. No need to panic. It was a figment of her overactive imagination. Her mother used to say it to her all the time. Then it paid off when she used it to write her books. And today, lately, it was working overtime and not serving any beneficial purpose.

Keeley allowed herself to exhale. "You're fine," she whispered. Glancing at the clock, she realized she had time to take a quick bath if she wanted to. It would do her good to try and soothe her nerves. She would take a quick, relaxing soak, then have just enough time to change into a nice comfortable outfit. The very idea already had put her mind at ease. She pushed the plug down and turned the hot water tap on. Right away she saw steam rising in wafting billows. Perfect. She dumped a scoop of lavender bath crystals into the stream of water. Then she added a little cold water and went to grab her water bottle and phone. Once she got to the kitchen, she saw that there was a missed call. It was an unfamiliar phone number with a local area code. Everyone of significance was recorded in her contact list and their names showed on the screen when they called. Even the newest people in her life, Dean and Tranise had been assigned to her contact list. She thought for a second that maybe it was Dean calling from his home phone. But if he were calling to change the time he was going to pick her up, or even to cancel, he would have left a message. There were no messages and the call had come in six minutes ago, according to her log. It was irrational to be concerned about this. She reminded herself that sometimes people called the wrong number and that it wasn't a sign she was in danger, but that didn't work. Fueled with new panic, she grabbed both her house phone and cell phone and ran back into the master, locking the door behind her.

***

Tranise was in bed, just waking from an unprecedented afternoon nap. She had been so worried about the Poe book left at her house that she hadn't managed more than a couple hours of sleep the night before. She was paying for it today. Jeff had volunteered to stay home from work today, against her protests. But when he emerged from the bedroom wearing his robe instead of office attire, she was eternally grateful, not to mention relieved.

The last thing she remembered was telling him she wanted to go lie down and read a bit. She looked at the clock and realized she had slept for a whopping two and a half hours. Her poor body was trying to make up for all the mental exhaustion piling up over the past weeks. Standing up and smoothing her blouse and capris, she realized Jeff was, of course, out chauffeuring the girls from school to practice. *Thank God he stayed home*, she mused. The girls would have been stranded. Then again, if Jeff weren't home she wouldn't be sleeping. She wouldn't be caught dead closing her eyes while she was by herself. Sadly, she didn't think she ever could again. But according to the bedside clock, she had done just that for about twenty minutes while he was out. And she'd survived. Nothing horribly wrong had taken place while she was asleep, alone in the house. She shuttered. The thought alone scared her to her core. Feeling uneasy, she crossed the master bedroom to the bathroom where she ran a comb through her hair and splashed a little water on her eyes.

Facing the bedroom door, she felt her knees begin to weaken. Here she was, a grown woman, in her own home, in broad daylight and afraid to open the door. She didn't have the courage. She had been by herself countless times since . . . the incident, but she stayed in the main rooms and mostly downstairs. And there was something different about having been shut away upstairs and suddenly having to face the unknown. She knew it sounded crazy, but sadly it made sense to her. For all she knew, the maniac was waiting outside for Jeff to leave and . . . she stopped her train of thought when she heard a thumping noise below her. She immediately locked the door and stepped back, haphazardly tripping over a laundry basket. She scrambled up, and dashed to the cordless phone located on Jeff's nightstand. She would call Jeff and tell him to hurry home. And if he didn't answer, she'd call the detective. Feeling a little less frantic, she picked up the receiver, only to find that the line was dead.

Chapter twenty-three

Tranise was overcome with terror. She' been a basket case since her attack, and now she actually thought she might die of fear, here in her own room. She was trapped. She was alone. The killer had won. She would die in her own house. She knew this because she didn't have any fight left in her. You couldn't cheat death twice. She scooted toward the window facing the street. She knew that Jeff wasn't due home yet, but maybe somehow she would get lucky and he would come to her rescue. When she stood and looked outside, she began to laugh through her tears. There were two large white utility trucks and a team of orange vested workers surrounding the green neighborhood utility box. The dead phone line was simply a fluke. This was a legitimate community problem, not a personal problem. She felt such a wash of relief.

But the thumping sound from downstairs hadn't been refuted. However, it now had less credibility. A noise and a potentially cut phone line was a sure sign of danger. The noise could have been anything, including the utility trucks. She gathered her courage and poised her hand above the locked door knob. She couldn't let fear control her. She was being overly paranoid and the last thing she wanted was for Jeff and the girls to see her like this – frantically boarded up in her room. She opened the door in one swift motion and walked down the hall. She tipped her head and listened at the top of the staircase. She heard nothing. Everything was fine. She descended the stairs, two at a time, then headed toward the front door. She would go outside and confirm that the lines were down. She unlocked the door and the deadbolt, her hand still shaking. *Calm down girl*, she warned herself.

With a turn of the knob she let out a blood curdling scream. "Oh," she wailed, steadying herself. "You scared the daylights out of me!" He simply smiled. Then reality set in. "What are you doing here?" *What was he doing here? At her house?*

***

Keeley was so frazzled that she couldn't even access the calling feature on her phone. She took a deep breath. Once her brain and her hands began to connect, she used her call log to call Dean on his cell. It went to voicemail after the second ring. Luckily he would call back quickly whenever he missed a call. For a spilt-second she wondered what she was even doing calling him. Was she over reacting? But on the other hand, she wondered if she shouldn't be calling 911. No one would consider her a total loon. There was a murderer on the loose for God's sake. She shouldn't be alone at all. She should have taken Bob up on his offer to let her stay there and she could commute. She felt so stupid for thinking she'd be okay on her own. Now here she was calling a detective over a missed call. Her next thought was to hang up, or even come up with a good excuse about why she was calling. Dean's prompt to leave a message ended her internal struggle. She felt a pang of guilt as she simply asked what time he was going to come by. She hated to lie to anyone, but he'd been so good to her, asking her to join in a family dinner and all. She didn't have the nerve to say she was afraid because her phone had rung. She was quite simply at the end of her emotional rope. He would understand that. And she would have to start coming to terms with that as well. After tonight she would be a guest at Bob's house. She was wanting to spend more time with him and she knew he could use the company also. Right away her phone began to ring. It was Dean. Time to face the music. She would tell him the truth. That she was a giant scaredy cat and she had had a panic attack.

"Hello?" she asked in a voice that even she didn't recognize.

"Keeley? Everything okay there?"

"Yes, I--" Dean jumped in before she could go through with her embarrassing confession.

"Good, because I think we may have a good lead on who our guy is. Hallelujah! There were prints on the Poe book, if you can believe that. The prints turned up a non-criminal, who needed clearance prints for work or something." She had never seen Dean so chatty before. He sounded giddy! "Anyway, we got really lucky. I'll pick you up in an hour and I can show you a copy of the guy's driver's license."

"That's wonderful. I assume it wasn't Professor Michaels?" At that moment, her phone emitted a low-pitched beep. It was dying. She had been sure she was charging it since she got home, but the plug was faulty. "I didn't hear that last part, Detective." She looked at her phone and the screen was black. Her phone was dead.

***

Ben was a friend, sure, but he was not a drop-by-the-house kind of friend. He was Tranise's head shot photographer two, maybe three times over the years. His charming smile didn't waver when she asked why he was at her home. He simply said, "I was in the neighborhood." It sounded practical enough until Tranise realized that Ben had never shot at her house. She worried for a minute, then remembered that he had flirted relentlessly at their first session. In fact, she had assumed he was gay because so many in the business are. In an attempt to quell the behavior, she had dropped Jeff's name, and status of husband, over and over. It was bothersome, yes. But when the proofs came back, they were the best she'd seen in her whole career. She couldn't deny that Ben was the best, so she had decided she'd have to endure the flirtations, which ultimately died down. He was certainly a good photographer and eventually someone she could call a friend after hours and hours of grueling and meticulous posing and staging and reviewing. But house calls? Not in their repertoire. Perhaps the old feelings had returned? She doubted that. He knew she was spoken for and it had been a good six months since she'd been on his radar.

"You knew my address?" she stated boldly, casually scooting behind the door so that less of her was exposed.

"Of course. You're in the database," he smiled. That smile probably worked on just about all the ladies. He was confidant and good looking. Probably not used to anyone saying no to him.

"Well it's good to see you. I'm right in the middle of something with a friend," she lied, "but I actually wanted to call you to get some current shots," she lied again.

"That's another reason I came by. I have some proofs from a few sessions ago that I couldn't find and then they turned up." He produced a manila envelope, holding it out toward her. She wrinkled her brow, but reached for the envelope. She didn't recall anything about missing shots. At that instant Ben grabbed her wrist and shoved her into the house. He pulled a cloth from his pocket and shoved it in her face. It was soaked in chloroform. She felt her knees buckling. And that was all.

***

Keeley quickly reached for the landline, but suddenly remembered she didn't know Dean's number by heart. She knew he had *her* number, but it was probably on the office computers. It wasn't like he had it handy in his pocket. But she was certain he would call. Until then she could easily run out and grab the charger from the kitchen counter and call him back. She could grab the plug and bring it in here and have Dean on the line within seconds. But it wasn't that easy. She'd have to leave the security of her room. But she really had no choice. Dean might feel like he didn't need to call her back since he was going to see her in just a little while. That should have provided a feeling of safety for Keeley, but it didn't in the least. An hour was a long time when you were scared out of your wits. She had to calm down. She didn't even have a legitimate reason for worrying. She had seen what she thought was movement in the mirror, then panicked over an unrecognizable number. *Get over it and go get your charger*, she told herself. So she got up and walked to the door, unlocking it. There was nothing to be afraid of. She opened it and there was no boogey man lurking outside. She let out a sigh of relief. She walked toward the kitchen and then lurched, cupping her ears. The stereo began blasting unintelligible music at an ear splitting volume, then it stopped. Then it started again, continuing in painfully loud staccato blasts. Knowing exactly what was happening, Keeley raced back toward the bedroom, where she once again locked herself in. She was crying in choking sobs, for this scenario was all too familiar. She had come up with it herself. Right now, against her will, she was staring as the heroine in her own horror novel. And she knew all too well that it was not going to have a happy ending.

***

The music blasts had come to a halt. Knowing what was next was the worst part. Keeley felt for all the women had had to endure the macabre plots, though she wasn't entirely sure they had all been cognizant of what was going on. Tranise had known. She had seen the book while she was struggling to escape. Had they all been privy to what was going to happen to them? Keeley shuddered, realizing she had written her own death. A horrifying, sickening way to die.

She tugged at the broken lock on her bedroom window in vain. It was always like that, and she wondered if the killer knew. Otherwise she would be able to escape through the window. She grabbed her bedside lamp, a heavy duty old piece from her mother's belongings. Maybe it would break the glass, though she knew it was most likely too thick. Just as she yanked the lamp's cord free from the plug she saw the axe break through the wood of her bedroom door, leaving splintering wood and an impossibly huge gaping slit. She used all her strength to slam the lamp against the window, but there was no damage except to the lamp. Unlike the door that looked like it might break away with a gust of wind. She hurdled her body toward the bathroom, half crawling, where she shut the door and began searching for a pair of scissors or something she could use to try and defend herself.

The tiny alcove which housed the toilet had a small sliding window covered with screen. It barely looked wide enough for her to fit through, plus the fact that it was too high for her to reach. It was worth a try though. Perhaps the killer wouldn't know that her bathroom lock was broken and he would have to spend his time axing that door down also. She stood on the toilet and opened the window. She used the scissors in her hand to tear away at the screen. She could hear the bedroom door fall opened. She had a matter of seconds. She tried hoisting herself, but lacked the strength to pull herself up. This was it. She was going to be drowned in her own bath tub.

***

Ben hoisted Tranise's limp body into a giant plastic bin. He put the lid on it and dragged it to his car. It was nearly too heavy to lift into the back of the rental SUV but he did it. He knew her husband would be home soon. And Keeley's story was unraveling at this very moment. He wanted to be there to see it through to the end. The look on her face would be priceless. That privileged bitch was so wrapped up in the successes of her books that she didn't give a damn about anything or anyone else. The irony was awesome. Recruiting help was the best idea he'd hatched since coming up with the plan. His associate served as a terrific asset and had been surprisingly easy to brainwash. And with an axe and a mask would go totally undetected. As promised. He would go to Keeley's for the grand finale, where Tranise would be able to watch her new best friend die, then he would drive her back up to the woods. It would happen in a different cabin all together, but it would still be exactly the way he had wanted it to go. She had made a huge mistake trying to escape her fate. And talk about a priceless look on one's face. Tranise hadlooked like she'd seen a ghost. Luckily Ben had been a jack of all trades in his youth. Exposed to one advantaged female after the next, starting with his mother. She was his first victim, unbeknown to his father who was probably relieved to see her go. Ben, only twelve at the time, had done an amazing job staging the poor old bag's suicide. He got such a rush that it became a passion which he honed over time. And now it would all come together. Now who was the award-worthy writer?

He would leave the two bodies and then take a private jet to Australia where his boss, whom he had blackmailed for inside trading, would vouch for his whereabouts, no questions asked. He would be the lead character in his *own* story, playing grieving fiancé to the popular new author. All the women who had blissfully thought they had it all their whole lives would have been punished, and Ben would feel that unmatched sense of accomplishment once again.

He drove to Keeley's, careful not to go more than a few miles over the posted speed limit. Glancing at his watch he realized it would be a good idea to further sedate Tranise, just in case. He didn't need her playing hero again. That was his job. He was the hero. Ridding the world of slime like Keeley. All of them. Entitled bitches who everyone else glorified. They were wrong. So wrong. And so unfortunate to have come across his path over the years. Every one of them.

***

She heard the axe make contact with the bathroom door. How many seconds did she have left? Twenty? Thirty? *Think*! She should know how to escape her own scenario! Praying it would work, Keeley jumped as forcefully as she could on the hinges of the toilet lid. The thing was old and threatened to snap off every time she shut it. This time though, the hinge on one side snapped. She jumped again on the other side, but it didn't budge as easily. She used the blunt end of the scissors she had tossed onto the floor, and then it cracked apart. She held the heavy duty lid in her hand, realizing it was not only a weapon, but a shield.

***

Dean was cleaning the grill in preparation for Terry's famous grilled garlic bread. It was always a hit. Terry was fluttering around the kitchen as if the Queen of England was coming over, instead of a few high school punks, most of whom she'd known since they were all in diapers. But it was a big night. Dean felt it too. It was a first, though sure to be one of many. Zoey's first semi-formal school dance, her first real date, her first group sleepover – God, he couldn't believe he'd agreed to this.

He glanced at his watch and realized he needed to leave shortly if he wanted to be at Keeley's on time and then be back when the kids, and pizza, arrived. The grill was pretty well scrubbed. He wished he could say the same for himself. He was wearing the same shirt he'd had on all day, pit stains and all; and his five o'clock shadow was more like a beard. He had just gotten home a few minutes ago to the frantic Terry, begging him to clear off the patio and scrub down the grill. Happy wife, happy life. Ah what he wouldn't do for his girls. Lately every time he felt sentimental toward his girls, he thought of all those victims and their families. And now, hopefully things were about to come to an end. The team at the station was sealing the deal on locating the probable perp, and there was a great chance he would be apprehended for questioning before the dance ended. It was going to be a great night. There was minimal room for error here, except of course if the fingerprints were planted. Dean still had the nagging feeling that this guy wouldn't have slipped up so easy, especially since he provided the item (complete with prints). But he also felt it in his gut that this guy was their man. He blended in, he was a functioning member of society, and attractive to boot.

Dean closed the lid on the grill and glanced at his watch one more time. It would be rude to keep Keeley waiting, but it would also be rude to show up at his little girl's party smelling the way he did. He lifted his arm and winced. *Whew*! He would take a quick shower, then call Keeley on the way to her house to tell her he would be running a little late.

"Honey?" called Terry from the kitchen. "You did the grill?"

"Yes Dear," he sang back.

"One more favor. I need help reaching the top of the windows facing the patio."

"Geeze Ter, we're having *kids* over. They don't give a damn what the windows look like."

"But I do care. I don't ask for much, and you're barely ever here to . . ."

"Okay, okay. It's what I live for," he smiled. Terry hardly ever pulled that card, so when she did, he obliged. Keeley wouldn't mind waiting a few extra minutes.

Chapter twenty-four

Ben pulled up alongside the curb, then re-membered his cargo. He had the code to open Keeley's garage, so he would back up the car as far as he could, then hoist the body out. Glancing at the console, he realized his timing couldn't be better. He felt confident in his assistant's willing-ness to help him with this "hoax," as he had called it. But at the end, when it was time to pull the metaphorical trigger, Ben would need to take over. And more than likely he would have one more person to eliminate. It wasn't every day you found someone willing to commit murder for you. So for now, pretending it was all an elaborate hoax that would end terribly wrong, made for the perfect scheme. Pleased with himself, Ben backed up against the garage door and pressed the numerical code into the box beside the door. Sure enough, it opened. He toyed with the idea of relocating his vehicle to the street, but it was a rental so there was no need to worry. Plus, Keeley had really kept to herself since moving onto this street. She was either at the shop or typing her pathetic little sto-ries. Ben's storyline blew hers out of the water: a copycat murderer. And it was a true story. He couldn't wait for the final headlines. He had been following his little game, clipping newspaper articles and savoring the nightly news, but the best was yet to come.

He nearly threw his back out lifting the plastic bin, which he basically let fall to the ground when his lower back cracked. Dammit. He would need his physical prowess for what lie ahead. There was zero room for error at this point. Dragging the large plastic bin toward the door, he smiled when he opened it and saw that the instructions had been followed to a tee. The door was unlocked and the shades and blinds had all been drawn. The stereo was on, but the volume was down. Perfect. Everything was working out. He knew it was a huge gamble to invite another person to join him, but it was necessary. And what was one more casualty if they weren't copacetic at the end of the day?

He pulled Tranise into the kitchen before opening the lid. He had the chloroform ready in his hand in case she had woken up. The woman was a force to be reckoned with, he gave her that much credit. She was still unconscious, and surprisingly, looked no worse for her ware. He stroked her cheek. She was strikingly beautiful on the outside. Too bad her ambition and strength got in her way. He stopped abruptly when he heard the sound of a struggle. He sealed the box again, knowing she would stay alive until he needed to punish her because of the small holes he had poked in the box.

Hurriedly, he pulled on his mask and tucked the neck of the plastic mask into his shirt. He caught a glimpse of the ghoulish face as he walked past the mantel mirror. He smiled, pulling up the corners of the plastic mouth. He couldn't wait another minute for the fun to begin, and then to end.

The door to the bedroom was completely destroyed. "A" for effort. His feelings of gratitude toward his little helper diminished the second he saw what was going on. He rushed in to help. Keeley was using the lid of the toilet as a lethal weapon. The blows of the axe were continually blocked, and both of them looked as if they were about to crumble to the ground.

"Give me the axe!" Ben ordered. "Now!" He took over, seeing a light of recognition flicker over Keeley's tired, wide eyes. Or at least he thought, but he could have been wrong. She was clearly in shock. Probably delirious. With the axe in his hand, he wielded it over his head, realizing he might just have to kill her before she made it to the bath tub. It would be less authentic, yes, but her escaping would be unacceptable. With luck on his side, once again, he landed the axe directly in the center of her make-shift weapon. It stuck to the blade and he casually pulled it from her. She began to cry. Plead, even. She finally let herself crumple to the ground. She had been defeated. It was about time she felt the harsh slap of reality. He dropped the axe and grabbed her by the hair, yanking it back hard. She screamed. "Please don't hurt me."

He moved his masked face within inches of hers and whispered, "Not a chance. You're going to die." He turned away from her and yelled out,

"Turn on the water and put the plug in. Now!" The masked assailant did exactly that. It was too late for Keeley. "Now go get the bag sitting by the big box. Hurry!" Keeley was struggling, but not as much as Ben had anticipated. It was more like gentle squirming. The poor thing had barely an ounce of energy left. *Where was the sport in that?* Ben smiled. She reached out and clawed at his mask, but he pulled away.

"What the hell? There's a dead lady in that box!" squealed the second masked attacker, re-entering the room. Keeley knew immediately who the voice belonged to – it was Summer.

***

Dean was finally finished with his honey-do list, which turned out to include more than cleaning the high windows. He was just stepping into the shower, planning to do the bare minimum – rinse what was left of his hair and a fast and furious scrub down to get the stink off. He was even dirtier and sweatier than before. Poor Keeley would be wondering where he was if he didn't get going. Plus he wanted to be there when the kids arrived to set the tone. Lenient Terry wouldn't put the fear into the hormonal young boys like he could. The thought really got to him. But if things went well, the killer would be behind bars by tomorrow morning and there would be no shenanigans under the Dean family roof. Terry always teased him that he couldn't protect the world. That he was obsessed. Well tonight his persistence had paid off. His little world, his family and community at any rate, would be safe from the bad guys. Just as long as he hurried the hell up. The water was taking forever to warm up, but time was not on his side. A warm shower wasn't a luxury he could afford. He figured the cooler water might help to wake him up. He was overtired.

With a final rinse, he stepped out of the shower and grabbed a towel. He was pleased to find that Terry had set an outfit out for him on his side of the bed. She was always looking out for him. He smiled at the pair of khaki slacks and dressy Hawaiian button up. Terry always said he was so busy taking care of everyone else that he needed her to take care of him. And he loved that more than she would ever know. She was his safety net.

Minutes later Dean was grabbing his keys off the kitchen counter. "Don't start without me," he called behind him. Without any traffic he could be there in ten minutes. He would just call her cell to give her the heads up. Poor girl was already expecting him, damn chore list. But he knew it was a give and take. What he wouldn't do for his girls.

***

Keeley couldn't believe her eyes. She was right – Summer slipped off the mask, wild eyes pleading. "What the hell is going on here? You said it was just a prank! Look how scared she is!" she wailed, gesturing at Keeley. "And now there's a body in the kitchen?"

"She's not dead, just sedated. Now you promised you'd help. Come over here," spoke the axe-wielding lunatic. He was altering his voice, but Keeley wondered for a moment if it wasn't Len after all. But Dean would have said it over the phone. Of course it wasn't him, but it was someone who knew Summer? She was so blinded by fear and pain that she couldn't make sense of much. She was nailed down by his knee and subsequent body weight and it felt like her spine was going to crack on the multi-level bathroom tiling below her. If he didn't let up, she would die from lack of oxygen. She let out a grunt, and tried to shove him off of her. "There's your fight. I was wondering where it went." This time he had forgotten to disguise his voice. And the moment Summer came to his side, Keeley realized who her captor was.

"Ben? Is that you?"

"I'm surprised it took so long for the super sleuth to figure it out."

"You can't seriously be doing this," she gasped. "And Summer?" Her eyes went from her fiancé to one of her dearest friends.

"He said it was a joke," yelled Summer. "A hoax. That was all. I had no idea . . ."

Just then, Ben picked up the axe and swung it through the air. Keeley averted her eyes, but knew what happened. Summer made a garbled sound before her body slunk to the ground. He had killed her. Keeley screamed, opening her eyes. Summer lie dead on the ground. And who was the dead body in the kitchen? This was all too much for Keeley to comprehend. Ben was the killer. Summer was helping him. And today she was going to die.

"There. One less complication," smiled Ben. "Guess I don't need this anymore," he said, removing the grotesque mask. The handsome, caring face that she loved so much had been replaced with a wild-eyed demon. His gaze was virtually unrecognizable. He was totally insane. Ben was completely gone.

"Come on," he said casually, hoisting her body and yanking her by the hair. "Let's get you a nice warm bath, shall we?" In reality he had done that for her on numerous occasions. Their entire relationship had been a charade. She tried resisting him, but he was stronger. He was always working out and lifting weights on the weekends and during lunch breaks. She found his strength so appealing, but now it stood as a reminder of how he had effortlessly strong-armed all those women. Ben was the common thread, not Keeley. He had known who Adrienne was. He had known Amy through her book club. *My God*! If only Dean could realize everything that was coming about. *Dean*! He should have been here by now!

Ben was clumsily fighting to get Keeley in the tub, her feet slipping beneath her, when there was a sound from the other room. "Tranise!" grunted Ben.

"Tranise?" Keeley mouthed, wordlessly. Ben reached as far as his arm would allow and grabbed the marble soap dish on the counter top. He swung it hard into her forehead and that was the last thing she remembered.

Ben positioned her body as if she were taking a nice relaxing bath, then turned the faucet higher. Water rushed from the tap. It would be full in minutes, covering her face. The deed would be done while he dealt with Tranise who was no doubt coming out of her stupor. Things were actually running pretty smoothly, despite the bumps in the road. He rounded the corner; and, instead of coming face to face with an incoherent super model, he was looking down the barrel of a gun.

***

An EMT was sitting next to Keeley on her own bed. She was draped in a towel and had a monster headache. "She's awake," he announced.

She looked up to see Detective Dean standing beside her.

"Hey kid. I'm sorry I was late." She winced, but smiled. "Hey, someone get the light. She's getting blinded over here." Another EMT rushed over with an icepack and the first began to take her vitals.

"Where is he?" Keeley mumbled. "Where's Ben?" Then she started to sit up, but winced and put her head back on the pillow. "Tranise. Where's Tranise?"

"Ben's cuffed and on his way to the station and Tranise is on the couch, perfectly fine. You did good, Keeley."

"And poor Summer."

"Yeah, poor Summer; but she made a poor choice in who she was fraternizing with," said Dean, somberly.

"I can't understand it." Keeley just wanted to go to sleep and block everything out. And her head hurt so badly.

"Miss, we're going to start an IV and get you some relief," explained the first EMT.

"Keeley, you just rest. I want you to know I'm so sorry. If I had been on time . . ."

Dean swallowed around a huge lump in his throat. He had let her down. He was trying too hard to be everyone's hero.

"You didn't know. *I* didn't know. I was planning to marry him." She felt the tears running down her cheeks. But she wasn't crying for herself and her misfortune. She was crying for the victims. Over time she would be able to come to terms with everything, but right now it was as if she had betrayed each and every one of those women. "How could I have been so naïve?"

"Ben is the guilty one, not you." He set his hand on hers. "The worst part is that I had his picture with me. I should have driven straight to your house. None of this would have happened."

"Take your own advice Dean," smiled Keeley, through the pain. She was alive. The killer was captured. Just then Tranise walked into her room. She looked rattled, but relieved. And despite everything, had kept her model good looks. She walked cautiously to Keeley's side and knelt down. The two new friends didn't have to say a word, but they both cried tears of joy and exhaustion as they embraced.

Epilogue

Now that everything about Ben was out in the open, his many personas and his personal vendetta as a result of his domineering mother, life was starting to look up. Keeley had moved some of her things into Bob's place where she planned to stay until she sold her house. Too many memories. Not only was it now a gory crime scene, but the local media had become fixated with the famed and fictional murders. As soon as Keeley, deemed a "minor celebrity," became a part of it, it exploded nation-wide and with its popularity came a following of bazaar, blood-thirsty weirdoes who camped out alongside her curb.

The bookstore was now constantly abuzz and Keeley was forced to trust human-kind once again and she hired two more girls in addition to Regina, who began taking on more responsibility. Business was booming, but naturally Keeley had mixed emotions about it. She hated that it was on the heels of such disaster. But luckily, she was in the works with a major publishing company to write her very first non-fiction novel. The popularity from her version of the story would be re-earned on her own merit soon enough. The novel would describe her role in the fictional copycat killings, as it had come to be called. During her quick recovery and forced time off, she had also come up with an ending for her untitled novel. Her real life brush with death had inspired her. As for Bob, he was happy to have closure on everything. Jess would never stop being the love of his life, but he was doing a good job of starting to enjoy life again – just as Jess would have wanted.

Tranise was doing better than ever and was in a place she thought she'd never return to. With her assailant's death, she could finally breathe again. She was in a happy, safe, healing place. The whole media frenzy had sparked a new interest in the model-mom. She was contracted as the new face of a career-minded woman's clothing line. The only thing about her life that was different from before the two attacks was her strong friendship with Keeley. Their bond began under horrific circumstances, but it survived and thrived. It was like they'd been friends their whole lives.

Detective Dean was in close communication with both of the women. After his initial feelings of failure over the case, he learned to give himself a little slack . . . and allow himself a little more time for the main ladies in his life. He decided to also cut Zoey's boyfriend, Ryan a little slack. A few backyard BBQs in and Dean was actually starting to like the guy. As much as he'd ever like his only child's crush, he supposed.

For him the despair and horror of homicide would never die down, at least for a while. But he wouldn't have it any other way. He liked knowing when there was one less bad guy roaming the streets. It was his way, whether he liked it or not. And right now, he was happy. He was getting ready to clean off the old grill. Tranise, Jeff and the girls and Keeley and Bob were on their way over. And so was Ryan.

~*~*~

Also by Pamela Malz

*****

The Reunion
ISBN 9780984619504

"He was sitting on the patio of a busy restaurant during lunch
hour with a glass of Chardonnay. The fizzling embers at the
end of his cigar created an eye catching design, though no one
was looking. He opened the Sierra Palma 1999 yearbook to
the colorful rows of senior portraits and set it in his lap. He
was making a mental list of his soon-to-be victims."

It's almost time for the Sierra Palma class of 1999 reunion.
Homecoming week will bring about nostalgia, regret, the re-
kindling of old flames, and for some, murder. It all begins
when the police find Mr. Olivares, washed up coach, beheaded in his living room. Beside his body lay the killer's calling
card- a cutout of his photograph from the 1999 yearbook.

Someone's about to get their revenge on an elite group of
students who graced the gilded halls of Sierra Palma: the Prom
Queen, the Valedictorian, the jock, the juvenile delinquent.
There is someone who will stop at nothing to make *The Reunion* a horrifying trip down memory lane; a week that will rock
the hallowed halls of Sierra Palma High to its core . . .

With the help of unlikely heroine and former Prom Queen,
Jaime Carrere, who must now face the demons of her past,
The Reunion is a page turning action-adventure-romance-
thriller from start to finish, complete with all of the mystery
and suspense that any avid reader could ask for.

*****

Secret at Oak Knoll Pass
ISBN 9780615576862

Bella Horn reluctantly returns to her hometown one year after her father's tragic death. Oak Knoll Pass is the picture perfect place to raise a family: a general store where everyone knows your name, holiday parades, breath taking centuries old homes... and hidden SECRETS that may cost some their lives. Bella will quickly learn that some small town SECRETS should remain buried. From the author of action-adventure-thriller, *The Reunion*, *Secret at Oak Knoll Pass* is filled with mystery, suspense and romance, and this action thriller will keep the reader guessing until the very last mesmerizing word.

As Bella continues trying to prove that her father's death was no accident, she comes face to face with a past she longed to forget and a dangerous killer on the loose who will stop at nothing to silence her. Amongst threatening letters and vanishing neighbors, Bella tries to mend a broken relationship with her stepmother and finds herself falling for a mysterious stranger.

Meet our Author

Pamela Malz

Pamela Malz lives in San Diego, California, with her husband and daughter. She has taught high school English and has always had a love for reading and writing. When she's not writing, she enjoys spending time with family and friends. She is currently working on her next mystery, *Mirror Mirror*.